"TONIGHT WAS GREAT. THANKS FOR SAYING YES."

"Thank you." Wynn smiled. "I don't get many opportunities to go out without my kids. It was fun."

"We'll have to change that. Check your calendar and let's shoot for something next week."

Wynn hesitated. Did she really want to do this again? Was she asking for trouble? "We'll see." She took a step closer and raised up on her tiptoes, placing a steadying hand on his shoulder. Wynn kissed his cheek and then turned away, fumbling with her keys.

Suddenly, Adam's hand encircled her arm. He spun her around to face him, taking a step closer. Surprised, she gasped, gazing into his face. Her heart almost stopped in her breast. His eyes were dark with intent.

He's going to kiss me. And she wanted him to.

I Can Make You LOVE ME

KAREN WHITE-OWENS

Kensington Publishing Corp.

http://www.kensingtonbooks.com

DAFINA BOOKS are published by

Kensington Publishing Corp.
119 West 40th Street
New York, NY 10018

All Kensington Titles, Imprints, and Distributed Lines are available at special quantity discounts for bulk purchases for sales promotions, premiums, fund-raising, and educational or institutional use. Special book excerpts or customized printings can also be created to fit specific needs. For details, write or phone the office of the Kensington special sales manager: Kensington Publishing Corp., 119 West 40th Street, New York, NY 10018, attn: Special Sales Department. Phone: 1-800-221-2647.

Dafina and the Dafina logo Reg. U.S. Pat. & TM Off.

ISBN-13: 978-0-7582-2959-5
ISBN-10: 0-7582-2959-3

First mass market printing: October 2009

10 9 8 7 6 5 4 3 2

Printed in the United States of America

I Can Make You
LOVE ME

Prologue

"And they lived happily ever after," five-year-old Adam Carlyle chanted along with his babysitter, Wynn Evans. They glanced at each other and burst into a round of giggles. Wynn shut the book of fairy tales and placed it on the nightstand next to the bed.

"We watched *Star Wars*, plus you've had two stories." The eighteen-year-old Wynn straightened his Spider-Man pajama top. "I think it's time for my favorite little superhero to go to sleep."

"Don't want to go to bed," he muttered sullenly.

Concerned, Wynn leaned back, watching the child closely. Adam rarely acted out. Generally, when his bedtime came, he went down without a fight. Tonight, he'd insisted on movie after movie until his brown eyes fluttered shut when the bewitching whisper of blissful sleep enticed him. Each time Adam shook himself, fighting off the lure of sleep.

"Sweet pea, what's going on?"

"When I wake up, you'll be gone just like my sister."

Understanding dawned and Wynn tried to explain. "Not in the morning. We're leaving in the afternoon."

His bottom lip quivered and tears pooled in his eyes. Sherry, Adam's sister, was starting her third year of college and had left days earlier.

"I know what we'll do. You and I will visit the park and then go have Buddy's Pizza tomorrow. How's that?" Wynn suggested.

Adam nodded solemnly.

Confident she had hit on the perfect diversion, she smiled. He never turned down a trip to his favorite pizza hangout, although the look of misery remained deep in his eyes.

"But you're still going to leave me."

"Only for a few months. I'll be home for Thanksgiving and then back at Christmas for a longer stay," she promised, pulling the blanket to his chin. "Come on. It's past your bedtime. Your mom and dad will have a fit if they come home and you're still up."

As he pouted, the little boy's thick eyelashes glittered with tears. "I don't want you to go. Who's gonna read to me and play with me?"

Tears pricked Wynn's eyes and she hugged him. "Oh, Adam. I'll miss you, too."

"Wynn?"

"Hmm?" she muttered, wiping away the moisture from her face.

"Will you marry me?"

Surprised, she drew back and looked into Adam's serious face. "What?"

"I said, will you marry me?" Adam asked the question a second time with more confidence and determination than Wynn expected from any five-year-old. Left speechless, she grappled for an answer that respected and protected Adam's feelings but let him down easy.

"Don't you think you should wait until you're old enough to date?" she teased.

"No. I love you."

"And I love you," Wynn replied. "Tell you what. When you're a man, you can ask me again. Okay?"

Adam's forehead crinkled into a frown as he considered her suggestion. "When I get big, I'm going to marry you. Then you'll never leave me," he promised, snuggling into the blanket and turning on his side.

"Good night. Sleep tight, sweet pea." She tucked the blanket tighter around his shoulders.

My first marriage proposal, Wynn thought, sitting for several minutes on the edge of Adam's mattress.

It was time to grow up, move on, and take charge of her life. As far back as she could remember, she knew that she wanted to help people. Now she was headed to Michigan State University to work toward her degree in nursing.

Wynn reached out and turned on the nightlight next to the bed before switching off the lamp on the nightstand. She waited until Adam's deep, rhythmic breathing signaled that he had succumbed to sleep. Seconds later, she tiptoed across the room and stood in the doorway, watching her favorite little man for a moment longer.

She giggled softly, turning away from the door-way and heading to the staircase. Maybe her boyfriend, Jim, would miss her as much as Adam and she'd get a second proposal. That was one she'd have to seriously consider.

Chapter 1

Adam Carlyle checked his watch and then leaned to the left, counting the number of people in the line ahead of him. He grunted, debating whether he should give the clerk a chance to catch up or head back to the office and have his administrative assistant pick him up a sandwich. If he didn't have a taste for a New York–style hot dog, he'd step out of the line right now.

His glance wandered around the beige walls and open space of the New Center One building, focusing on the woman standing in line in front of him. *Nice curves,* he thought, taking a more leisurely second stroll along her frame. The blue-green suit caressed every delectable line. The jacket hugged her waist and stroked a path along her hips.

He grinned devilishly. She had the sort of curves he liked to hold on to while making love.

Beethoven's Fifth Symphony chimed from the interior of the woman's purse. She unzipped the

No way. Not after all these years. Adam took a step closer, examining her. The slim shape, height, and breadth of the woman seemed right. But he wasn't sure if his suspicions were correct. After all, his Wynn didn't have a copyright on the name.

I'll wait until she's done with her call and then I'll ask her, he decided, fighting the urge to interrupt. Instead, Adam eavesdropped on her one-sided conversation to glean more information. It wasn't his shining moment, but he'd never use anything he heard against her.

"Sounds good. How many shifts? Well, I'm on the road right now. You'll hear from me when I get back to the office. Great! Talk to you soon," she promised in a husky voice reminiscent of Kathleen Turner. Tiny shivers danced up and down his spine as he listened to the achingly special sound of her voice.

The woman snapped the phone shut, slipped it back inside her purse, and took a step closer to the counter.

shoulder. She turned, facing him with a polite but curious expression on her lovely face.

Pure joy swept through him. Wynn! A smile spread across his face. His childhood babysitter stood in front of him.

Wynn's beauty was timeless. A short pixie hair-cut replaced the long ponytail she used to wear. Wisps of auburn hair feathered around the sides of her oval face. One silver lock fell across her forehead while long dark brown lashes shielded Wynn's almond-shaped eyes. Adam's gaze skipped over her straight nose before moving lower, settling on her full, lush, and kissable lips. She looked great; different, mature, but incredibly appealing and sexy.

He put on his most charming smile and said, "I'm sorry to bother you. I heard you when you were on your phone and I wanted to ask you a question."

Wariness replaced the pleasant curiosity of a moment earlier, but she answered cautiously. "Yes?"

"You said your name is Wynn Evans. Did you grow up in the Rosedale Park area?"

Wynn's forehead crinkled into a frown. She gave him a second, more thorough inspection. "Yes."

"I don't know if you remember me." He stabbed a finger at his chest, feeling the blood pound through his veins with anticipation. "I'm Adam. Adam Carlyle."

For a moment, there was no recognition, and then she gasped. Her eyes opened wide. Wynn threw her arms around his neck, hugged him, and then stepped back. "Adam from Outer Drive. My sweet pea."

Instantly, his body reacted to the softness of her slim frame. His arms dropped to his side and he took a step back to get a better look at her and give himself a moment to get his raging hormones under control. The intervening years had been very kind to her. Grinning, he answered, "That's me."

She grabbed his hands and squeezed. Adam almost purred like a cat with pleasure. "It's good to see you! You look fantastic!"

"Next!"

Startled, Wynn jumped and turned to the counter. "Sorry. Excuse me." She brushed her bangs from her eyes and turned to the clerk, placing her order. As she reached inside her purse, Adam touched her arm, feeling her skin leap to life under his fingers.

"I've got it."

"No. I'm fine," she protested.

Adam didn't intend for Wynn to get away without giving up her telephone number or address. "My treat."

Wynn started to protest, "Oh, but—"

"How many times did you feed me back in the day? We've got to sit, talk, and catch up."

Wynn caught her bottom lip between her teeth. She glanced around the open space and then back at him, smiling hesitantly. "Okay."

He grinned. "Good."

She zipped her purse and slung it over her shoulder. "You're right. It's too good an opportunity to pass up. I want to know how your family is doing."

Adam placed his order and paid for their meals. He turned to Wynn. "Why don't you find us a table."

Nodding, she headed through the lobby to a table near the entrance for the Detroit Public Schools.

He picked up the tray of food and followed, admiring the sway of Wynn's hips in her fitted skirt as she strolled ahead of him across the beige tile floor. She chose a table in an area of the building that offered a bit of privacy but was within reach of others. As she seated herself gracefully on one side of the table, Adam removed the food from the tray and placed the tray on a nearby tray holder.

He slid into the white plastic chair opposite her and studied her. "You look great."

Self-consciously, she arranged her plastic-ware around her plate and took special care to place the paper napkin in her lap. "Thank you. It's been a long time."

"Yeah. It has."

"What's going on with you?" Wynn reached for the yellow packet, added sweetener to her cup of green tea, and stirred. She stuck the red-and-white plastic stirrer into the corner of her mouth and chewed on the end. "Are you married? Do you have kids? What do you do for a living?"

"No middle ground for you. Just the facts."

She laughed.

The sound filled his heart and head with wonderful memories of the times she had spent with him, reading stories before putting him to bed.

"You know me. I always want to know how things tick."

Adam added mustard and ketchup to his hot dog before biting into it, chewing slowly as he considered her questions. "Not married. No kids. I'm a real estate attorney and VP of Legal Services for Gautier International Motors." He wiped his mouth with a paper napkin and took a sip from his Pepsi. "What about you? Married? Kids?" His gaze rested on Wynn's ringless fingers. "I heard you say something about shifts when you were on the phone. What's that all about?"

"Divorced," Wynn stated and then shrugged a little sheepishly.

Adam let out a relieved sigh. *Good,* he thought. *That's what I wanted to hear.* "I'm sorry."

She smiled sadly, tearing a piece of lettuce from her chicken salad sandwich and nibbling on it. "Don't be. It happens. Besides, things worked out for the best. My only regret is my sons don't have a full-time dad."

"Sons?"

"Mmm-hmm." She wiggled two fingers at him. A loving expression replaced the sorrow of a moment earlier. "Two. Eight and six."

"You were always good with kids." Adam tossed his hands in the air, grinning. "Look at me. I'm a prime example of your skills and know-how."

"Babysitting you came easy. You were always sweet."

"Thank you," he answered, with a slight bow of his head. "What do you do for a living? I remember you were going to be a nurse. Did that happen?"

"Yes, it did," Wynn answered, picking up her sandwich and taking a bite. "I finished my degree at Michigan State. After I got my license, I decided to go back to school and get my master's and I became a nurse practitioner."

"Nice. Where do you work?" Adam asked, then polished off the last of his hot dog and reached for his soda.

"I worked for Harper Hospital for a while. When my husband and I separated, I needed a regular schedule. I wanted to spend more time with my sons. So I kind of changed careers. Now I run my own nursing and home health care agency. I provide pool nurses to the hospitals and CNAs to seniors."

"CNA?" Adam questioned.

"Certified nursing assistant," Wynn explained.

He smiled approvingly. "Entrepreneur. Very impressive."

A hint of red crept into Wynn's cheeks as she muttered modestly, "Something like that. What about you? Are you still in the Detroit area?"

"No. I moved to West Bloomfield. Bought a house and I commute downtown to work."

"How about your mom and dad? What's going on with them?" she asked before taking a bite out of her sandwich.

"They split up a few years ago."

Wynn gasped. "No way!"

"Way," he responded. "Believe me, it shocked the hell out of me, too. It was hard for me to keep my mouth shut. They sold the house, split the profits, and Dad moved to South Carolina. Mom lives in Farmington Hills."

She leaned back in her chair. "Really! I would never have thought your parents would separate. They seemed so happy together. I can still remember how your family and mine celebrated birthdays together. And they were always going places with my parents."

"I remember that," Adam admitted, still feeling a twinge of betrayal at his parents' separation and divorce. It didn't seem possible that the two people he loved the most couldn't find the common ground to live together and had instead chose to call it quits. "Yeah, they did. Like you said earlier, things happen. People change. What about your parents?"

"They sold their house on Outer Drive and moved to Beverly Hills. They live a few blocks from my place."

His eyebrows rose and nodded approvingly. "That's handy."

"Yes, it is. Mom's a lifesaver. She picks my boys up from school and stays with them until I get home from work."

"Hey! What about your sister? Where is she these days?"

"California."

Adam sighed. "Don't tell me she's pursuing an acting career."

She laughed. "Oh, come on. You were way too young to remember how goofy Kayla was."

"I remember," he replied.

"Originally she moved west to act. But, she met her true love and soul mate and got married. She has five girls and they own a horse ranch."

Laughing heartily, Adam shook his head. "She was always the one doing her own thing."

"Yeah, you got her. Let's talk about you for a minute. I mean, look at you. You're a grown man with a great career and a life of your own. You're not my little Adam anymore."

No. I'm not, he thought, deciding to get to the point. "We have to get together."

"That would be nice," Wynn answered. "Why don't you come to my place for a barbecue? Bring your girlfriend and I'll cook for you guys."

"No girlfriend right now," Adam responded quickly as the image of Vivian Manning, his colleague and dinner companion, entered his head. Taking Vivian anywhere constituted a problem. Her jealousy and demanding ways had caused Adam to put an end to their blossoming relationship before it got too intense. Shaking off those thoughts, he returned to the present. Vivian was the last person he wanted Wynn to meet.

"A barbecue would be great." Adam opened the briefcase at his side and removed a business card and fountain pen. He turned the card over and scribbled a note. "Here's my home number. When you decide on a date and time, give me a call."

She smiled, finishing the last of her tea. "Will do."

"How about you? Can I get one of your cards?"

"Sure," Wynn muttered, putting down the styrofoam cup and wiping her hands on a napkin before reaching for her purse. She extracted a card, using two fingers to keep from smearing it with mustard from her sandwich, and handed it across the table to Adam. "My office and cell phone are listed."

Adam accepted the card, glanced at the numbers, and slid the card into the breast pocket of his suit jacket.

They finished their meal with a minimum of conversation. Leaning back in his chair, Adam watched her, enjoying spending time with her.

After a few minutes, Wynn checked her watch, stood, and took his empty paper plate and her own. She moved to the trash container, discarded the items, and returned to the table.

"Well, I have to get back to work," she announced, gathering up her purse.

He stood and picked up his briefcase, smiling down at the woman. "Wynn, it was great to see you. Don't be a stranger." He tapped her purse. "Call me."

"I will," she promised softly.

Adam grabbed her hand and squeezed it reassuringly, promising, "I'll talk to you soon."

Wynn took a step away and Adam released her hand. She headed for the West Grand Boulevard exit. For the second time that day, he enjoyed watching the seductive sway of her hips as she made her way to the exit. At the door, Wynn turned and waved before leaving the building through the exit.

He reached for his briefcase and strolled across the lobby in the opposite direction. Thoughts of Wynn Evans filled his head as he stepped onto West Grand Boulevard and made his way across the street to the parking lot.

Wynn looked beautiful. Everything Adam

would have expected and more. He pulled the card from his pocket and glanced at it, taking a look at her business address and telephone number. *You'll be hearing from me,* he promised silently, sliding the card back into his pocket.

Chapter 2

Wynn and her assistant, Helen Jenkins, worked steadily throughout the afternoon. Between interviewing potential employees and matching several customers with clients, Nursing Solutions had a very productive and financially successful day.

Around five-thirty Wynn stuck her head out of her office and looked around the empty office lobby. Mozart's Piano Sonata in C Major swirled around the outer office. "Is it safe to come out?"

Laughing, Helen ran her hands over her silver, shoulder-length braids, allowing them to slip through her fingers and feather around her shoulders. "Yes, finally."

Tired from their busy schedule and happy to see the end of the workday, Wynn sauntered across the room with a bottle of Evian water. She opted to sit on the beige-and-rose-striped chair next to Helen's cherrywood desk instead of the rose three-cushion sofa against the opposite wall. Wynn massaged the tight muscles at the back of her neck, kicked off her shoes, and dug her nylon-covered toes into the plush beige carpeting. "This has been one busy afternoon."

"Yes, it has. Good for business though."

"True." Wynn reached for the applications on Helen's desk and quickly sifted through them. "Do me a favor."

"Sure." Helen reached for a scratch pad and pencil.

"When you get in tomorrow, call Harper University Hospital and talk with Purchasing. I had a call from Linda while I was at lunch." She returned the files to Helen's in-box, twisted the cap off her water, and took a long swig. "The Nursing Office is scheduling for the weekend and wants to know who we have available to work twelve hours in CCU."

"Will do." Helen scribbled down Wynn's instructions. "Anyone in particular you want to send?"

"Don't send any newbies. We don't know enough about them. Send our old faithfuls."

"Got you." Yawning, Helen rose from the desk and made a beeline for the coffee machine. "I need one final dose of caffeine before I make the trip home." She filled her mug with the last ounces from the pot, hit the Off button, and reached for the cream and sugar.

"I know how you feel. I'm whipped. But the day has been good. Business has really picked up."

"You're right about that. Let me get back to something you said earlier. Tell me about your lunch date."

Wynn's heart lurched in her chest. Adam was still forbidden territory. She felt conflicted over the boy she remembered and the man she met today.

A mental image of Adam materialized. As if he were standing in front of her, she felt his intense gaze warming her insides and causing all manner of havoc within her.

This particular question didn't surprise her coming from Helen. In some ways, Helen and Wynn were closer then Wynn and her mother.

"It wasn't a lunch date, per se. More like a casual encounter that included lunch. After my meeting with Ford Hospital, I stopped at the New Center One building for a sandwich. While I was standing in line, I felt this tap on my shoulder and this guy asked if I was Wynn Evans who grew up in the Rosedale Park area."

Helen leaned back in her chair with her coffee, softly blowing on the streaming brew between sips. "Interesting. You're getting picked up in sandwich shops. Tell me more."

Laughing, Wynn picked up a red file folder and lightly slapped Helen on the wrist. "Cute."

Grinning, Helen shrugged. "It's just an observation. Seriously, who is he?"

"A kid I use to baby-sit while I was in high school."

Gasping, Helen lowered her mug. "You're kidding."

"Nope."

"You haven't been a teenager for a long time."

Wynn moaned. "Tell me about it. Twenty-five years to be exact."

"What's this guy doing now?"

Wynn found it impossible to keep the dreamy

expression off her face. "He works for the auto companies."

"Doing what?"

"Adam's an attorney."

"Wow! That must be something. Is he married? Does he have kids? A live-in girlfriend that we should kill off?" Helen asked.

"No. No. And why would I want to kill his girlfriend?"

"So that you can take her place, silly," Helen answered as if it were the most logical thing in the world.

"You are too silly."

"Oh, come on. Single with a great career. Sounds like love to me."

Wynn made a buzzer sound. "Wrong answer. I'm not looking for love in the right or wrong places."

"What about sex with a cute, fun guy?"

"No, thank you."

"Wynn, we've had this conversation before. I know Jim treated you like crap. But you can't judge all men by his standard." Helen sneered. "Actually, Jim didn't have any standards. Which is why you're not with him today. I'd say that's a good thing."

"Helen!"

"Okay. Okay. I'll leave Jim alone. But seriously, this Adam sounds nice, interesting. Hell, at least he bought you a meal."

"And he's almost fifteen years younger than me. I'm way too old for this very cute baby."

"Don't think that way," Helen said, and then

swallowed the last of her coffee. "You know what they say. Raise them the way you want them."

Groaning, Wynn shook her head. "Thank you. I really needed that visual."

"Don't dismiss it."

Wynn sighed. "Anyhoo, Adam bought me lunch and we caught up on old times and our families. I gave him my card and he gave me his. If we're lucky we might get some business from the automaker." She shrugged. "You never know."

"So what does this paragon look like?" Helen asked, rising from the desk and locking the black metal file cabinets.

A little smile touched Wynn's lips. "I never use this phrase because teenagers use it so often but it fits Adam. He's hot." She said with a little smile on her face. "Handsome. He's tall, dark chocolate skin with light brown eyes with a hint of hazel. I remember his dad's eyes were the same color." She took another swig of water. "Close cut dark hair. Eye candy."

"Do you think he'll call?"

"I don't know," Wynn admitted, silently thinking it was a long shot at best. "I'm not betting on it. But, if there's business to be had, hopefully Adam will remember us."

"No. That's not what I'm talking about." Helen returned to her desk.

Confused, Wynn stared at her confidante, friend, and employee. "What?"

"Do you think he'll call and ask you out?"

Her heart jumped in her chest. Would he? Probably not. "Hello. Did you hear me a few minutes ago? I'm almost fifteen years older than he is. I'm sure a hottie like Adam has plenty of women to keep him company. He doesn't need or want a divorcee with two small children."

"How do you know? You might be just what he wants. Besides, you need an adventure."

Laughing, Wynn shook her head. "And that's all it could be."

The telephone interrupted Wynn's next comment. She glanced at the console. "Oops! You forgot to switch to voice mail."

Helen waved her away as she picked up the receiver. "No biggie. I'll take this one and then switch over. Nursing Solutions. How may I direct your call?" There was a pause as she listened to the caller. One arched eyebrow curved sharply. "Just a moment. Let me check to see if she's available."

Quickly hitting the red Hold button, Helen turned to Wynn with a big cheesy grin on her lips. "It's him."

Shuffling through a pile of mail, Wynn glanced up. "Who?"

"Your babysitting kid is on the phone."

Oh Lordy! Wynn thought. Gathering her composure, she rose from the chair and moved across the room. *Maybe this is about doing business together.* "I'll take it in my office."

She entered her office, picked up the phone, and sank into her chair. "Wynn Evans."

"Hey, Wynn."

She thought she was ready to talk but the sound of his sexy drawl sent shivers coursing down her spine. "Hi, Adam. What can I do for you?" *Is that my voice?* She wondered. *I sound so normal. Yet I feel as if I might crumble into a zillion pieces right here, right now.*

"First of all, I wanted you to know how much I enjoyed seeing you today. A little old school time together made my day."

"Mine, too."

"Second, let's not wait for a barbecue," he said confidently. "So, how about dinner?"

Her heart kicked into a gallop. Dinner with Adam? Seeing each other had been a great experience, but she wasn't sure what dinner with him really meant.

"Wynn?" he prompted.

"I'm here."

"It got real quiet on your end. Did you hear me?"

"Yes."

Adam chuckled. "In case you didn't realize it, I'm waiting for an answer."

"When?"

"Saturday night."

Jim had the boys this weekend. No problem with babysitting. Why not? There weren't any outstanding obligations holding her back. Except this nagging feeling that there was something more behind Adam's invitation.

Taking a reckless leap, Wynn answered, "That would be nice."

"Great! I thought you might like to go to Seldom Blues for dinner."

Wow! She mouthed the word silently. Seldom Blues was no greasy spoon. It was one of Detroit's premiere and very expensive jazz and supper clubs. Once a year, she took Helen out to celebrate the success of the company.

"It sounds wonderful. What time?"

"Mmm. I'm going to make reservations for eight. So, I'll be at your place around seven-thirty."

"Good! I'll see you then. Bye."

"Bye. Oh, Wynn?"

She returned the receiver to her ear. "Yes?"

"Thanks. I'm looking forward to seeing you."

"Me, too." As soon as the words were out of her mouth, Wynn realized that she meant them. She liked Adam. Always had. And she was looking forward to learning more about his life.

Wynn glanced up from the telephone to find Helen in the doorway with a knowing expression on her sepia brown face. "What?"

Folding her arms across her chest, Helen barely suppressed a grin. "Nothing. I'm glad you're going out for a change."

That silver-haired devil didn't fool Wynn. "Mmm-hmm."

"So." Helen sauntered into the room and slid into the empty chair, facing the desk. "Where's he taking you?"

"Seldom Blues."

Wynn held her breath, waiting for Helen's over-the-top reaction. The older woman didn't disappoint. She whistled long and loudly. "My. My. The babysitting kid has money and he's willing to spend it on you. Nice."

"Possibly, I don't know. It could all be because I used to take care of him." She grabbed her purse out of the bottom desk drawer and reached for her briefcase, resting on the floor next to her desk.

"Anyhoo, Saturday night I'm going to have a great dinner with an old friend."

Helen opened her mouth to say more. Before the words formed on Helen's lips, Wynn halted her with her hand. "No. It's not anything more. I'm a forty-three-year-old divorcee with two kids. Adam's thirtysomething. It's not that kind of dinner. And trust me. He's not that into me."

"What kind of dinner is it? Men don't spend chunks of money on their former babysitters. He's looking to impress you."

"And why would he want to do that?"

"Maybe Adam likes what he sees. And he wants you to see him as a man. A single eligible man."

Ignoring Helen's comments, Wynn slung her bag over her shoulder and started for the door. "Oh! Look at the time. My kids will be looking for me. Mother has her yoga class this evening, I'd better hurry. See you tomorrow."

"Wynn?"

"Yes?"

"You can act like you don't hear me all you want. But I'm pretty sure Saturday night, Mr. Adam Carlyle is gonna show you a thing or two." Helen followed Wynn out of the office and into the reception area. "Have a good evening. I'll lock up."

Yeah, Wynn thought. *The only thing I have going with Adam is the years when I babysat him.*

Wynn marched across the room and out of the office. She shut the door, and started down the hall to the stairwell, and exited the building. As she approached the vehicle, she hit the remote and opened the car door, slipping behind the wheel to start the engine.

The best thing she could do was enjoy the evening with Adam. It wasn't often she got the chance to spend time with a handsome, younger man who wanted to spend money on her. Wynn planned to enjoy her evening with Adam at Seldom Blues and forget about everything else.

Chapter 3

The melody of Alexander Zonjac's jazz flute serenaded the restaurant patrons as Wynn and Adam stepped through the entrance of Seldom Blues restaurant and approached the hostess station.

"Reservation for Carlyle," Adam stated with confidence, resting his hand on the lower portion of Wynn's back. A black dress caressed her curvy figure. The bodice fitted against her breast and waist and flared into a full skirt. His fingers moved seductively against the silk fabric covering her back.

"Good evening, Mr. Carlyle, ma'am." The young woman gathered three leather-bound folders. "Your table is ready. Please step this way."

Wynn and Adam trailed the hostess along a dark blue hallway, past the central dining room and stage to a separate curved corridor.

Surprised, Wynn glanced back at Adam with a question in her eyes. Adam's encouraging hand at the base of her spine urged her forward.

The hostess halted at a frosted glass door

etched with a swirling pattern. "This is our River Room," she announced, opening the door and stepping back. Adam and Wynn entered. The young woman placed menus and a wine list on the single table set for two. "Enjoy your meal." With a smile, she turned toward the hallway, shutting the door softly behind her.

Amazed, Wynn moved around the elegantly decorated room. Blue, tan, and cream created the central color scheme for their private quarters. Wynn strolled around the room, examining and touching every item. She admired a painting of a trumpeter and ran a gentle finger across a silver twisted metal wall hanging.

Watching her, Adam stood near the table and shoved a hand inside the pocket of his trousers.

"This is beautiful," Wynn said.

"I thought you might like it."

"I do." Wynn glanced out the window. The room faced the Canadian border, providing a spectacular view of downtown Windsor. Lights from the business district glittered off the Detroit River. Casino Windsor's white structure loomed large and majestic on the water's edge, facing the Detroit shoreline.

Wynn moved across the room toward the man. She halted several feet away. "You sure know how to 'wow' a girl."

"I aim to please." He offered up a gentle smile and asked, "Are you?"

"Very."

"Good. I plan to make certain the evening stays that way," he promised, reaching for her hand.

Adam led her around the table, helped her

into her chair, and then took the seat opposite hers. Her gaze swept over her dinner companion. Adam's aura practically bragged of wealth and power. Dressed in a raven silk jacket and matching trousers, he looked absolutely gorgeous tonight. A cream cashmere V-neck sweater provided a splash of color and a glimpse of dark hair generously sprinkled across his chest.

He leaned back in his chair, studying the wine list. "Is there anything in particular you'd like for a cocktail?"

"No. I'll leave that decision to you."

"I appreciate that," he replied, perusing the wine list before setting it aside. His gaze did a lazy slide from the top of her shiny auburn head, slid lower, and lingered on the swell of her breasts above the bodice of her black silk dress. Something intense flared in his eyes, causing Wynn's nipples to tighten in response. His gaze returned to her face. A broad smile of approval spread across his face. "You look beautiful."

"Thank you." Pleased and a bit nervous, she focused on his face. Yes, Adam had grown into one striking man. One question lingered in her mind: Why had he chosen her company tonight? Wynn understood her potential and limitations. Honestly, she knew that she paled against the current flock of twenty- and thirty-something women who would kill for a chance to get close to a man like Adam.

A tap on the door caused those thoughts to dissipate. A gentleman dressed in a black suit, white shirt, and royal blue tie entered with a crystal water pitcher in hand. "Good evening. Welcome to Seldom Blues." He crossed the carpeted floor and filled their water goblets before turning to Adam. "It's good to see you again, Mr. Carlyle. How have you been?"

"Very well. How about you, Eric?"

"Great!" He moved around the table, stopping next to Wynn's chair. He shifted the silverware from under the napkin and shook out the linen, draping it across Wynn's lap.

"It's getting close to your wedding date." Adam picked up his water goblet and took a drink. "Is everything under control?"

"Three weeks," Eric replied.

"I wish you and Amelia the best."

"Thank you. We appreciate it."

Listening to this exchange, it became obvious to Wynn that Adam frequented Seldom Blues on a regular basis. She tucked that thought away for future examination and turned her attention back to the men.

Hands linked behind his back, Eric asked, "Have you had a chance to review our wine selection?"

"Yes." Adam handed the list to the server. "We'll have a bottle of champagne. Also, two lump crab cakes for an appetizer."

Nodding slightly, Eric complimented, "Excellent choices, Mr. Carlyle." He started to the door. "I'll be back in a moment with your wine."

The beat of Ramsey Lewis's piano softly filled the room. Adam placed his hand over hers, caressing the tender skin with his thumb. "Thanks for coming out with me."

Uncertain what all of these soft caresses truly

meant, she eased her hand from under his and placed it in her lap. *Time to start the small talk. Keep things light,* she thought, "Thanks for asking. You seem to know the staff here pretty well. Do you come here often?"

"Often enough. Gautier's offices are in the RenCen," he explained. "We do a lot of business in here."

"How long have you worked for Gautier?"

"Reynolds hired me right out of law school. Actually, once I accepted the position, I moved to Paris for a couple of years."

"Wow! Paris! What are you doing back in Detroit?"

"I missed my home. Don't get me wrong; Paris was exciting and fun. It's one of those once-in-a-lifetime adventures. But there's nothing like your mom's home cooking, and living in your own country or sleeping in your own bed."

"I know what you mean. It's a comfort zone you need to cross every once in a while."

"Exactly."

Before he could add another thought, there was a light tap on the door and then Eric returned with a bottle and a silver wine carafe. He held the bottle for Adam to see. Adam gave his approval with a quick nod. Eric twisted off the wire and pushed the cork from the bottle. Champagne flowed freely from the top and into the carafe. After a second, the foam morphed into liquid and he poured wine into Adam's glass. "Here we are."

Adam lifted his glass and took a sip. Nodding a second time, the young man filled Wynn's glass.

Eric returned the bottle to the carafe and

headed for the door. "I'll be back in a minute or two with your crab cakes."

Adam lifted his glass. "Let's make a toast."

Toast? Should they be making toasts? "Sure. What are we toasting to?"

"The start of a new friendship."

Friends? Maybe. She picked up her glass and touched it to his. "To old buddies and new friendships."

"Excellent," he stated, sipping from his glass. "Topic change. Who'd you marry?"

Wynn felt heat flood her cheeks. "I don't know if you remember him. He used to come to your house when I baby-sat. Jim. Jim Harrison."

"The jock?"

Nodding, Wynn answered, "You remember him?"

"Yeah. I never liked him." Adam sneered. "He always treated me like a pest."

"I'm sorry."

Adam waved away her apology. "No problem. Trust me. I'm way over that."

Wynn smiled.

Concern replaced the laughter on Adam's face. "What happened?"

She stared out the window, feeling her good cheer disappear. Honestly, she didn't know how to answer Adam's question. "I don't know. Things were good for a while and then one day our marriage changed. We didn't seem to like similar things. Jim and I couldn't watch a television show together without arguing. The kids didn't help our situation. Jim ignored them and me. About two years ago, he moved out and in with his secretary. I'm almost embarrassed to admit it." Her voice trembled. "My family became a cliche."

"I'm sorry. I didn't mean to bring up bad memories."

"That's all right. I could never regret having my boys." Wynn waved her hands in front of her. She gave herself a mental shake. "Let's talk about you. No girlfriend. No kids. How come?"

"Well, I'm not gay if that's what you're asking."

"I didn't think so. You're very handsome. Upwardly mobile, and from everything I've seen, you've got your life headed in the right direction. What's going on?"

"Fair question. I was involved with someone for a while. I thought we would be together."

"And?" Wynn prompted.

"It went something like what happened to you. One day everything was fine and a couple of months later we were headed in different directions."

"I think I know what you mean."

"Let's talk about more interesting stuff. Tell me about your boys."

"That's my favorite topic. They're six and eight. I'm very lucky. They're good kids. I've got one math whiz and one artist. Both are interested in Xboxes, basketball, and the movies. My weekends are spent at the Boys Club, movie theatres, and the mall."

"It sounds like you've got two winners. But I'd expect nothing less from you. Is your husband involved with them?"

"Some. Not as much as I'd like. I know they miss their dad and would like to see more of him.

But I can't help that. It's Jim's choice whether he plays a part in their lives."

"Trust me, they do need it. Having that male role model in a boy's life is so important. It's good that you keep them involved with different programs; it'll pick up the slack of what your husband isn't doing."

"Ex-husband."

"Sorry."

"No problem. It's good to hear from a male point of view."

Adam shrugged. That sensual flame blazed from his eyes and she responded to it.

"Anytime. What do you do for yourself? How do you relax and enjoy yourself?"

Her heart began to race in her chest. *Get a grip,* Wynn warned silently. *Just because you haven't been with a man in two years doesn't mean you should fall all over the first man that shows you any attention.*

"I don't have a lot of free time," she admitted. "Between the kids and Nursing Solutions, that's my life."

"We're going to have to change that."

Before she could respond, the door opened and Eric appeared with plates filled with crab cakes and a black wire bread basket. The aroma of seafood, onion, and a hint of garlic made her mouth water.

Grinning at her, Adam said, "You're going to love this. It's almost impossible for me to come here and not order crab cakes."

Eric placed the food in front of them before topping off their wineglasses. After returning the champagne bottle to the carafe, he headed to the door. "I'll come back and take the rest of your order in a few minutes. Take your time and enjoy."

Adam reached for the wire bread basket and offered it to Wynn. She chose one of the softly steaming rolls and buttered it. "Let's enjoy the rest of the meal and leave the family history for another time," Adam suggested.

"Sounds good to me."

Once dinner concluded, Adam and Wynn returned to the main dining room and occupied a table near the stage. Richard Elliot performed a series of selections from his repertoire. For Wynn, this was a special treat because she seldom got a chance for an adult evening without her children. She kicked back and had a great old time.

Curious gazes from other patrons rested on them throughout the evening. Their scrutiny made Wynn feel a bit uncomfortable and on display. As the evening progressed and the music lulled her, she relaxed and forgot the people around them and concentrated on Richard Elliot's sax.

Adam rested his arm on the back of her chair and she found herself leaning close to him. He ordered drinks and they sipped sparkling wine while listening to the music.

On the ride home, they chatted about their shared past and what plans they had for the future. Wynn had to admit, she hadn't enjoyed herself so thoroughly for a very long time.

When they reached her house, Adam got out of the car, followed her up the walk and halted at the green front door. Wynn fished her house keys from the dark interior of her purse before facing Adam. The expression in his eyes made her stomach flutter. "W-w-would you like to come in for a cup of coffee?" she stammered.

"No. It's late." He grabbed her hand and linked their fingers. "Tonight was great. Thanks for saying yes."

"Thank you." Wynn smiled. "I don't get many opportunities to go out without my kids. It was fun."

"We'll have to change that. Check your calendar and let's shoot for something next week."

Wynn hesitated. Did she really want to do this again? Was she asking for trouble? "We'll see." She took a step closer and raised up on her tiptoes, placing a steadying hand on his shoulder. Wynn kissed his cheek and then turned away, fumbling with her keys.

Suddenly, Adam's hand encircled her arm. He spun her around to face him, taking a step closer. Surprised, she gasped, gazing into his face. Her heart almost stopped in her breast. His eyes were dark with intent.

He's going to kiss me. And she wanted him to. All evening they had tiptoed around each other, trying to gain their footing. Now Adam was taking charge and she liked it. He was an attractive man who excited Wynn.

Ohmigod! Helen was right. *Adam is interested in me,* Wynn realized.

His head lowered and his hand settled on her cheek, tilting her chin up. He claimed her lips in a tender but passionate kiss.

All of her talk of friendship and reacquaintance disappeared the moment Adam's lips touched hers. It was obvious that he wanted to be more than a casual friend. And at this moment she wanted nothing more than to learn the taste and texture of his kiss. The soft tangling of tongues shot through Wynn, surprising and thrilling her. Adam tasted of champagne and seafood. His kiss spoke of desire and passion. She raised her arms and wrapped them around his neck, pressing her body against his.

After a moment, he released her, looking deep into her eyes. He gave her one additional tender kiss before saying, "Good night. I'll give you a call later this week."

Nodding, she focused on opening the door and getting inside the house. All of a sudden she was all thumbs and couldn't get the door open. He removed the ring from her hands and inserted the proper key into the lock. Within seconds the door was open. Wynn hurried inside and entered the code to deactivate the alarm system.

Adam gave her arm a quick caress before jogging down the walkway to his car.

Wynn stood in the doorway. She felt the weight of his lips on hers and a lingering hint of his cologne rose from her dress while she waited for him to drive off. She turned away when she could no longer see the red from his taillights.

Content in a way she hadn't felt in a long while and filled with giddy nervousness, Wynn shut and locked the door before activating the alarm. She climbed the stairs to the second level, made her way to her bedroom, and crossed the floor to sink onto the comforter. She crossed her legs and removed her earrings, dropping them on the nightstand next to the bed.

Her gaze fell on the framed photo of her children. What would they think of their mother's date?

This had been a night of surprises. The last thing she expected was to find such passion with Adam. It had astonished her to learn that he wanted and expected more than friendship. Wynn drew her legs up on the bed and settled her back against the headboard. More important, what did she want from him?

Chapter 4

What am I going to do about Adam? Wynn wondered for the hundredth time as she removed a load of laundry from the dryer. *Hell, what am I going to do about the feelings he stirs inside me?* All morning a goofy grin kept appearing on her face whenever she allowed her thoughts to stray to Adam and the previous evening.

Wynn folded a dozen white T-shirts belonging to her son, Kevin, contemplating where this attraction might head. Yes, Adam was handsome and certainly prosperous. Yes, Wynn found him incredibly charming. And yes, if she were younger, she'd love to see where all of the attraction and sexual tension might lead. Someplace really enjoyable and fun, she felt certain. But she wasn't ten years younger.

Come on, woman. Get real. Why would someone like Adam want to be with her? Adam had the looks, money, and power to get anything and everything he wanted. Wynn had little to offer. All she had was herself and two children. On the flip side, Adam's world included the young and nubile women of today with their body adornments and tramp stamps.

The doorbell chimed as Wynn stuffed the boys' school uniforms into the washer. Surprised, she glanced at her watch. *Who in the heck is that?* She wondered, adding laundry detergent to the cold water and lowering the lid on the machine before leaving the laundry room.

Her heart sank when she opened the front door. *Not again,* she silently moaned.

"Hi, Mommy." Six-year-old Kevin dropped his overnight bag on the floor in front of his mother, wrapped his short arms around one of his mother's legs, and hugged tight.

Eight-year-old Jimmy shifted to Wynn's opposite side and duplicated his younger brother's gesture. "Hey, Mom."

Wynn wrapped an arm around each child, hugged them close, and kissed the top of each dark brown head. She beat down her irritation at her ex-husband and focused on her children.

"I'm hungry," Jimmy stated.

Laughing softly, Wynn thought, *That's no surprise.* "There's fruit on the counter in the kitchen. Where's your father?" She asked, finding it difficult to keep the exasperated note from her voice.

Jimmy jerked his thumb at the door. Wynn's ex-husband Jim Harrison sat in the Evans's driveway behind the wheel of his cherry Jeep Grand Cherokee. Her eyes focused on him as he climbed from the SUV and headed up the walk.

Both boys grabbed their canvas bags and moved past their mother toward the stairs.

"Hey! Hey! Hey! You know the drill," Wynn scolded in a stern voice. "Take your bags to the laundry room and empty the dirty clothes into the hamper."

"'kay," Jimmy answered.

Kevin nodded.

Both boys changed direction and headed for the back of the house.

Wynn listened to their soft murmurings as her sons did her bidding. Minutes later, Kevin emerged from the kitchen with a handful of small peanut butter cookies while Jimmy munched on an apple. The brothers made it down the long hallway to the den and then the theme music from the Teenage Mutant Ninja Turtles cartoons floated into the hallway.

Jim slithered through the door and landed in the foyer. "Hi. How you doin'?" He leaned down to kiss her cheek.

"Fine." Wynn took a hurried step back, avoiding any contact with him. They did not have that kind of relationship. "Whoa! What are you doing?" she asked.

"Saying hello," Jim answered.

"Do it from over there."

Jim always had an excuse for bringing the kids home earlier. Wynn wondered what tale he'd spin for today's early arrival.

"Let's hear it." She folded her arms across her chest. "What happened to three o'clock?"

Sheepishly, he shrugged, shutting the door after him. "Sorry."

Frustration mounted inside Wynn. Her voice registered impatience. "Well?"

"No food," Jim explained. "Besides, Jimmy and Kevin wanted to come home."

She let out a gush of hot air, dropping her hands to her sides. "Jim, this is your weekend. You knew they were coming. Why didn't you buy groceries?"

"The boys don't like what I have. Besides, it's Sunday. I know you cook a good dinner for them. Hey, there's an idea. Why don't we have dinner together? I think the boys would love to see us at the dinner table as a family." A hopeful gleam entered Jim's pale brown eyes.

Not today. Not ever again, Wynn thought. "What about Lorraine?"

Jim's face flushed a dull red under the maple brown of his skin.

Wynn smirked, enjoying his discomfort. He'd left his family for Lorraine. Wynn wondered if his face would turn the same shade of red as his Jeep if she asked a few more pointed questions. "How's the shop doing?"

This question was also met with silence. Interesting. Something wasn't right here. Jim's sports equipment shops had always been very profitable. This might explain why she hadn't received a child support payment in three weeks. She made a mental note to call her attorney and have Debo-rah check it out.

The doorbell chimed for a second time. *Saved by the bell,* Wynn thought, twisting the handle and opening the door.

A young man with curly blond hair and a gray uniform stood on her porch. *Keith* was stitched into the front of his shirt in yellow thread. He cradled a long white box under one arm. "Ms. Wynn Evans?"

"Yes." She glanced beyond him at the van from Viviano's Flowers parked behind Jim's SUV.

The delivery man thrust a clipboard and pen into her hands. "Sign here, please."

She complied.

He swapped the clipboard for the box. "Have a nice day, ma'am."

"Thank you. You, too," Wynn responded, shutting the door.

Brows drawn together in a frown, Jim studied the box. "What's that?"

"My guess would be flowers." Wynn tucked the box under her arm and moved down the foyer to the living room.

Jim followed, asking, "From who?"

Ignoring her ex-husband, Wynn sank onto the silver blue three-cushion sofa and dragged the red bow along the box and off the end. She pushed the top off and found long-stem roses garnished with baby's breath nestled in a bed of white, crispy tissue paper. "Ohh!" Wynn cooed, lifting a yellow rose to her nostril and inhaling its sweet fragrance. "These are beautiful."

"Where'd you get those? Who sent 'em?" Jim pushed the tissue paper aside to peek inside the box.

Wynn lightly smacked his hand away. "Your name wasn't on this."

His fingers touched the stem of each rose. "Ten. Eleven. You have cheap friends. There's only eleven roses. Couldn't even afford a whole dozen? Who does that?"

Wynn shut Jim up with a look. She recounted the flower and found that Jim was correct. There were eleven yellow roses. In addition, one long stem red rose rested among the yellow ones. She removed the scarlet flower, rubbed it against her cheek, enjoying the way the velvety petals felt against her skin.

An ivory envelope laid within the folds of the tissue paper. Wynn's hands shook with anticipation as she retrieved the note and opened it.

> *Wynn,*
> *Although we have plenty of shared history, I feel that we're just beginning to know each other. Yellow roses symbolize friendship and red is for passion. I believe we share plenty of both emotions. I enjoyed the evening. Thank you. I'm looking forward to another wonderful evening.*
>
> *Adam.*

Wynn smiled. *Adam, you are good. You know what to say to a woman while wooing her.* She tucked the card inside the pocket of her shorts and rose from the sofa, making her way to the kitchen with the roses.

Jim dogged her every step, assaulting her with questions. "Was it a client?"

"No," she responded.

"It's not your birthday. So I don't think your parents would have sent them." Jim hurried behind her. He leaned one hip against the sink and crossed his arms over his chest, running through a checklist. "What about your sister? Are they from her?"

"No."

"Who else would send you flowers?"

Annoyed by Jim's lack of tact and his annoying questions, Wynn turned to him, ready to read him the riot act. Out of the corner of her eye, she caught a glimpse of the beautiful spray of flowers and all of her anger dissolved. *I'm not going to let you destroy Adam's wonderful gift and my enjoyment of it.*

"None of your business," answered Wynn, reaching under her kitchen sink for a vase. She ran warm tepid water into the glass vase, placed it on the countertop, and dropped in a packet's worth of crystals to make the flowers last longer before arranging them in the vase.

Wynn smiled, thinking of last night. Adam was right. They had shared a beautiful evening, culminating in a series of passionate kisses. Her pulse quickened. She gazed up to find Jim's speculative gaze on her. Wynn didn't want him to know what was going on in her head.

Uncomfortable with his sharp assessing glance, she decided to put an end to it. "Since the kids are home, I'm sure you have things to do. Let me see you out."

"Nah. I've got time." To prove his point, Jim strolled slowly across the kitchen, opened a cupboard, selected a glass, and returned to the refrigerator. He added ice from the door dispenser and then filled the glass with water. Jim took his time, swallowing every drop. Once he finished, Jim placed the glass on the marble countertop. "I thought I'd stick around and spend a little more time with the boys."

"I don't see the point in that," she dismissed. "You had all weekend to be with your children."

Jim admitted, "They don't feel comfortable with me. Jimmy and Kevin are polite. But they don't want to be at my house."

"Maybe you should talk with them and learn more about them. Find out what they like. My boys are easygoing kids. It doesn't take much to please them. An afternoon tossing a ball or going to the park is all they require. They love that stuff and it doesn't cost much."

"This has nothing to do with money," Jim snapped.

"I never said it did."

For the third time in less than fifteen minutes the doorbell rang. Wynn shook her head and sighed. "Good grief. It's Sunday. I've had more company today than I normally have all week." She strolled down the hall to the front door and opened it. Peg Evans stood on the porch.

"Hi, Mom." Wynn stepped back. "Where's Daddy?"

"Home watching the baseball game."

Peggy Evans took a step closer and kissed her daughter's cheek. "I went to early service and decided to drop by."

"Come on in." Wynn pointed toward the back of the house. "The kids just got home."

"Is that the idiot's car?" Mom asked.

Wynn nodded.

"Mmm!" Peg Evans grimaced. "Never mind about him. My grandbabies are here."

"Yep."

"Let me go get my kisses." With purposeful

steps, Peg moved through the house on high-heeled feet and turned into the family room.

Wynn heard cries of pleasure from her children. "Nana!"

"Come give your Nana a hug and kiss."

"Where's Granddad?" Kevin asked.

"At home. You'll see him tomorrow. What are you watching?"

Jimmy answered, "Cartoons."

"Oh, you shouldn't watch mess like that. It'll rot your brain."

"Nana, no they won't!" Wynn oldest child responded in a logical tone.

"Well, it could. Your nana's going to have a cup of coffee with your mom and then I'll come back and sit with you for a while."

Peg stepped from the family room and followed Wynn to the kitchen. Wynn shook her head. Peg Evans was an anomaly to her daughter. The socialite spent much of her time at charity functions, always making a point to get her photo in the local metro section of the Detroit area papers.

"Jim." Peg nodded at the man from a safe distance. "I saw your truck outside. Where's your live-in love?"

Jim's cheeks flushed red under his brown skin. Smiling, Wynn watched the game, loving her mother's slice and dice of Jim.

"At home," he muttered, turning toward the window, pretending to study the foliage in the backyard.

Dismissing the man, Peg fingered the petals on the red rose. "These are gorgeous. Who are they from?" She turned to her daughter. "Wynn?"

Wynn strolled passed the counter and took a seat at the island. "Remember the Carlyles?"

Mom's forehead crinkled into a frown as she made the connection. "The family who lived next door to us on Outer Drive?"

"Yeah. Them. I ran into Adam in town a few days ago."

Her mother took a seat at the island and placed her Coach bag on the countertop. "Really! How are the Carlyles?"

Wynn eyed Jim. He stood listening to every word. His pea-size brain was working overtime. She turned in the chair to face her mother. "Adam's doing quite well for himself. He's an attorney for one of the auto companies."

"That's wonderful. What about his parents?" Peg scooted closer to the countertop. "How are they?"

"Oh! This was a surprise. They're divorced," Wynn replied.

Peg gasped. "No! I don't believe it. They seemed so devoted to each other. I wonder what happened."

"The news surprised me," Wynn admitted.

"So what about Adam?" asked Peg.

"Single. No kids. He lives in West Bloomfield."

Impressed, Mom's eyebrows rose. "Very nice. Wait a minute. You got all of this from one conversation?"

Now Wynn felt heat prick her cheeks. "No. Adam told me some of this when we ran into each other. But I learned the rest at dinner last night."

"Mmm," Peg mumbled, glancing back at the

bouquet sitting on the island. "And now you have roses. Interesting. Where did Adam take you?"

Wynn chuckled silently. This would rock her mother. "Seldom Blues."

"Oh! I love that place."

"Do you know they have a private dining room that faces the riverfront? It's beautiful."

"Oh my. Adam went all out," Peg muttered, playing with the strap of her purse. "I wonder why?"

"I think he meant to impress me."

Peg Evans absently tapped a nail against the counter's surface, a thoughtful expression on her face. "Why?"

"I'm not sure," Wynn hedged.

"You're not thinking of getting involved with Adam, are you?"

"No, Mom. We're friends. Don't make more of it than there is." Wynn turned away from her mother's penetrating gaze. *Boy, was that an understatement.*

Peg blew out a relieved puff of air. "Good! You two would definitely turn a few heads."

"Why, Mother? Because we make such a great-looking couple?"

Exasperated, Peg waved a hand at her daughter. "Oh stop, Wynn. You know what I mean. What would people think? You're what? Fifteen or sixteen years older than that boy?"

"Thirteen," Wynn corrected. "And he's a man."

Peg shrugged. "Whatever."

Until this moment, Jim had silently stayed on the sidelines, listening but not commenting. Now, he added his two cents' worth. "You can't seriously be considering going out with this guy. I mean, he's a baby compared to you."

Furious, Wynn stood, facing her ex-husband. "Let me walk you out."

Jim put down his glass, raising both hands in a deliberate act of surrender. "Don't shoot me. I thought this was an open forum."

"It's not."

Nodding, he left the room. Wynn started after him but her mother caught her hand.

"Don't get mad at Jim," Peg defended. "He's just considering how everything looks to an outsider."

"His opinion doesn't matter," Wynn stated in a fierce tone.

"Honey, you're going to have to think seriously about this." Peg moved to where her daughter stood and placed a reassuring hand on Wynn's shoulder.

"Mom, there is no this."

"How do you think a relationship will look to your friends? Your colleagues? Your children? You've got a business to run. Are you going to take Adam to business dinners with you? Introduce him as your boy toy?"

"First of all, Adam and I went out once." She wagged a finger at her mother. "One time. I don't understand why you are so concerned."

"Honey, I don't want you to make another mistake. You're still paying for this one."

Wynn shook her head and restated the question with a twist. "Don't you mean, what will your friends think?"

With a delicate shrug, Peg admitted, "That, too."

"Mother, leave it alone. Adam probably won't call me again."

"Then why are you so feisty about something that's not going to happen?" Peg tilted her head to the side and studied Wynn. "There's got to be a reason."

This conversation is over. Wynn reached for the coffeepot. *Whatever I decide to do with Adam is my business. No one else's.*

Wynn filled the coffeepot with water. After clearing her throat, she asked, "I've got some new specialty coffees. Would you like to try one?"

"That would be lovely," Peg answered, letting the conversation drop.

But the gleam in her mother's eyes made Wynn's stomach cramp. This wasn't over.

Chapter 5

Monday morning, Wynn hesitated outside the office to Nursing Solutions as she listened to Ramsey Lewis's piano notes floating from under the closed door. Wynn sighed, feeling her pulse accelerate. The moment she stepped through the door, the mother of all interrogation would begin and she wasn't sure she was ready for it. Helen wouldn't rest until she'd extracted every detail about Wynn's date with Adam.

Wynn squared her shoulders, turned the doorknob, and entered the room. The reception desk sat empty. Instantly, she searched the office for Helen. Wynn found the older woman, standing at the coffeemaker with a mug perched under the spout and a grim expression on her face as she waited for her mug to fill.

Wynn grinned, shutting the door. Helen didn't function well until she had her first cup of morning coffee.

"Mornin'." Helen slipped the glass coffeepot in place to catch the last drops of the brew.

"Good morning." Wynn strolled across the room to her door, entered her office, deposited her briefcase on the corner of her desk, and opened it. She extracted several folders and arranged them on her desk surface before flipping the calendar to Monday's date. She sank into her chair and pulled it closer to the desk.

Helen stood in the doorway, silently watching as she stirred her coffee. "I know you didn't think you were going to get away without telling me about Saturday night." The older woman moved farther into the room and took the guest seat next to the desk. Helen took a long swallow of coffee before placing the mug on the edge of the desk. "How was your date?"

Wynn tried to control her smile, but she lost the battle miserably. Surrendering, she shrugged, grinning like a fool. "Real nice."

Nodding, Helen stretched her legs in front of her and then crossed them at the ankles. "Tell me more."

How much did Wynn want to tell Helen? If she excluded anything, Helen would know. Sometimes she was like a bloodhound on the trail of an escaped convict. She always knew. "What do you want to know?"

"Did you go to Seldom Blues?"

Silently, Wynn nodded.

"Nice dinner?" Helen queried, eyebrows lifted.

Nice everything, Wynn thought, but answered, "Yes. Did you know there's a private dining room at Seldom Blue?"

"Really."

"Umm-hmm." Wynn leaned back in her chair,

visualizing the room. "It's called the River Room. Intimate. Almost seductive. I must say, it was quite the perfect experience."

"It sounds like Adam went all out to impress you," Helen surmised, bringing her mug to her lips.

"He did," Wynn admitted, remembering the hungry way Adam devoured her lips and how passion had flared between them. "I had a great time."

"What else did you two do?"

Boy, was that a loaded question. "After dinner we stayed for the show. Richard Elliot performed with Alexander Zonjac." Wynn's smile grew larger and brighter. "I really had a wonderful time."

"What time did you get home?" Helen asked.

"Near midnight."

"Ohh! Very nice."

"Actually, it was nice to go out without the kids and have the full attention of a handsome man." Adam's gorgeous face appeared in Wynn's mind. "Yeah. I enjoyed myself."

"You don't get many opportunities to escape your kids. Who had them this weekend?"

"Jim."

"Ooo!" Helen's face scrunched into a mask of disgust. "Couldn't you find anybody else to take care of them? Somebody with some sense. Hell, you could have called me."

Laughing, Wynn answered, "No. Besides it was Jim's weekend."

"I know," Helen said. "But your ex-husband is such an ass. You are too nice a person to have married a fool like him."

Wynn sighed and rested her chin on her fist. There was no love lost between Jim and Helen. The kids' father was the one person Helen refused to make any effort to be civil to.

She shrugged. "It's an old story. I fell for the football captain. I did my best during my marriage. It's a time I don't want to revisit. Now it's over and I can move on with my life. All of that was over a long time ago. I try to get on with him for my children's sake."

"That's exactly what you should do, and Adam is a perfect place to start." Helen took another long swallow of coffee.

Groaning, Wynn shook her head and opened the folder in front of her. *Here comes the lecture.*

Helen pushed the file shut. "Did Adam make a second date?"

"No."

"Wynn?" The older woman's eyes narrowed. She gave Wynn a second more thorough once-over. Wynn squirmed under the intensity of Helen's gaze. "What aren't you telling me?"

"He sent flowers."

"Excellent! What kind?"

Grinning, Wynn thought of the beautiful bouquet. "Roses. Eleven yellow long-stem roses and one red rose."

"A man with style. I like that. He'll call," Helen said confidently.

"Maybe."

"Definitely," Helen stated. "You need to think about what you're going to say. Actually, you should call him. Thank Adam for the flowers."

"I don't want to do that."

Frowning, Helen examined her boss. "What's going on in your head?"

Wynn fidgeted with the edge of her file. "There's issues."

"Yeah. And? Life is full of problems. That doesn't stop most people from doing what they want to do."

Wynn felt all of her insecurities and worries rise to the surface. "Come on. Look at me. I'm not sweet sixteen."

"Well, that's for sure," Helen agreed. "Neither is he. What's that got to do with anything?"

"There's thirteen years' difference between us. Do you believe someone like Adam could truly be interested in me?"

"Absolutely. That means the boy will have a lot of stamina."

Shocked, Wynn gasped. "Helen!"

"Come on. You're a beautiful woman. Lots of men have been after you. Some of our clients ask about your personal life. They want to know if you're married or seeing someone."

Wynn hissed. "It's none of their business."

"Whoa! Don't get huffy with me."

"Sorry. My life is complicated enough without this."

Helen frowned. "How so?"

"Adam's a VP at Gautiers. There's a lot of life ahead of him—"

"And you, too," Helen inserted, swallowing the last of her coffee.

Ignoring her assistant's comment, Wynn said, "What do I have to offer him?"

Shaking her head, Helen added, "Girl, you

have officially lost your mind." She put down her coffee mug, ticking off items on her fingers. "Number one. Stop worrying about the future. It'll take care of itself."

"I have to worry. I've got kids."

"Number two," Helen continued, "everyone gets first crack at you. The boys, your parents, and Nursing Solutions, even that old stupid ex-husband of yours."

"Not all of the time," Wynn defended.

"Jim gets too much of your time. What does Wynn need? Do you ever ask yourself that? When was the last time you did what you wanted? Put yourself first? I can answer that. Never."

"I have to be careful. Anything I do can affect my children."

Helen waved a dismissing hand at her boss. "Please. Your kids are fine. They'll be great no matter what you do. Think about yourself for a change."

"I don't know."

"Here's a bit of advice. Enjoy Adam. Let him enjoy you. Don't worry about the future or his motives. Carpe diem. Seize the day."

"Are you telling me I should make Adam my boy toy?"

"Nothing so crude. There's feelings between you. So it won't be just sex. Let go. Have fun."

"How do you know what I feel?"

Helen laughed, leaning back in her chair. "Girl, I know you too well. Adam would never have gotten to your front door if you weren't interested in him. You would have tossed his business card in the trash and never answered his calls."

"We do have a little bit of history."

"So." Helen stretched her legs out in front of her. "There's another reason. You wouldn't be fretting over what he feels and thinks about you. I know you. It's Monday morning. You'd be on the phone making cold calls, checking the newspaper to make sure our ad ran, not sitting here with me telling me about the lovely time you had Saturday night."

Wynn shrugged and then stated, "I like him."

Helen grinned broadly. "I know you do. But you're afraid to take a chance. There's nothing in life that doesn't come with a risk."

"I've had to put my family first."

"That's all well and good. It's time for you to have a little fun. What are you going to do about it?" Helen pushed the phone toward Wynn. "Call Adam."

"I don't know."

"Listen to me and listen good. This is not about love or marriage. It's more like comfort, closeness, and a whole lot of sex. Let go. Have fun. The future will take care of itself. Live in the present for a while. Now, what are you going to do?"

"Call Adam and thank him for the flowers."

Helen rose and patted Wynn on the shoulder before leaving the office and shutting the door after her. "Good girl!"

Wynn reached for her purse and removed her wallet. Adam's card was wedged between her American Express card and driver's license. She studied the card, turning it over and over in her hands.

Should she? Wynn tapped the edge of the card

against the top of her desk. Helen had a point. Why shouldn't she have a little fun? This wasn't a love match. Physical attraction—yes. Long-term commitment—no. Chances are that's all Adam wanted from her. Her thought shifted back to Saturday night. Adam had made her feel things she hadn't felt in a long time—maybe ever—and she missed and craved the closeness of a relationship.

No guts, no glory. Wynn picked up the receiver and dialed the number for his office. The telephone was immediately answered. "Office of the General Counsel. Tia speaking. How may I direct your call?"

For a moment, Wynn didn't know what to say. Did she have the correct number? She checked the card against the number appearing on the display. Yep. It was the right number.

"Hello?"

"Hi. I'm looking for Adam Carlyle."

"May I ask who's calling?"

"Umm. I'm Wynn Evans. Is Mr. Carlyle in?" God! *I feel like a fool,* she thought. *I bet lots of women call him.*

"Oh. Ms. Evans. Just a moment. Let me see if Mr. Carlyle has returned from his meeting. I'm sure he wants to speak with you."

The line went silent. Within seconds Tia returned. "Mr. Carlyle is still away from his office. I'll leave a message for him to call you when he returns."

Disappointed, Wynn swallowed loudly and left her number. "Thank you."

She hung up the phone and swiveled the chair to face the window, staring unseeingly into the bright morning. *Well, Lady Mae, you tried*. Maybe it wasn't meant to be. She reached for the folder and opened it, focusing all of her energy on the words in front of her. After several difficult minutes, Wynn's concentration returned.

The ringing of the telephone pulled her away from the work spread across the desk. She picked up the receiver and absently answered, "Wynn Evans. How may I help you?"

"I could think of a few ways," Adam responded in a sexy drawl that made something deep inside her quiver like a teenager on her first date.

He called back. Her heart kicked into a gallop as her hand tightened around the telephone.

"Hi," she whispered.

"How are you this morning?" he asked.

"Good. And you?"

"Busy. As usual. But let's not talk about that," he dismissed. "I want you to know how much I enjoyed Saturday night."

Wynn couldn't help smiling at his remark. "Me, too."

"Glad to hear it."

There was a moment of stiff silence and then Adam asked, "So, why did you call? Do you need something?"

Instantly, Wynn's thoughts returned to Saturday night. The feel of Adam's lips on hers. The heat of his body pressed against hers. *You*, she thought.

"Wynn?" he prompted, snapping her from her wonderful dreamy state.

Shaking her head, she replied, "I'm sorry. I

wanted to thank you for the lovely flowers. They're beautiful."

"You're welcome. I'm glad you liked them."

"Maybe I could repay you." She swallowed loudly and pumped up her courage.

"How so?"

"Dinner. This Friday night at my place."

Another long, uncomfortable silence followed. Maybe she'd misinterpreted the signs and body language. Her nerves screamed for him to say something, anything.

"That would be nice. But I've got another commitment."

"Oh," she muttered softly. Helen was wrong. He wasn't interested in her that way. Who could blame him? Wynn was so caught up in her own misery, she almost missed Adam's next comment.

"My secretary just received her bachelor's degree and is moving into a new position. We're having a celebration for her at Flood's. I have to go. Why don't you come with me?"

"You want me to go to the party with you?" she asked.

"Yes. Tia's great. She worked hard to get her degree. I think you'll have a lot of fun."

Her heart lightened and a smile spread across her face. "I have to check on a babysitter. Let me call my mother. I'll let you know this afternoon."

"You do that. I really want you to come with me."

And I really want to be with you, Wynn thought. "I'll give you a call later today."

Chapter 6

The driver parked the long, black limo on the corner. He jumped out of the driver's seat, rushed around the hood of the car, and opened the rear passenger door of the limousine. He extended a hand to Wynn. She took his hand, stepped grace-fully from the backseat, and stood on the sidewalk of St. Antoine and Lafayette Streets. Flood's Bar and Grill loomed large and foreboding in front of her.

Wynn giggled, remembering the shocked ex-pression on her mother's face when the chauffeur appeared on her doorstep and rang the bell. Peg Evans wasn't easily impressed. The society queen prided herself on being in the middle of every-thing and knowing how to handle herself in every situation. This scenario stopped her dead.

On the other hand, Wynn didn't know what to make of Adam's invitation. Had she made the right choice in attending this party? Should she be here? Did she and Adam have enough history for her to be invited to company parties? She stood under the Flood's sign, watching the passing traffic as the glittering lights from Greektown Casino winked suggestively at her from the opposite side of Lafayette Street.

Wynn smoothed a nervous hand over her outfit. "Thank you," she said to the driver, reaching inside her purse to remove her wallet.

The man took a step away from her, shaking his head. "No, ma'am. That's been taken care of. It's my job to make sure you arrive in good order." He extended his arm.

"Okay." She slipped her hand into the crook of his arm and allowed him to escort her through the bar's front door. Once inside he bid her good night and left the club.

I hope this works out, Wynn thought, clutching the strap of her purse in a death grip as she studied the crowd. Where should she go? The bartender might know something.

Music hummed through the club, creating a low buzz. Dancers moved to the primal beat of the live band. Tables were packed with customers, hooking up and separating, forming new alliances. Young business professionals populated the place on a Friday night. They mingled, danced, and merged into social groups. The dance floor lay beyond the central room.

With a gentle stroke of his finger along her arm, Adam drew her attention away from the crowd. Her skin tingled as her pulse raced from his touch. He kissed her briefly on the lips, sending her thoughts into a million different directions.

"Hey," he muttered close to her ear. His warm

breath caressed her cheek, sending a shiver of delight surging through her.

Sighing with relief, she smiled and answered softly, "Hi. I was just thinking about you."

"Good thoughts I hope," he said.

"Oh, yeah."

Wynn felt the warmth of Adam's gaze as it skipped along her frame, lingering on her breasts cupped in an empire style top in hot pink. He glanced lower, checking out Wynn's black Capri pants. Dark leather sandals covered her pink-painted toes. His heated gaze returned to her face and Adam gave her a sexy smile of approval.

"You look wonderful," he whispered in a husky drawl.

"Thank you," Wynn replied shyly.

"How was your ride?" Adam asked, brushing away the silver lock of hair falling into her eyes.

"Good. Riding in a limo is exciting. Thank you for the opportunity."

"You're welcome. I really wanted you to come. Plus, this way works out better for me. I got you downtown without leaving my meeting, and I get the pleasure of taking you home."

She examined the goings-on for a beat. "Where is everyone?"

"Private room in the back." He intertwined his fingers with hers and tugged her away from the doorway. "Come on."

Following him, Wynn strolled along the edge of the bar. "You like those private rooms, don't you?"

He grinned. "They can be handy."

Her eyebrows lifted suggestively. "Really?"

"Here. Let me show you."

Adam and Wynn picked their way through several rows of occupied wooden tables across from the main room to the back of the club. They moved down a long hallway and stopped outside a closed door.

"This is the place," Adam announced.

Panic, sharp and unexpected, roared through Wynn. Her transparent expression couldn't be hidden.

Adam frowned and gently ran his hands up and down her bare arms. "Chill! We're all friends here. Kick back and enjoy the evening. Eat, drink, and have fun. There's no pressure. Honest. That's why I invited you."

"I know," Wynn said, feeling foolish. "I feel like the new girlfriend going home to meet the family for the first time. I want everyone to like me and find me witty and charming."

"You're all of those things and more," Adam said. He took her lips in a swift, explosive kiss. The taste of him rattled her and sent coherent thoughts into the next century.

Grinning at Wynn, Adam held her hands. "FYI. The only person that matters in this group is me. And I like everything about you. So, come on. Let's do our thing and have some fun."

He opened the door and pushed Wynn inside ahead of him. Professionally dressed men and women filled the room. Many stood in groups, holding wineglasses or beer mugs as they conversed.

Adam steered her through the maze of people to a table. A pretty African American woman with light brown hair tied in a ponytail stood among a group of partygoers playing court to her. Wynn found herself mesmerized by the gold-green twinkle in the woman's eyes.

The woman studied Wynn for half a second and then grinned broadly. She stood, extending her hand. "Hi. I'm Tia Edwards. And you must be Wynn. It's nice to put a face with the voice."

Wynn instantly liked Tia. "Congratulations on your promotion. Thanks for inviting me."

Grinning, Tia waved her away. "You're welcome. Adam has said nothing but good things about you."

"That's good to know."

Adam, Tia, and Wynn stood at the table. The trio talked quietly, getting to know each other.

An attractive woman in a tailored two-piece rose-colored suit joined them. Her hair was pulled into a bun at the back of her head. The severe style accented her long, angular face and walnut-colored skin. She was beautiful. The woman stroked her hand down Adam's arm. "Hey, Adam."

He turned, removing the woman's hand from his shoulder. "Hi, Vi. Let me introduce you to my friend. Vivian Manning, Wynn Evans. Vi is one of the acquisition attorneys on my staff. She does a lot of traveling for the company."

For a moment, Wynn watched the pair, noting Vi's body language and familiarity with Adam. He stiffened when Vi touched him. Wynn sensed something more in Vivian's casual gesture. Were they more than colleagues? Did they have history together? Wynn couldn't tell from Adam's expression. But there was definitely something more.

For now Wynn was a guest and she planned

to play her part. "Nice to meet you," Wynn said, offering her hand.

Vi took her hand in a limp shake that lasted less than a second. She gave Wynn a smug smile and said, "Do you mind if I steal him for a moment?"

Confused, Wynn shook her head.

"What's up?" Adam asked, rubbing his hand up and down Wynn's bare arm.

"That Bradford business. I need a word with you."

Adam kissed Wynn's check and promised, "I'll be back in a minute."

Frowning, Wynn watched the pair walk away.

Tia studied Wynn's face for a second and then pointed to the opposite wall. "Can I get you something? There's food on the table against the wall. Open bar at the back of the room and lots of conversation and opinions flying around the place."

A gentleman dressed in an expensive pair of Armani trousers, cashmere loose-fitting sweater, and handmade leather shoes approached the group. Tia turned to him, asking, "Do you need me?"

"Nope." The man shook his head. Golden locks whipped across his cheeks. Fascinated by the sheer beauty of the man, Wynn stared. He was the most striking man she'd ever seen. Tall with an athletic build, he stood silently. His angular features would have been considered pretty on a woman, yet, he wore them well. It made him more alluring and appealing.

Tia gestured to Wynn. "Attorney Christophe Jensen, Wynn Evans."

"Pleasure," he replied in a slightly accented voice, kissing Wynn's hand.

"Chris just transferred to Detroit from the home office in France," Tia explained. "I'll be working with him once I find my replacement."

Adam returned, sliding an arm around Wynn's shoulders and pulling her against his side. "Hey. Stop with the French charm. You've got my secretary. Stay away from my girlfriend."

Everyone laughed. Wynn studied Adam. *Am I?* She wondered. Did he think of her as something more than friends? This was going to be an interesting evening.

Another man joined the group. "Hey, Adam. Who's the pretty lady?"

"They're all trying to charm you," Adam whispered into her ear. "This is Wynn Evans. Brennan Thomas is part of our advertising team." Frowning, Adam glanced around the room. "Where's your better half?"

Brennan pointed toward the door. "She's in her favorite place."

What was he talking about? Wynn wondered.

A few minutes later, Wynn understood. Krista Thomas entered the room. The young woman was approximately five or six months pregnant. Now Brennan's statement made sense. She strolled over to the group and looped an arm around Brennan's shoulder. "Hi."

Brennan stated. "Wynn Evans. This is my better half and soul mate, Krista Thomas."

Grinning, Krista said, "D-d-doesn't he say the sweetest things?"

"Very nice," Wynn answered.

Chapter 7

Wynn and Adam stood on the sidewalk outside Flood's, exchanging good nights with the last of the partygoers. "Where's your car?" Wynn asked.

Adam tipped his head to the flashing lights on the opposite side of the street. "Greektown Casino. I figured it was easier than dealing with Flood's little parking area."

"Oh." Wynn watched several Gautier employees head down the street to their cars.

Adam glanced at his watch. "It's a little after eight. Do you need to get home right away?"

Wynn shook her head. "My mother is with the kids. They're fine."

"Great." Adam laced his fingers with hers and tugged. "Come on."

They ran across Lafayette Street together. But instead of stopping at the valet station, Adam steered her past the line of cars to the entrance. He ushered Wynn through the doors and inside the building, stopping in the lobby. Jingles blared from every direction and lights flashed against the burgundy carpeting. Wynn stared at him. "What are we doing?"

"Playing. The night is young and we're going to hang out for a while. You need more fun in your life."

"Aren't you enough?" Wynn asked in a sassy query.

He stroked her cheek with his fingertips, sending a riotous shiver racing through her veins. "Yes, I am. For now, we're going to have a good time."

Wynn crossed her arms across her chest and stared back at Adam. "Have you been talking to my assistant?"

Frowning, he mumbled, "No. Why?"

"You sound just like her."

Chuckling, Adam reached into his trouser pocket and withdrew his wallet. He removed a hundred dollar bill and handed it to Wynn.

"What am I supposed to do with this?" She eyed the bill.

"Spend it."

"What!" She tried to push the bill back into Adam's hand. "No! This is too much. I'll use my own money."

"No. You won't. If I asked you to dinner, you wouldn't pay for your meal. This is my idea and you're out with me." He curled his fingers around hers, folding the money into her palm. "Relax. Use it. Enjoy. I'm going to."

Confused, Wynn turned the bill over and over in her hands. "Adam, I have some money with me. You don't have to spend your cash this way to impress me."

"I'm not trying to. I plan to play a few hands of blackjack and then head over to the roulette table for a few spins of the wheel. I want you to entertain yourself." He took her arm and led her farther into the casino. After a few quick steps she found herself seated in front of a slot machine with a white bucket in her lap. Adam removed the bill from her hand and loaded it into the slot machine. He took her hand and placed it on the one-arm bandit and pulled the level.

Worried, Wynn confessed, "I don't know about this."

"You don't need to know anything. Just have fun."

Multiple lights flashed, music played, the wheel spun, and a few seconds later five dollars were deducted from the hundred.

"It didn't work that time. Keep playing. I'll be back to check on you in a little while." Adam gave her a quick kiss on the lips before strolling off.

Uncertain what course of action to take, Wynn sat at the machine for a few minutes, staring blankly at the slot machine. Should she return the money to Adam or have fun like he insisted?

A woman with a bucket filled with coins approached Wynn and asked, "Honey, are you done here?"

Wynn shook her head and turned back to her machine. Adam told her to play and maybe she needed to. If she won any money, she'd give him back his hundred dollars. If she didn't win, she'd give him a home-cooked meal for his trouble.

For the next twenty minutes Wynn won, lost, and won again. She found herself ahead by twenty dollars. Wynn looked up to find Krista Thomas at her side with a small bucket of her own.

"Do you mind some company?" the pregnant

woman asked as she arranged her large bulk on the stool next to Wynn's.

· "Not at all." Wynn smiled. "What are you doing here?"

"Brennan wanted to play the craps table before we head home."

"Ah," Wynn muttered. "Adam's at the roulette or blackjack tables."

"They've probably met up by now," Krista said. "Brennan keeps telling me, we have to enjoy ourselves before the baby comes. Life is going to change drastically once junior makes his appearance."

"Brennan's right," Wynn stated. "I've got two boys and they have definitely changed my life."

"How old are they?" Krista asked, hitting the button on the console.

"Six and eight," Wynn replied, doing the same thing on her machine. The machine played loud music as it dispensed her winnings.

"They're at good ages."

"It can be. I think every age can be difficult. They present new and very different challenges. When are you due?"

"18th of September," Krista answered.

"You've still got a little time."

"Yeah. I'm going to need it. I haven't done anything with the baby's room. No shopping or baby purchases."

"Why not?" Wynn asked. "That's the fun part, especially with a first baby."

Krista shrugged. "I - I - I had a miscarriage before and I'm afraid to let things get too permanent."

"I'm sorry. But don't let that color what you do

now. You look pretty healthy to me. Enjoy your pregnancy."

"Thanks for the words of encouragement." Krista scooped the coins from the bin and dropped them in her bucket. "I need them."

"Give me a call. I'll help you with the baby's room. I haven't done anything like that in a while. I think it could be fun."

"Don't be surprised if I take you up on your offer."

"Do it. I mean it." Wynn realized that she did mean it. She liked this woman with her gentle voice and quiet demeanor.

"I'm a little scared about the whole labor thing," Krista confessed quietly. "But I'm really looking forward to having my own little person to love."

"I was very afraid with my first. Those fears quickly faded. Don't worry about labor. It's not the easiest thing, but you'll do just fine. Once it's over you have your baby."

"Yeah. That's what I keep hearing."

Wynn glanced at the woman's round belly. "Do you know what you're having?"

Krista shook her head. "We want it to be a surprise."

"That's how I was with Jimmy." Wynn noticed several people with their buckets combing the area for a machine. "We better focus on our machines before someone asks us to get up."

"You're right." Krista added twenty dollars to the slot and hit the button on the machine, and instantly the cards began to spin.

They slipped into a companionable silence as they played, enjoying the comfort of having someone they knew playing beside them. When Krista hit for fifty dollars, they both cheered.

Gentle and familiar hands massaged Wynn's shoulders. "How'd you do?" Adam asked.

"Not bad."

Smiling, he glanced into her bucket. "Good. Did you have fun?"

"Yea." Surprised by her answer, Wynn realized that she had indeed enjoyed playing the slots and talking with Krista. He'd been right. She did need to spend time playing with friends her age.

"How about a glass of wine before we head home?" Adam suggested. Glancing at Wynn's companion, he added, "For you a glass of milk."

"Gee, thanks." Krista giggled softly, collecting her winnings. When she rose from the chair, Brennan stood at her side, providing a helping hand.

"Stay here. I'll cash you out." Brennan reached for the bucket.

Krista eyed her husband suspiciously and held on to her winnings. "Can I trust you?"

Brennan pretended to be offended. A playful display of hurt feelings appeared on his face as he pressed a hand to his chest. "I'm crushed. Who do you sleep with?"

"You."

"Then I think you should trust me with your money. After all, you trusted me with your body and I believe it's the most precious thing you own."

"You know what to say to a woman." Krista leaned close and kissed Brennan on the cheek. "I'm sorry, sweetie."

"You should be," he offered in mock reproach. "I'll be right back."

"Wait up." Adam turned to Wynn. "Do you want me to cash you out?"

Wynn handed over the bucket. The women stepped away from the machines and waited for the men to return.

Minutes later, Adam and Brennan reappeared. Adam pressed the bills into Wynn's hand. Without looking at them, she shoved the money in her pants pocket.

The couples made their way through the casino to the row of restaurants at the rear of the first floor. After a few minutes of debate, they selected an eatery that served drinks and were quickly seated.

Adam ordered appetizers for everyone and then selected a bottle of wine for the alcohol-indulging group and an orange juice for Krista. They settled in for light conversation and food.

"Where do you guys live?" Wynn asked.

Brennan jabbed his thumb toward Jefferson Avenue. "Harbortown."

"Nice," Wynn said.

"We like it," Krista said.

They spent an hour or so discussing current events, life in Detroit, and several extra minutes on Gautier business. As they spoke, Wynn noticed how quiet Krista got and caught her eyelids lowering on her eyes before she shook off sleep and returned to the topic.

Brennan leaned close to his wife, speaking to her in quiet tones. He rose from his chair and helped his wife to her feet. After dropping several twenties on the table, he said, "I've enjoyed the evening. It's time to get this lady home to her bed."

Nodding, Adam rose and added money to what

was on the table. He reached out a hand and cupped Wynn's elbow, helping her to her feet. "It's been a good evening. We should do it again."

"I'm up for that. Let us know," Brennan replied.

Krista reached for her purse, hanging on the back of her chair. "We've got a busy day Saturday. Our nephew, Joshua, is turning three. We're all going to Chuck E. Cheese's for his party."

"Oh yes. I've done those and will probably have to do more," Wynn replied.

"Yeah. It's going to be quite a weekend. Joshua's fraternal grandparents and some of Steve's family will be driving here from Ohio. Some are going to be staying at our place."

Wynn slipped her hand through the crook of Krista's arm and the pair walked toward the door. "That's a lot of work for you. Are you sure about this?"

"I'll be fine. My sister-in-law Liz will come and help me. Liz and Steve live in the complex."

"Good. Don't overdo."

Smiling, Krista hugged Wynn. "I won't."

Wynn turned to Brennan. "It's been fun getting to know you guys."

"Call us. We're trying to get everything in before the baby arrives."

"It's time for me to get you home." Adam wrapped an arm around Wynn. They made their way to the front of the building and the valet brought the car around. He tipped the clerk before heading to I-75.

Chapter 8

Adam pulled into Wynn's driveway and switched off the engine. "Is that your mother's truck?"

Wynn shook her head. "No."

"Your mother must have company."

She eyed the brightly painted SUV. What was Jim doing here? He barely showed up when it was his weekend with the kids. And he never made pop visits to her home without calling first. "My mom drives a Lincoln."

"Nice."

"Yes. She's very much the social butterfly."

He glanced at the clock on the dashboard. "It's kind of late for company. Do you know who that truck belongs to?"

"Yeah," she answered in a dry tone. "That's my ex-husband's SUV." A wayward thought hit her. Fear shot through her. Maybe something was wrong with her kids. Instantly, she scrambled for the door handle. She turned the handle preparing to swing her legs out of the car and run up the walkway to the door.

Suddenly, the voice of reason took control. *Calm down. Mom would call you if something had happened to the kids. Peg Evans would never call Jim Harrison before informing you.*

Forestalling her, Adam grabbed Wynn's arm. "Don't get upset. Maybe your sons called their dad and invited him over. Boys need their father."

She shrugged. "Maybe so." Holding on to those words of logic, Wynn relaxed, contemplating how her mother would react to Adam in the flesh. She didn't really care. Adam was right. It was time to have some fun and enjoy. "You want to come in for coffee?"

"No. I don't want anything to drink. But I'd like to come in for a little bit. I'm not ready for our evening to end."

Wynn wanted to laugh out loud. Adam would stir up trouble. Big time. Peg Evans would have plenty to say about how things looked. What would her friends and family think of Wynn dating a younger man? During the course of the evening, Wynn had decided she wanted to take a chance on Adam. She knew Adam couldn't possibly love her and their future was limited, no marriage or happily ever after. But maybe she needed to have some fun and play like Adam suggested. Have her fling and then move on. Wynn planned to keep this little affair separate from her real life. Her sons could not get attached to this man. There wouldn't be an Uncle Adam. Whatever Adam and she did together, it wouldn't touch her children.

Grinning, she reached for the door handle. Before she had the door opened, Adam had left the car and reached her, offering a supportive hand. Hand-in-hand, they slowly strolled up the drive.

Wynn removed her keys from her purse and opened the front door. They entered the house and stood in the foyer, listening for sounds of life. Except for the television blasting from the family room, the house was silent.

"Mom?" Wynn called.

"Hi, honey. We're watching the news," Peg Evans called.

If the news was on, Jimmy and Kevin had to be asleep. "We?" Wynn called back, although she knew the answer to her question.

"Mmm-hmm. Jim and I," Peg replied. "We'll be out in a minute."

Puzzled, Wynn turned to Adam and shook her head in disbelief. Her mother disliked Jim with a passion that surpassed anything Wynn understood. The pair rarely remained in the same room for more than a few minutes without sniping at each other. And this feud went back to before she and Jim got married. Now, they sat in the family room, watching the news together like old cronies. What was up with that? Had she entered the Twilight Zone?

The local news anchor's voice was abruptly cut off. Seconds later, Peg stepped from the back of the house into the hallway. Jim followed, smiling sheepishly at Wynn before focusing a curious gaze on Adam.

Peg studied her daughter for a moment before moving to the man at Wynn's side. Her mother gave Adam a thorough onceover from the top of his head to his handcrafted leather shoes.

"Adam?" Peg asked.

He squeezed Wynn's shoulder and walked to Peg with an outstretched hand. "Hello, Mrs. Evans. It's good to see you."

She shook his hand, all the while checking him out. "Wynn said she had run into you at work. How's your family?"

"Good. My mom and dad divorced a few years back. Dad moved down south and my mother lives in Farmington in one of those assisted living apartments. How's Mr. Evans doing?"

"Doing fine," Peg answered, and then added, "You know he still loves his antique cars. Our garage has two he's working on right now."

Grinning, Adam nodded. "I remember that. I'd love to see him. Maybe Wynn will take me over for a visit and I can check out his car collection."

"We'd like that." Peg stepped around Adam. "Maybe I'll plan a barbecue and everyone can come. How does that sound?"

"Perfect." Adam grinned. "Name the date and I'll be there."

Throughout this exchange, Jim stood on the sidelines. He glanced at Wynn with a knowing smirk on his face.

You don't know Jack, Wynn thought, annoyed by the smug expression on Jim's face. When they split, she'd made a point of keeping him out of what went on in this house. All he needed to do was arrive every other Friday and pick up the boys, drop them back at home on Sunday afternoon, and keep going. Jim had a new life and

Wynn understood and accepted that. What he did with Lorraine was his business and what went on in Wynn's life was hers.

Jim stepped forward and took Adam's hand. "Jim Harrison."

"Adam Carlyle."

"You're the kid that lived next door. Wynn's girlfriend's little brother? Right?"

Adam's eyes narrowed, but the tone of his voice remained deceptively pleasant. "Correct. Good memory."

"Honestly, not really. When Peg mentioned your parents, some of it started to click. What are you up to these days? Still in college?"

"Been there. Done that. I work for Gautier International Motors."

Frowning, Jim asked, "Aren't they supposed to be moving to the U.S.?"

"That's what we're doing," Adam responded.

"What do you do for them? You work on the line?"

"No. I'm head of the legal counsel for international operations and real estate," Adam answered. "What about you? If my memory serves me correctly, you were the jock. Basketball. Football. Something like that. Do you still play?" He glanced pointedly at Jim's protruding belly.

Instantly, the older man sucked his gut in. "I own a couple of sporting stores."

"That makes sense. Use your skills." Adam leaned against the wall and folded his arms across his broad chest. "Good way to incorporate your knowledge of the game and love of sports. Where are your stores located?"

"Royal Oak, Southfield, and Lincoln Park," Jim boasted.

"Gautier's has basketball and soccer teams. I'll have to check you out one day soon. Do you have a card?"

Always on the lookout for a sale, Jim eagerly removed his wallet from his back pocket. Adam took the card and glanced at it before sliding it into his pocket. "We'll keep you in mind."

Enough chitchat, Wynn thought. "Mom, is Daddy coming to pick you up? If not, Adam can take you home."

"Sure," Adam said.

"Oh no, honey. Jim's already offered to take me home." Peg retraced her steps to the den. Seconds later she returned with her sweater and purse. "Are you ready, Jim?"

He dug in his pocket and produced a car key. "Sure am."

Peg hugged Wynn and kissed her cheek. "Talk to you tomorrow."

"Bye, Mom."

"I need to move my car." Adam followed the pair out of the house.

Standing on the porch, Jim examined Adam's car. "Nice. What is it?"

"It's called 'Deceptive.'"

"Why?"

"It's our version of the Jaguar. It's really a sports car with the comfort of a sedan."

"What's its top speed?" Jim queried.

"200 mph."

"No way." Laughing, Jim started down the

stairs. "You won't do that in the U.S. unless you're on a raceway. You'll end up with a ticket."

"This isn't the only country where we sell the car."

"Oh," Jim muttered stupidly.

Adam held Peg's arm and helped her down the stairs, leading her to the passenger side of Jim's SUV. He opened the door and helped her climb into the passenger's seat before shutting the door. Through the open window, Adam said, "Take care, Mrs. Evans. It was good to see you."

Peg touched his arm. "You, too, Adam. Say hello to your parents for me."

"Will do, Mrs. Evans," Adam promised.

Wynn stood in the doorway, watching the trio. That was a surprise.

Wynn turned to the den. She wanted to make sure the boys hadn't fallen asleep on the floor. That was their habit on Friday night. Sure enough, wrapped in blankets, her sons lay on the floor, sound asleep. She lifted Kevin and left the room, starting for the stairs. Adam reentered the house, shutting the door after him.

"Is your other son in the den?" he asked.

She nodded. "I'll get him in a moment."

"Wait." Adam hurried down the hall. Seconds later, he returned with Jimmy in his arms. "Where to?"

Wynn answered, starting up the stairs, "This way. Come on."

Adam followed. At the top of the stairs, Wynn pointed to a door. "That's Jimmy's room." Adam nodded and pushed the door open with his foot.

She tossed back the covers and laid Kevin

in the center of the bed. Through the whole process, Kevin slept. After untangling and straightening her son's limbs, Wynn kissed his cheek, covered the child with the sheet and blanket, and quickly left the room. She crossed the hallway to Jimmy's room.

Adam pulled the blanket over the child and turned. Wynn entered the room and leaned down, then kissed her oldest son on the forehead. Adam reached for her hand and they left the bedroom together.

They returned to the first floor and Adam led her toward the front door. "I'm going to go."

Nodding, she followed him. "Thanks for helping."

He grinned down at her and pulled her close. "Any time."

At the door, she turned, settling against the door frame. Anticipating his kiss, Wynn raised her arms and wrapped them around his neck, fitting her body against the strong, male planes of his. She lifted her head to meet his lips. Adam took his first sweet taste of her lips before venturing further. His tongue slipped between her eager lips and found hers. The kiss was sweet, lingering, and filled with promise.

Adam slowly released her and took a step away. His hand caressed her cheek and he leaned down for a brief but equally tantalizing second kiss. "Good night, sweetheart."

"Good night," she whispered back.

He stepped into the night and down the stairs, waving when he reached his car. "I'll call you tomorrow."

Nodding, Wynn shut the door and locked up. On her way to her bedroom, her hand slipped inside the pocket of her slacks and touched a scrap of paper. Curious, she withdrew the sheet and laughed out loud. She removed a crisp one hundred dollar bill. "That turkey."

Chapter 9

I can't believe I'm going to do this, Wynn thought, swirling the last bite of salmon into the spicy tartar sauce. She glanced around the elegant formal dining room of Adam's West Bloomfield home and then took a quick peek at her dinner companion before quickly looking away. Her stomach churned.

Stop freaking out. Put this evening in the proper prospective, she advised silently. *You're taking the plunge and going for everything Adam has to offer. It won't last long. When it's over, you'll go back to your life. For now, remember, this is sex, companionship, and fun. No permanent commitments. Just a good time, great sex, I hope, until it ends.*

It had been almost two years since she'd been sexually active with anyone. Jim had been her first and only lover. Her dry spell was almost at an end.

After weeks of being wined and dined at every turn, Adam had checked the date and asked if the boys were going to their father's this weekend. Wynn had nodded, equally fearful and hopeful of what he might ask of her. With an enticing smile, Adam had wrapped her in his arms and then invited her to dinner at his home, adding that she might want to stay the night.

Excited and frightened, she had agreed, understanding that it was time for their relationship to move in a different direction. Here she sat, after another delicious meal and plenty of wine, waiting for Adam to make the next move.

"Do you want to do dessert now? Or wait until later?" Adam inquired.

Smiling seductively, she shot back a sassy retort, "I thought you were going to be my dessert."

Adam's eyes widened a fraction and then he grinned approvingly. "I am. But I thought you might enjoy a little something sweet."

"What you got?"

"Cherries Jubilee."

"Wow! Did you make it?" she asked.

"No. Bakery near here."

"Interesting."

"Are you impressed?" Adam asked.

"Very."

His eyes were intent as his gaze held hers. "Good. That's part of the plan." He pointed at her plate. "Finished?"

Wynn felt herself growing warm. "I'm done. I'll load the dishwasher." She retrieved her plate and returned to the kitchen. *Yeah, I want something else,* she admitted silently. Anticipation sent hot blood surging through her veins. Her feelings had nothing to do with food and everything to do with expectant sexual gratification.

"You don't have to." Adam trailed her into

the kitchen. "Leave them in the sink. I'll do them tomorrow."

Wynn needed a little time to regain her balance. "I'll rinse them. It's the least I can do. You cooked. It's my turn to help out." Adam shrugged, heading back to the dining room. A minute later, he returned with serving trays and used cutlery.

Wynn scraped the remains of her meal into the garbage disposal. "Dinner was delicious. Are you a closet chef?"

Grinning, Adam shook his head. "Not me. I like to cook. Right now, Gautier's business keeps me too busy to do much of anything other than order takeout."

"Poor baby." Wynn opened the dishwasher door and turned on the hot water. She stuck a finger under the running stream, testing the temperature before rinsing a wineglass.

He leaned against the counter, watching her. "I thought we'd stretch out in the family room and watch a movie."

"Sound good." Images of them getting busy on the sofa flashed through her head. The telephone rang, interrupting Wynn's erotic fantasy.

"Excuse me." Adam crossed the floor and picked up the receiver. Instantly, his back stiffened.

She concentrated on the dishes, halfheartedly listening to his deep, sexy drawl. Adam's tone identified it as a Gautier call.

"What do you need, Vi? I'm busy."

Wynn grimaced. Vivian again. What was it with this woman?

"You know better than that. Have him sign

the promissory note. If he refuses, pay the bill and leave."

Wynn sighed. Since Tia's party, Vivian made it her life's work to interrupt Adam and Wynn's dates. It seems as if every time they were out, Vivian had drama that needed Adam's immediate and complete attention. How in the world did Vivian work before this?

From the moment Adam introduced them, Wynn had felt an undercurrent of something personal between Adam and Vivian. Maybe it was a long-dead relationship on Adam's side, but Vivian wasn't going gently into the night. Wynn understood that Adam was a grown man with a previous life. But Vivian always ended up in their faces. Maybe that would change after tonight when Wynn felt as if she held a stable role in Adam's life.

"Come on, Viv. You know the drill. Think logically. Look, do what you need to do and I'll talk to you Monday. Bye." He hung up the phone and returned to Wynn's side, standing behind her.

"Everything all right?" She placed a damp plate in the dishwasher.

Adam placed his hands on her shoulders, gently massaging the tense muscles. "Yeah."

She leaned into his soft caresses, enjoying the warmth of his fingers through the thin fabric of her blouse.

"I don't know what's going on with Vivian," Adam complained. "She can't seem to close a deal without calling me. It's getting really old. I'm trying to give her a little time to get herself together. But if she doesn't come up to speed soon, I might have to reevaluate her assignments."

"Talk to her first," Wynn suggested. "She could be going through something at home and it's affecting her work."

"You're probably right." He shook off his gloomy mood and wrapped his arms around her waist, drawing her back against the hard planes of his body.

Adam peppered the gentle slope of her neck with tiny kisses, nibbling his way to her ear, making it almost impossible for her to think clearly. It felt so good to be in his arms. She tilted her head, moaning softly.

"You taste delicious," Adam whispered close to her ear. With a hand on her shoulder, he eased her into his arms.

Wynn wrapped her arms around his neck. Adam lightly brushed his lips against hers. Not satisfied, he deepened the kiss, sweeping the recesses of her mouth with his tongue. She met his tongue with her own while pulling his closer. Adam tasted so good. Wynn couldn't get enough of him.

They continued to kiss until the spray from the faucet hit Wynn's rear. "Mmm." She grunted, turning in his arms.

Dazed, he gazed down at her with hunger in his eyes. "What?"

"Let me finish the dishes."

Nodding, Adam stepped back and she returned to her task. "The movies are in my car. I'm going to grab them. Meet me in the entertainment room." He kissed the side of her neck and then headed toward the attached garage.

"Okay." Taking in a shaky breath, she glanced over her shoulder at Adam, studying his delectable rear end as he strolled way.

Ten minutes later, Wynn found herself relaxing on the cream leather sectional in Adam's entertainment room. The L-shaped sofa surrounded the HD television mounted on the wall.

Adam slipped the disc into the player and grabbed the remote. He dropped into the spot next to Wynn and switched on the television.

"What movie did you get?"

"Political thriller."

She snuggled against Adam's warm side. His fingers curled around her upper arm, stroking the bare flesh, causing her heart to flutter.

Wynn faced the television and tried to focus on the screen. The political thriller's beginning credits rolled by on the screen, but her thoughts remained on the man at her side. Slowly, her hand settled on Adam's thigh, feeling the skin under the trousers leap to life.

With a warm hand on her shoulder, Adam urged her closer. It felt like sweet torture, being so close and yet not close enough. She wanted bare skin against bare skin. Eager for the taste of him, Wynn wrapped her arms around his neck and drew his head down.

His hand moved from her arm to her shoulder, kneading the lithe muscles before slipping lower and palming one of her breasts. Wynn practically moaned out loud with pleasure as he kissed his way down her throat to the breast.

She stood, taking Adam's hand and pulling him to his feet. Adam and Wynn made their way hand-in-hand to the second floor. He pushed open a door and they entered his bedroom.

Adam took her lips in a kiss, deep, and passionate. Panting softly, Wynn wanted to touch him and her thoughts turned to action, slipping her hands under his sweater and stroking the warm, smooth flesh.

Like magic her clothes landed in a heap on the floor. Wynn stood nude in front of Adam. She felt vulnerable and wanted to cover herself. After all, thirteen years separated them. Adam's sharp gaze wouldn't miss her flaws or imperfections. Slowly, Wynn crossed her arms over her breasts, hiding them from his heated gaze.

"Don't. I want to see all of you." Adam pulled her arms away, sliding his hands down her arms to link his fingers with hers. His gaze made a thorough perusal of her naked flesh before returning to her face. A delighted grin spread across his handsome face. "You're beautiful," he whispered in a reverent tone. Adam's lips touched hers, setting her soul on fire.

"Your turn." Wynn's hands hovered near his belt.

"True enough." Starting with his sweater, Adam began a slow striptease. Seductively, he pulled the cashmere garment above the line of his trousers, revealing a flat belly. Wynn's mouth watered at the sight of his tight abs as he drew the sweater over his head. Caught in his lure, she caressed his nipples, pleased when they beaded to hard pebbles. Wynn stroked her way down his belly to the leather belt at his waist.

She stopped, gazing uncertainly at him.

"Don't stop now," Adam coaxed in a low, teasing tone. "Things are getting interesting."

Fueled by his words, Wynn unhooked his belt and unzipped his trousers. Her heart did a little dance inside her rib cage as the garment hit the floor.

With thumbs hooked inside his jockey shorts, Adam slid the garment over his hips and down his legs in one fluid movement. The silk pooled around his feet.

Riveted to the spot, Wynn gasped. How did he keep all of that from plain sight? Adam was a beautiful male specimen and for tonight, he was completely hers.

"Come here," he commanded, taking her hand and leading her across the room. As he passed the nightstand, Adam grabbed a small foil package from the surface. He stopped, leaned back against an empty space, and reached for her.

"Here, let me." Wynn took the condom from his hand and used her teeth to tear it open. She removed the latex from the foil and took his shaft in her hand, rolling the protection along the length of his flesh.

She took his face between her hands and leaned close, and covered his mouth with hers. Wynn's tongue slipped into his mouth, sliding across Adam's, tasting the fresh scent that was uniquely his alone with a hint of the Riesling they shared at dinner. Her hands found their way around his neck as she drew him closer.

Their hunger grew stronger and bolder until they were close to the breaking point. But Adam wasn't done with her. He released her lips, peppering light kisses down the slope of her neck. His head dipped lower and he caught a nipple between his lips. His tongue swirled around the nub as his hand expertly caressed her other breast.

Then Adam placed his hands on her waist.

Puzzled, she glanced across the room. "What . . . what . . . what about the bed?"

Adam grinned, showing white, even teeth. "We can do that any old time. Tonight requires something special." His lips gently slid across hers. "Something memorable."

Adam rained tiny kisses along Wynn's throat, nipping here, lapping there. He twirled her around and backed her against the wall. The coolness seeped into her skin. His tongue led an enticing path across her collarbone to her right breast. He cupped the warm flesh within his palm and flicked his tongue across her brown nipple, causing her to moan out loud. Instantly, it responded, hardening into a tiny bud.

Until that moment, Wynn's arms had remained stationary at her sides. She enclosed his head between her hands, holding him at her breast. Her eyes drifted closed, savoring the sensation of his tongue lapping across her nipple.

It had been so long since anyone had loved her. She planned to enjoy the attention, feelings, and heat of this young, virile man.

As he sucked on her nipple, his hand caressed her flat stomach and made its way down to the slit between her legs. His fingers separated the flesh and found the quivering button, waiting for his touch. His thumb stroked the button in time with the motion of his tongue at her breast.

Adam lifted her off the floor. "Wrap your legs around my waist."

Wynn did as he directed and felt the pulsating heat of his shaft searching for her core. Wanting him within her, she reached between their bodies and captured the steel warmth in her hand and guided him to her opening. She rubbed the head of his shaft against her opening, using her wetness to coat his flesh.

Groaning, Adam surged upward, entering her completely with one thrust. "Don't move." Adam's hot breath caressed her neck. He traced the shell of her ear with his tongue and wrapped his arms around her waist, holding her still as he experienced being inside her.

She gasped, feeling her body quivering, stretching, and adjusting to having him fully inside her passage. She locked her feet at the ankles, keeping him deep within her. They stayed that way for a moment, savoring the feeling and excitement of being intimately joined for the first time.

Adam began to move, guiding her movements with his hands on her waist. Adam thrust upward and Wynn pushed downward, meeting each thrust of his body. They quickly established a fierce, pleasurable rhythm.

Wynn kissed and licked Adam's neck and nipped at his shoulders as he moved inside her hard and fast. Head thrown back, she gave herself over to the pleasure. "More," she moaned, grinding her hips against his.

He kissed and sucked the tender slope of her neck before he reached her lips and took her mouth in a deep kiss. Locked in her, Adam spun on the heels of his feet and pinned Wynn against the wall. Adam pumped into her repeatedly. The solid surface was cool against her back. She didn't care. She wanted Adam and everything he had to give. They rocked together, giving and receiving pleasure as they moved higher and higher. Adam and Wynn's tongues tangled together as they carried each other closer to the edge of completeness.

His rod grew thicker, and moved deeper as he pumped into her, spreading her wide and leading her in a wild dance of their bodies. He filled her, stroked her vaginal walls, and coaxed Wynn closer to her orgasm. She couldn't hold out much longer. She felt her interior walls begin to quiver and she knew her climax was close.

Finally, she took the plunge over the edge, screaming his name as she squeezed him tight, drawing every drop from him. Adam joined her, moaning and groaning as they climaxed together.

Chapter 10

After making love with Adam most of the evening, Wynn had fallen into an exhausted but satisfied sleep. Now she was having the most erotic dream of her life. Her body was on fire, striving to reach another orgasm before she fully woke up. Wynn's body swayed to the movement of his hands. Everything felt so good and real. She hated to wake up and lose this moment.

The gentle lapping of his tongue against her breast created a pool of heat between her legs. Adam's fingers found a different treasure at her junction, sent her pulse into an erratic gallop. His fingers separated the lips and his thumb began a gentle stroking of her nub. The movements back and forth against this tender flesh had her hips dancing on the bed wanting to keep up with his movements.

This was one hell of a dream. If she wasn't enjoying enough pleasure, a finger found its way into her canal, moving in and out, copying the rhythm established by his tongue on her breast.

This triple invasion had her hot and on the edge of exploding. God, it felt so good. Wynn didn't want it to stop.

A second finger joined the first. Wynn gasped. Unable to control the sensations taking charge of her body, she arched her body to take the digits farther in. The lapping became an insistent tugging on her breast, echoing and amplifying the increased movement of his fingers. In and out. In and out. Just enough to keep her on the edge and wanting more, but not enough to make her jettison like a rocket into space.

Wynn rocked against the fingers, seeking release. She rose to meet each thrust, wanting, needing the invasion to continue, but at the same time knowing it must end. Hopefully with a powerful, soul-wrenching orgasm for her trouble.

Wynn's vagina walls sucked greedily at his fingers, pulling them farther within her canal. Eyes still closed, she lifted her hips off the bed. She reached between her legs to catch the hand that offered her such mind-shattering pleasure, forcing it farther into her. The first tingling of her vaginal walls indicated that she was close. The sensations grew. Her legs trembled as the invasion continued. His lips at her breast sucked harder, drawing the hard nipple into the dark and moist recesses of his mouth. Her sheath quivered violently, caught up in the rhythm of Adam's sweet, erotic music.

Heaven. That's where she was. She'd found heaven on earth.

Wynn exploded, with a final flick of his thumb across her nub. She raised her hips completely off the bed and cried out Adam's name. Spent, she floated back down onto the mattress, and slowly opened her eyes. Adam lay at her side, licking moisture from his fingers.

He smiled. "I love the way you taste."

Without missing a beat, Adam turned on his side, removed a package from the night side table, and tore open the foil. He quickly rolled the latex protection on his engorged sex and climbed over her, sliding fast and hard into her passage.

"Adam!" she cried, filled to the hilt with him. "I love the way you feel inside me."

"I love being inside you. Wrap your legs around me," he ordered, showing her how he wanted her to hold him. Obeying, Wynn wrapped her legs around his waist and linked them at the ankle, opening her body fully to his invasion. Adam began with a gentle stroking, in and out, slow and sure, stroking her inner walls with a tender, easy rhythm. Eagerly meeting each downward stroke of his shaft, Wynn lifted her body, allowing him to fill her completely.

Capturing her head between his strong hands, Adam kissed her, licking the moisture from her lips. He nibbled his way along her jawline, outlined the shell of her ear with his tongue, and then tenderly bit on the edge of her earlobe before whispering, "Come on, sweetheart. You know the route. You've been down it a few times tonight. This time let's go together."

Suddenly, his gentle invasion became fierce and demanding. He pumped into her with renewed and varied energy. One moment he moved, slow and steady, rocking back and forth in a rhythm that made her believe she could stay like this forever. The next, his strokes were hard and fast, moving so quickly that she was lost in a sea of aching sensations. And yet a moment later, Adam allowed only the tip of his shaft to enter her, rotating his hips so that she almost died from the pleasure.

Wynn cried out in frustration. He was driving her crazy with his lovemaking. But she wanted all of him and was not about to let him stop her. Gripping his butt cheeks, she pushed him all the way inside her core, working her hips to hold him deep within her. Not satisfied, she ground her hips against his.

Enraptured by the feelings, Adam moaned, giving her exactly what she wanted. He swept in and out of her, faster with longer strokes. Her canal swelled and contracted with each downward beat, savoring the feeling of him deep within her. Wynn drew Adam's head down for a soul-shattering kiss.

"Come on, baby," he muttered against her neck. He sucked the scented skin into his mouth. Letting go, he whispered, "It's almost time. Let's do this together."

His wish was her command as she felt the familiar quivering of her legs and vagina walls as she reached for another climax. The quivering intensified. Her canal tightened instinctively around him and covered his flesh in her juices as she ground her hips against him. She couldn't wait another moment and she climaxed, crying out his name. Her orgasm triggered his, and she heard the harsh cry of Adam's release. Together, they sailed above everything, lost in their lovemaking. Hovering in their own world, Wynn and Adam slowly crashed back down to earth together.

Adam slipped from her body and turned away, working the condom from his flesh and then dropping it on the floor next to the bed. He pulled her into his arms and held her close, caressing her damp skin. Tiny kisses peppered her cheek, jaw, lips. "Thank you."

Wynn offered him a tired but sated smile. She reached out to touch his cheek with her limp hand. "No. Thank *you.*"

He tucked her into his embrace and planted another kiss on her forehead. "Let's get some sleep."

Nodding, Wynn rested her cheek against his chest and fell asleep against the steady and reassuring beat of his heart.

Wynn woke to the lingering aroma of sex. She shifted to her right, opening her eyes to find Adam propped on his elbow, watching her.

"Good morning, sweetheart," he greeted, giving her a swift kiss on the lips.

She kissed him back. "Good morning to you."

"Want some breakfast?" he asked.

"Sure. What you got?"

Shrugging, Adam flipped onto his back and took her with him. Wynn settled between his legs. "Pancakes, waffles, or eggs. You choose."

"Mmm. Poached eggs, sausage, and toast works for me."

"Done." With another swift kiss, he shifted her to the spot next to him, rolled off the edge of the bed, and reached for a robe. "You can have the bathroom in here."

A little self-conscious, Wynn rose, shoved her arms inside the robe, and then tried to finger comb her short hair into some semblance of order. Adam draped her in the rich silk. His arms surrounded her and wrapped her in the silk against the hard planes of his warm body.

He reached for a pair of denims and stepped into them, leaving his magnificent chest bare. "Fresh towels are in the bathroom. I'll meet you in the kitchen with your breakfast."

"Okay."

Wynn headed for the bathroom as Adam moved to the door. "I'll see you in a bit," he called, strolling down the hallway.

After brushing her teeth, showering, and finding clean clothes, Wynn entered the kitchen to find Adam hard at work preparing breakfast. Weather and traffic could be heard from the radio as he buttered toast and turned sausage patties. He glanced up as she entered the room. "Hey. Breakfast is almost ready. Coffee or tea?"

"Tea."

"Coming right up." Adam took a mug from the cupboard and added hot water from the tap.

Wynn seated herself at the kitchen island, and moments later Adam placed a plate of steaming food in front of her. Within seconds a mug of hot tea accompanied the food. He slipped into the chair next to hers and spread strawberry jam on his whole grain toast.

"So what do you have planned for the rest of the day?" he asked, biting into the toast.

Wynn gave him a seductive smile.

Adam's eyebrows rose. "You haven't had enough?"

"I liked it so much that I want some more," she admitted softly. "Can you handle it?"

"Oh yeah. I'm up to the challenge. But I can see that I better make sure I take my vitamins. Find a way to keep up my stamina. I heard older women are insatiable. I see you're proving that theory correct."

"So what are you saying?"

"Are you going to allow me out for potty breaks and food?"

"Maybe after you've pleased me enough." Wynn giggled, pleased by the gentle sparring between them.

"I'll do my best."

"That's all I ask." They finished their meal in a comfortable silence punctuated by the news, weather, and traffic from the radio and a commentary or two from Adam or Wynn regarding the news.

Adam removed their dishes from the island, rinsed them, and placed them in the dishwasher. He leaned against the counter and said, "Seriously. Do you want to get the kids and go do something with them? We've got the whole day ahead of us. Maybe go to the park or the Science Center and then do dinner afterward. Buddy's Pizza is always good." He folded his arms across his chest. "What do you think?"

Wynn's good cheer flew out the window.

She didn't want to hurt his feelings or change the mood. But she didn't plan on their playing house like a family. Her children were off-limits. She didn't want Kevin and Jimmy to get too close to Adam or think that he'd be their new father. She needed to figure out a way to let him down easy.

"Actually—" Wynn ran her tongue across her lips, tasting the strawberry jam from breakfast— "the boys will be with their dad until late this afternoon. So it's just you and me for the present."

Adam leaned close and kissed her lips. "I don't mind spending the day alone with you. I just didn't want you to miss out on time with your kids. They're important and I understand that. I want us, you and me and even your boys, to be together and enjoy each other. And I know your kids are a big part of that."

Wynn felt tears prick her eyes. She flung herself into his arms and held him tight. Adam was so good to her. How had she gotten so lucky to have found him? It didn't matter. She planned to enjoy this relationship to the fullest and then let go when the time came for them to go their separate ways.

together this weekend, doing all manner of things, his kisses still caused heat to pool between her legs. She felt like a teenager discovering sex for the first time. He rocked her to and fro as he nibbled his way down her neck. "Why don't you come back to my place and stay a little longer. I'd love to have you."

"You've already had me." Wynn shifted so that she faced him and returned his kiss with one of her own. "Several times I might add. But who's counting."

He grinned. "Nobody. But there's always room for more. Come on back and let's try a different approach."

Laughing, Wynn shook her head. "Oh so tempting."

"How tempting?"

"Not enough." She sobered. "I had a great time this weekend. And it wasn't just the sex. Although that was a lot of fun, too."

"I liked having you at my place. I meant it when I said you're welcome anytime. Feel free to come on over and stay awhile."

"I'll remember that." Secretly thrilled by his invitation, she knew she wouldn't be taking him up on his offer. She'd never invade his privacy without at least calling first.

Releasing her, Adam moved to the center of the room and glanced out the window. "What are you going to do with the rest of your day?"

Wynn flopped down on the sofa and hugged a pillow against her chest. "I don't know. Probably do some laundry, fix dinner for the kids, and get ready for Monday."

"Want some company?"

"I'm not sure that's a good idea. My ex will be bringing Jimmy and Kevin home soon. I don't want him to see too much or get a hint about us. He's always threatening to start custody hearings. The less I have to deal with, the better."

"Sweetheart, don't worry about Jim." Adam slipped into the spot next to her and drew her against his side. "He doesn't have a leg to stand on. You're a great mother. There's not much he can get on you. Besides, you've got me. You know, I'm a lawyer." He squeezed her shoulder reassuringly. "I know how to take care of men like Jim."

Wynn sighed heavily. "But I don't want to chance it."

Adam nodded, planted a kiss on her forehead, and then stood. "I'm going to head home now. Call me later."

"Thank you. I know being involved with a woman with kids can be difficult."

"No problem. I told you Saturday morning that I understood, and I do. You're trying to raise boys and turn them into young men. That's very important and I don't want to hinder you in any way. If anything, I want to help."

Wynn saw the hope glittering from his eyes and realized Adam planned to interject himself into her children's life. She couldn't let that happen. Jimmy and Kevin were off limits.

He pulled her to her feet, resting his hands on her waist. "How are we going to do this? I do want to see you next weekend. And not just for sex. Although I wouldn't mind a lot more of that."

"I don't know," Wynn admitted cautiously. "I

can't arrange my schedule just yet. Give me a chance to work out the details and see what my kids are up to."

"Don't worry about it. Things will come together."

Silence filled the room as Adam evaluated the situation. "Tell you what, why don't we, we meaning you, me, Jimmy, and Kevin, have a family night out. Like I suggested yesterday, we can go for pizza and check out one of those superhero movies. It'll give me a chance to get to know them better."

"We'll see," she dodged, feeling on very shaky ground. "I don't want to commit to anything until I see what the week brings. Jimmy's known for waiting till the last minute to do his homework and school projects."

He frowned as if he'd missed something. "You sure?"

"Yeah. We'll talk later this week and see how my weekend comes together."

"You know," he began before the telephone rang.

After the second ring, the answering machine kicked in. "Wynn. It's me."

Her heart did a little twist in her chest. What was wrong? Jim only called when things weren't going according to his plans. She untangled herself from Adam and hurried across the room, searching for the cordless telephone. Where had the boys put it? She snatched up pillows and moved papers, but the receiver eluded her.

"Something's came up at the store and I need to be there. I've already dropped the boys at your mother's." The machine clicked off seconds before she found the phone stuffed between the cushions of the love seat.

"Damn!" she muttered.

"Is that a bad thing?" he asked.

Frustrated, she dropped the phone on the sofa. "No. It just means that he didn't spend much time with Jimmy and Kevin."

"Don't worry about Jim. Your boys are fine." He grabbed her hand and tugged on it. "Come on. Let's go."

"What are you talking about? I've got to go get my kids."

"That's what we're going to do. I'll take you to your mother's." Adam checked his watch, fishing his keys from his pocket.

"You don't have to do that."

"I know," he answered. Placing his hands on her waist, he guided her from the room and toward the front of the house.

She searched desperately for an excuse that would end this act of chivalry. "We've been together all weekend. I know you must have things to do before Monday. I don't want to keep you."

He silenced Wynn with a kiss, covering her lips. As he drew away, Adam stroked her cheek. "Hush talking trash. I want to be with you. If I didn't, I'd be on my way. Now, come on and let's get those kids of yours. I know they've missed you and want to see you now."

On cue, the telephone rang again and Kevin's pitiful voice filled the room. "Mommy, we're at Grandma's. Come get us."

Adam gave her a look that said it all. "See? Told you."

With no way out of this situation, she conceded the battle. She would just have to work harder to keep the kids from getting too close to Adam. Although she was enjoying having a man in her life, she knew their relationship was headed nowhere. It would reach a dead end and they would eventually go their separate ways. No way could or would he love someone like her. Besides, Adam was an upwardly mobile executive at a major corporation. She would not make the image management would want their top executive to have. There would come a time when he would want to marry and have children of his own. He wouldn't want to play surrogate father to her children indefinitely.

Wynn picked up her purse and headed for the front door. "Thank you."

"You're more than welcome." Adam followed her out of the house, shutting the door after them.

Monday turned out to be an incredibly busy day at Nursing Solutions. The phone rang consistently. Hospitals from across the tri-county area were in need of nurses and health care workers for all shifts. Orders were placed and filled throughout the morning. Near two o'clock, Helen and Wynn got their first real break of the day.

Coffee mug in hand, Helen followed Wynn into her office and took a seat at her work table while Wynn ordered lunch from Jimmy John's

Gourmet Sandwich Shop. Fifteen minutes later, their food arrived.

Helen placed the telephone on voice mail, locked the front door, and then returned to Wynn's office with a mug of fresh coffee in one hand. She held creamer and sugar packets in the other. "So tell me about your weekend."

Wynn stood at her desk, kicking off her shoes and wiggling her nylon-clad toes. She opened the white paper bag and extracted two sandwiches, potato chips, and an iced tea. She handed one of the sandwiches and a bag of chips to Helen and placed the other on her desk in front of her. Butterflies danced in the pit of her belly. Wynn knew this would be the topic of discussion today. But she'd hoped to avoid the conversation as long as possible.

"It was really fun. Adam's a great cook." Wynn slipped behind her desk and sat down.

Helen stirred cream and sugar into her mug with the end of a straw. "Was he everything you hoped for?"

"Yes." *And so much more,* Wynn thought, remembering their early morning truce on Saturday morning.

Helen's eyebrows lifted. "From the look on your face, there's much more. Am I right?"

"What do you mean?"

"Oh, come on, girl. The drought is over. The only man you've had in your life for the past fifteen years has been Jim. And I use the term *man* lightly when referring to that idiot." She popped her fingers in front of Wynn. "Wake up! You've got a virile, sexy, younger man who is ready and willing to be your boy toy. I'd say that's a call for celebration."

"Why don't you worry about your own love life?" Wynn unwrapped her sandwich.

"Can't." Helen opened her sandwich and removed some of the lettuce. "Yours is so much more fun and interesting. So give me the details. Was there fun to be had?"

Wynn couldn't help the smile that spread across her face. "Yes."

"And?" Helen asked, eyes bright with curiosity.

"Let's just say that he had me many times and in many ways. And that's all I'm going to tell you about my weekend because it's none of your business."

"That's all I need to know." Helen bit into her sandwich. "When did you come home?"

"Sunday afternoon."

Helen nibbled on a potato chip for several seconds and then asked, "Did you invite Adam for dinner?"

"No. Adam invited himself."

She laughed. "That's my boy. How did that happen?"

"Jim was being Jim. He didn't feel like being bothered with the boys, so he dropped them at my mother's. Adam was over when I got the call, so he volunteered to go with me to pick them up. He took us to dinner at Buddy's."

"I bet Jimmy and Kevin loved that."

"Yes, they did."

"I detect something. What's wrong?" Helen picked up a napkin and brushed off her fingers, watching Wynn carefully the whole time.

Wynn sighed, feeling a bit foolish. "I don't want my kids to get too close to Adam. I want to keep this relationship, affair, whatever it is, away from them."

"Why?"

"Because they're kids," Wynn stated, placing her sandwich on the plate. "It's far too easy for them to get attached to the current man in their mother's life. I refuse to have a parade of uncles in my children's life. It's too confusing and they could get hurt."

"You talk as if you don't expect this relationship to last." Helen sucked on the end of the straw. "Why not?"

"Let's look at this logically. I went into this with my eyes wide open. Adam is thirteen years younger than me. Plus, he's an executive at Gautier's. I'm sure at some point he'll want to settle down and have children. He'll be looking for some young chicky-poo who's ready to make babies. My baby-making days are over."

"No, they're not. Your reproductive organs work just fine. And what makes you think Adam doesn't see you that way?"

"I'm too old. And too much baggage comes with me."

Helen scoffed. "Like what?"

"Two kids, an ex-husband, and a busybody mother."

"So. What makes you think he can't handle that? Seems to me you're putting yourself down."

"No. I've got kids."

"What makes you think he can't love your kids and help your raise them?"

"That's not what we're doing. This is an affair. Remember, you suggested it. Good time. Sex. Fun."

"Yes, I did. But that doesn't mean you can't feel more than pleasure with him. Why not fall in love again? Adam's certainly a better catch than that loser Jim. I mean, he's everything Jim isn't."

Chapter 12

Wynn paused in the doorway to her youngest child's bedroom and caught him bouncing up and down on the mattress. She stepped inside the room and gave the boy her sternest glare designed to put a halt to the worst behavior.

"Oh, Mommy. You look fretty!" Kevin continued bouncing on his bed.

Ahhh! Wynn smiled. Her heart melted like ice cream in the microwave. Her baby was such a charmer. He knew how to sweet-talk a girl. When Kevin hit his teens he was going to win and break a lot of hearts.

"Thank you. Now stop jumping on the bed. You'll break it down." Taking his hand, Wynn swung him off the mattress and onto the floor and then planted a wet, juicy kiss on his cheek.

"No, I won't," Kevin answered, standing on the floor next to her. "Where are we going, Mommy?"

She chuckled softly. Jimmy and Kevin always assumed that they were going wherever she was going. "You and your brother are going to spend the night with Nana and Granddad." Wynn sank onto the bed and wrapped her little boy in her arms. "Remember, I'm going out with Mr. Adam. We're going to a party."

Adam had invited her to the event of the automotive season. A launch party hosted by Gautier's for its newest models would introduce the French automaker to the Detroit market. The Deceptive sedan would be the star of tonight's show. MSNBC, CNN, and all the local press and television stations would be present to offer their critiques and impressions of Gautier's new models.

"Oh yeah. I forgot," Kevin said. "Can we take Twinkies to Nana's?"

"No. You want your grandmother to have a fit, don't you?"

"No."

His little solemn face almost made her laugh out loud. But she knew he was serious, so she kept it under wraps.

"I think your grandparents have everything you need." She glanced around the room. "Where's your brother?"

"Downstairs watching Transformers."

Wynn shrugged. "Of course." Jimmy was addicted to television. She had to threaten him with bodily harm to get him to do his homework before television time.

"Get your brother and then get your backpack. I want you to put them next to the door. Your grandpa will be here to pick you up soon."

"'Kay." Kevin ran from the room. He stood at the top of the stairs and yelled, "Jimmy!"

Shaking her head, she thought, *I could have done that*. Wynn rose, picked up denims from the floor, and tossed them into the hamper.

"Mommy?"

Wynn swirled around. There was a note in Kevin's voice that bothered her. "Yes?"

"Can I ask you something?"

"You can ask me anything." She returned to the bed and sat on the edge of the mattress, patting the spot next to her. "Come here." Kevin sank onto the bed and leaned against her side. "What's up?"

"Do you like—" He paused, twisting the edge of his T-shirt around his finger.

"Go on," she encouraged.

Kevin ducked his head. "Do you like Mr. Adam more than me and Jimmy?"

Wynn gasped. Shocked beyond words, she stared at her child. Where in the world had Kevin gotten an idea like that? First things first. "No. I don't. Where did you get that idea?"

"Well, do you?" Unconvinced, he asked a second time.

"I said no. Jimmy and you are the most important people in my life. You are my children and—" She stretched an arm around him and drew him close. "I love you and your brother more than anyone else."

Embarrassed, Kevin muttered into her side. "You go out with him a lot, Mommy. And you don't take us with you."

"True. Mr. Adam and I do go out," she admitted, searching for the truth behind her son's words.

"How come we can't go?" Kevin questioned.

"Honey, sometimes adults need time alone without their kids."

"I don't understand. Before Mr. Adam came, you took us with you."

"I didn't all the time. Sometimes you guys stayed with Nana and Grandpa."

She ran her tongue across her dry lips. "Remember how your daddy and I used to go out sometimes without you?"

"Yeah."

"Well, it's sort of like that."

"Mommy?"

"Yes." She dreaded his next question.

"Are you going to marry Mr. Adam?"

"No. Where did you get that idea?"

"Daddy."

Wynn bit her bottom lip to keep from calling her ex-husband a few choice names. Jim always stirred up crap. Why would he make a statement like that in front of the kids? It upset and worried them. *Oh come on, Wynn. You know why.* He liked to stay in the middle of her business.

"Kevin, you and your brother come first with me. No one else. Mr. Adam and I go to places that I can't take you. We do grown up things together."

A mental image of her and Adam making love flashed through her head. She flushed hot all over at the thoughts.

"Daddy said you wanted to be with Mr. Adam more than us. He said that we would probably have to come and live with him and Lorraine when you get married."

Bastard! she thought. Jim kept sticking his

nose in places where it didn't belong. "No," she answered firmly, placing a finger under her son's chin and lifting his head so that Kevin gazed into her eyes. "You won't be doing that. This is your home."

Wynn stood, grabbed Kevin's hand, and started from the room. "Come on. I want to talk to you and your brother." She marched down the stairs to the family room. Her oldest son lay stretched across the floor on his belly, gazing attentively at the television screen.

She stepped over his body, picked up the remote and switched off the television, and then tossed the remote on the floor.

"Mom!" Jimmy exclaimed.

"Yes!"

"I was watching that." He shifted into a sitting position.

Wynn sat on the sofa, pointing to the spot on the floor next to Jimmy. Kevin complied, dropping down next to his brother.

"I want to talk to you both. And since I don't want to repeat myself, I decided to get the two of you together." She placed her shaking hands together in her lap and focused on her children. "Jimmy, what has your father said about Mr. Adam?"

His little body stiffened. He refused to look at her.

"Jimmy," she prompted in her most stern, nononsense tone.

Picking nonexistent stuff out of the carpeting, Jimmy murmured, "Dad said you'd probably marry Mr. Adam and that he wouldn't want little kids like us around."

She wanted to scream her frustration. But her children weren't responsible for the workings of her ex-husband's twisted mind. "What do you think?"

Gazing at the floor, Jimmy hunched his shoulders.

"Come on. Don't give me that 'I don't know' mess. I know you have an opinion. You always do. I want to hear it. Now!"

"I think Mr. Adam likes us okay."

She turned to her youngest child. "What about you?"

"I like Mr. Adam. He plays games with me."

"What else, Jimmy. I know there's more." Wynn didn't like her son's tone. It closely mimicked his father's.

Jimmy muttered sullenly, "He's not my dad." He picked up the remote and punched the color keys.

"No, he's not. Has he told you that he was?"

Jimmy shook his head. "How do we know if he'll even want us around? Mr. Adam acts like he likes us. He could be pretending in front of you."

"First of all, Adam and I are not getting married. So you don't have to worry about the rest."

"Yeah but," Jimmy added, "Mr. Adam could be acting nice so that you'll go out with him."

"Did your dad say that?"

"He said we could come and stay with him any-time we wanted. That Lorraine likes us a lot and that she'd love to have us live with them."

Lips pursed, Wynn nodded. "Well, your father

has gotten things wrong. Adam and I are not getting married. We're friends who go out and do things together like go to dinner, see a movie, and visit friends."

"We don't have to move?" Kevin asked, hopefully, worry clearly visible on his young face.

"No! You live here." She stabbed a finger at the floor. "This is your home and always will be."

"But Daddy said," Jimmy began. Wynn held up a hand. Jimmy instantly went silent.

"Your father doesn't know what goes on in this house. He's guessing. And he is wrong." She emphasized each word clearly and concisely. "Nothing is going to change. We are a family and will remain that way. Am I making myself clear?"

Jimmy and Kevin's heads bobbed up and down.

"Good." She turned to her oldest son. "Jimmy, Mr. Adam is not pretending that he likes you. He does. Trust me, if he didn't I'd never let him anywhere near you guys. You and Kevin are my life. You come first. You always will. Understand?"

There were still hints of disbelief in both boys' faces, but Wynn could tell that they had heard and understood what she was telling them. If Jim had been in the room at that moment, she would happily have gutted him like a Christmas turkey. That man was a constant pain in the rear. Why couldn't he go about his business and leave them alone? He had deserted them and started a new life. Why wouldn't he let them get on with theirs?

The doorbell chimed. She rose from the sofa and headed toward the front of the house. It must be her father.

Once this evening ended, Wynn planned to have a nice, long talk with Jim Harrison. He needed to hear a few home truths. Wynn planned to put an end to whatever scheme Jim had in mind. The boys were off limits. She'd tear him apart if he continued to play havoc with their young lives.

Chapter 13

This was going to be some evening, Wynn thought as Adam helped her into the limo. The first of several surprises had hit Wynn when she opened her front door and found a black limousine parked in her drive instead of Adam's car. He grinned now, noticing her raised eyebrows.

Once she settled into the backseat, Wynn took note of the available space. "Are we picking up anyone else?"

Chuckling softly, Adam leaned in the seat and shook his head. "Nope. It's just you and me tonight."

"Not that I mind. But why didn't you drive your car?" She frowned, stroking the soft steel gray leather seat. A full bar, flat screen television, and digital sound system completed the limo's setup.

He hunched his shoulders and scooted closer to her. "It's Deceptive's night. Driving my car might give the media a sneak peek before we're ready. Besides, I don't want to take from the car's debut."

Wynn giggled. Adam spoke as if the car were a

real, live person instead of a piece of machinery. "Tonight we're playing second fiddle to a car?"

"Pretty much."

Going with the flow, she tossed her hands in the air. "What the heck."

The sun was a huge orange ball in the sky as the limo sped down Jefferson Avenue past Belle Isle. Enthralled, Adam caressed her hand as his gaze lingered on her.

"You look beautiful. I like my lady in red," he whispered enticingly close to her ear. He lifted her hand from atop her white beaded bag and kissed the palm.

Dressed in a red crepe dress with a tight empire bodice and full flowing skirt, she felt thrilled to be out tonight. His touch and kisses made her feel beautiful. She studied her dinner date and silently admired how well he wore his tux. He looked pretty grand. Tonight Adam looked every inch the epitome of the successful businessman.

The limo turned down St. Clair Street, leading to the Roostertail and Sinbad's. The car halted at the gate leading to the banquet hall. A security guard stepped into their path, holding a clipboard. Adam hit the window button and then displayed his employee badge. "Hi, Fred. How's it been this evening?"

With a smirk on his lips, Fred glanced at the crowd gathering near the Roostertail entrance. "Busy. Real busy."

"You take care," Adam warned.

"Head in, Mr. Carlyle. Stop near the door and then the limo can find a place to park."

"Thanks." Adam saluted the guard. "Take

care and don't let the media get to you. We'll see you later."

The limo rolled toward the entrance. Wynn got her first close look at the pandemonium awaiting them, and the scene sent her head into a spin. Her mouth dropped open and her heart began to pound in her chest as she studied the crowd, which was as compelling and intense as any Hollywood premiere.

Shocked, Wynn turned to Adam with a question in her eyes. She expected a little crazy, but this was overwhelming and far more then she imagined.

He shrugged. "Told you."

Worried by the intensity of the crowd, Wynn drew closer to Adam. Arm wrapped around her, Adam held Wynn against his side, murmuring reassuring nonsense to her. People and news crews packed the parking lot. MSNBC, CNN, and the Detroit newspapers were gathered outside the Roostertail. News personalities who stood near vans featuring station logos were broadcasting using the Detroit River as a backdrop.

The driver crept along as the crowd pushed forward, peeking inside the smoked glass windows of the limo. Adam got out first and placed a hand in the small of her back and urged her forward. Bulbs went off in Wynn's face. Startled, she froze, reaching for his hand. He propelled her past the flashing lights and microphones to the entrance. "Watch your step," Adam warned, guiding her up the stairs and into the lobby.

Instantly, a woman approached them. "Welcome to The Roostertail."

"Thank you," Adam stated.

"Can I offer you directions?"

"No. Thank you," he responded, scanning the lobby for a familiar face.

"Adam! Wynn!" came Krista Thomas's voice.

Wynn turned and found Brennan and Krista headed their way. Happy to see a friendly face, Wynn sighed softly and hugged the very pregnant Krista. "Oh wow! You look like you're ready to pop any minute."

Krista rubbed a hand across her protruding belly. "No such luck. I've got another month to go."

"That's a whole lot of baby in there."

"Tell me about it."

Adam and Brennan shook hands. Adam studied the commotion going on around them and said, "You did a great job on this shindig."

"It's quite a show. It's going to be bigger." He held onto his wife and steered her in the opposite direction. "Come on. Let's get to our spot before we find ourselves stuck in traffic."

They moved slowly through the crowd, heading to the head tables. Tia jumped up and hugged Wynn. "Hi. It's been a while. It's good to see you."

Adam cleared his throat.

Tia blushed. "Hi, Adam."

"Have you seen Reynolds?"

"Not so far." She glanced at her watch. "It's still early. Don't forget getting into this building is a major project."

"I can agree with that," Brennan muttered. "Adam, let's get our ladies something to drink." He rubbed Krista's back. "Honey, orange, grape, or cranberry juice?"

"Cranberry."

Brennan nodded.

Adam touched Wynn's hand. "What about you, sweetheart?"

"White wine."

"Be back in a couple of minutes," Adam said, slowly moving away.

Krista and Wynn stood together, watching their men disappear into the crowd.

"You need to sit down." Wynn stared pointedly at Krista's belly. "Come on. This is going to be a long evening. Pace yourself."

Nodding, Krista turned back to the table where Tia and Christophe sat.

Twenty minutes later, Adam and Brennan returned with drinks. This time they brought an addition to the group.

"There's somebody I want you to meet," Adam said, placing Wynn's drink on the table. "Reynolds Gautier, this is my friend Wynn Evans. Wynn Evans, Reynolds Gautier."

She extended her hand to the distinguished-looking, white-haired gentleman. "It's nice to meet you, Mr. Gautier."

"Call me Reynolds. Mr. Gautier is my dad. He lives in France." He spoke in a heavy French accent, a pleasant smile on his face.

"All right. Reynolds."

"Excellent." In an elegant gesture, Reynolds took her hand and kissed it. "I've heard good things about you."

Surprised, Wynn's eyebrows rose. "Really?"

"Oh, yes. You've been keeping our friend here in line."

Scowling playfully, Adam slapped the French

man on the back. "Hey! Don't talk about me like I'm not here."

"My boy, you stay away so much that all I see is your coat tails. Sometimes I forget that you work for me."

Chuckling, Adam suggested, "Stop sending me all over the world and I'll spend more time in the office." Frowning, he halted as if he'd just realized something. "Where's Michelle?"

"My wife said she didn't want to be in this circus. Michelle told me to wave at her because she planned to watch us on CNN."

Everyone laughed.

Brennan stepped in. "I hate to break up this group when we're all having so much fun, but we have to take care of some business. Reynolds, do you have your speech?"

Gautier nodded.

"Good." Brennan, the ad man, turned to Adam. "What about you?"

He reached inside his breast pocket and retrieved a sheet. "I'm ready."

Brennan placed hands on the shoulders of Adam and Reynolds. "Let's go do the interviews and get that out of the way." Brennan turned to his wife. "Sweetie, would you keep Wynn company while we're gone?"

Krista stepped closer to Wynn and hooked her arm with Wynn's. "Absolutely. Come on, Wynn. Let's check out the buffet."

Wynn dodged a group of partygoers as she returned to the party in the main ballroom after spending some time on the deck. The music, people, and hustle of the evening had overwhelmed and worn her out. She had grabbed a moment of solitude to regain her balance before returning to Adam and his group of friends.

Wynn noticed Vivian's alluring form strolling a few feet ahead of her. Vivian's stunning black dress with the plunging V-neckline had been a major hit at tonight's event. Many of the single fellows had taken time to dance and talk with the attorney. Wynn couldn't blame the guys; Vivian looked great. Suddenly, Vivian stopped midstream and ducked into a small private room.

The sound of Adam's voice caught Wynn's attention. Not quite sure how to take this development, Wynn stopped, backtracked, ready to call his name. What were they doing together? She bit her bottom lip. Maybe she didn't want to know.

Curious, Wynn peeked through the crack in the door and listened to the conversation. Yes, she knew it was wrong to eavesdrop. And yes, she understood that generally eavesdroppers never heard anything good about themselves when they did things like this. But she couldn't help it. She wanted to know what was going on between Adam and Vivian. After all, forewarned was forearmed and where Vivian was concerned, Wynn needed all the ammunition and help available. Besides, Wynn couldn't go to Adam and ask, "What's up with Vi?"

"How you doin', Adam?" Vivian moved into view.

"I'm good." He waved his cell phone in Vivian's direction and then stuffed it in his jacket pocket.

"I needed to take a call and the ballroom was too noisy."

"Anything I need to know about?"

"No. Business for Reynolds. I'm good."

"Mmm," Vivian muttered. "I saw you arrive with your date." She practically spit the last word out.

"Did you?" he said cautiously.

"Yeah. I've got a question for you."

"Go ahead." Caution quickly turned to curiosity. "Shoot."

She came close to Adam and placed a hand on his arm. "How long do you plan on punishing me?"

Wynn gasped softly. Every muscle in her body went stiff as her heart kicked into a gallop. Why would Adam be punishing Vivian? She studied Vivian's expression and then focused on Adam.

A puzzled note entered Adam's voice. "Punishing? I don't know what you're talking about."

"Oh, come on." Vivian tossed her hand in the air and paced the confines of the small room. "Don't pretend with me. We both know that you're only going out with that woman to get back at me."

He chuckled. The sound had a cruel, unpleasant edge that grated on Wynn's nerves like a car door needing oil. Wynn got the impression that Vivian had stepped over an invisible line. Wynn would hate to be on the receiving end of Adam's anger if she ever crossed the invisible boundaries he'd established. "What makes you think I'm doing anything to you?"

The other woman placed her hands on Adam's

chest, imploring him to understand. "Look, I made a mistake. I don't love Jensen. It was a quick thing that happened."

Shaking his head, Adam removed her hands from his chest and took a step away from the woman. "I don't care about you and Jensen. That's your business. And I prefer to not hear it."

"Don't play with me," Vi pleaded. "We were close. Very close for a while."

"No. We worked together, period."

The other woman moved into the small door frame and Wynn saw Vivian raise her hand to caress Adam's cheek, stroking it tenderly. "Honey, we meant a lot more to each other. You can't deny that."

"Actually, I can." He folded his arms across his chest and said, "Vi, a kiss or two and a couple of dinners does not make a relationship."

"Don't tease me." She smiled seductively at Adam. "You know it's much more than that. We broke up and now you're with that woman. When are you going to stop torturing me?"

Adam hunched his shoulders. "I guess never. Vi, my kissing you was a momentary lapse. A mistake. Nothing more."

"No!" Vi almost yelled, and then caught herself. She lowered her voice and said, "Don't call it that."

Somewhat bored, he answered, "That's what it was."

Viv opened her mouth to say more, but Adam cut her short, touching his hands together in the classic time-out signal. His voice dropped to a dangerous octave. "Stop. You're delusional. This has gone on long enough. We don't have a relation-ship. We're colleagues. Professional colleagues. Don't make it into anything more, because you and I are not going to happen. Get it? Have a good evening. I'm out of here."

I better move on. I don't want Adam to catch me lis-tening to his conversation, Wynn thought, hurrying down the hallway. She smiled, feeling more confi-dent than she had since she began dating Adam. There might be a little history between Adam and Viv, but nothing that she couldn't handle. This was a good thing.

Chapter 14

With Sade's sultry lyrics playing in the back-
ground, Wynn entered her son's bedroom with a
stack of clean sheets. She stripped the bed and pillows, determined to get through a list of house-
work that needed to be completed.

Wynn dropped what she was doing when the
doorbell chimed. Wiping her hands on her denim
shorts and straightening her white T-shirt, she
bounced down the stairs, opened the door, and
resisted the urge to shut it again immediately. Jim
stood on the porch. Didn't he have a home to go
to? Why did he keep popping up on her doorstep
whenever the spirit hit him? Barely hiding her frustration, Wynn asked, "What are you doing here?"

"I came by to check on you." Jim opened the
storm door and waited for Wynn to invite him in.
She stood her ground. He took a step closer and
waited for her to step aside.

Came by to check on her? Wynn almost laughed
out loud. She didn't think so. Since when did he

care what happened in her house? To her? Or even the boys? "Did you? Why?"

"You didn't answer the phone when I called the other day. I wanted to make sure everything was going okay on this end of town." Jim dropped his keys in the pocket of his chocolate Polo shirt, shoved his hands into the pockets of his tan Dockers, and kicked the cement flooring with his leather-covered toe.

Shaking her head, Wynn turned away from the door and headed back to Jimmy's room. Jim entered the house and closed the front door, hurrying up the stairs after her.

"Jim, that was three days ago. You just decided to find out if we're okay. I'd say you're a little late."

Wynn entered the blue room, picked up the sheet, and fanned it open before laying the cotton over the bed. She tucked the edges under the mattress and reached for a pillowcase.

"I knew you'd handle whatever came up. You and your mother always take good care of the boys."

Wynn didn't say a word. She gathered the soiled sheets and stuffed them into the hamper. As she moved around the room, she picked up game pieces and books, placing them on the dresser and nightstand.

Watching her work, he asked, "Where were you?"

"Out."

Jim took a step closer and reached out a hand to touch her. He said in a soft persuasive tone, "Don't be that way."

Wynn quickly shifted out of touching range, appalled by the notion that Jim believed he could touch her. "That's what you used to tell me."

Stains of scarlet appeared on his cheeks. Good. Every once in a while he needed a wake-up call. A little payback never hurt. Jim had abandoned their family, moved in with his girlfriend, Lorraine, and begun a whole new life. Yet he still wanted to barge in and control her household. Wynn refused to allow him to do it.

"Why are you concerned about what I'm doing?" Wynn asked.

"I just wanted to know," he muttered.

"It's none of your business."

"That's where you're wrong. Think about it. What if the kids needed something? How was I supposed to get in touch with you?"

"Cell phone." Wynn added the red, royal blue, and yellow comforter and fluffed the pillows at the head of the bed.

"Yeah, well," Jim paused dramatically, "what if you didn't have it on?"

"I always have my phone on when my children are away from me." She exited the bedroom and started down the stairs to the kitchen. "Is there a reason for your visit?"

"Jimmy wanted some information about bats."

She faced him and gazed pointedly at his empty hands. "They'll be home after four."

He frowned. "Where are they?"

"Karate lessons." She removed the dirty dishes from the sink and placed them on the countertop. Wynn opened the dishwasher door and turned on the faucet.

"I wanted him to know that there will be a program at the Mount Clemens Public Library in a couple of weeks. You might want to take him."

"Since you know about the program, why don't you take him?" she suggested, rinsing the dishes before placing them in the dishwasher.

He shook his head. "Can't. Too much going on at the shops."

Wynn wanted to scream. This was so like Jim. The idea man never had time to follow through on his suggestions. As usual, Wynn would be left with the motherload of responsibility while Jim breezed in and out of their children's life.

Ignoring him, Wynn systemically loaded glasses and plates into the dishwasher.

"How's the boy toy?"

"I don't have a boy toy. If you mean how is my friend Adam, then he's fine." Wynn smiled thinking, *Adam certainly is fine and in more than one way.*

Jim scowled. "Whatever." A devious smirk appeared on his lips. "I saw you in the news."

"Did you?" Unperturbed, she dropped silverware into the dishwasher basket.

"Yeah. You and the boy, I mean Adam, showed up in the Metro section of the *Detroit Free Press.*"

"That's nice."

Jim moved across the kitchen, opened the cupboard, and removed a glass. He crossed the ceramic tile floor and filled his glass with water, swallowing half the water in one turn. "You looked good."

"Thank you," she responded automatically.

"You're moving in expensive circles these days." Jim cackled like an animal. "High society. Your boy must be a hotshot at Gautier's."

Now it was Wynn's turn to smirk. She faced him, folded her arms over her chest, and stared him down. "He is."

Over the top of his glass, Jim's eyes narrowed. "So how old is Adam anyway? Twenty-five?"

Wynn felt her pulse leap and heat surge up the back of her neck. *Don't let him get to you,* she silently warned.

"He doesn't look thirty. What is there fifteen, sixteen years between you guys?" he asked.

Wynn turned her attention to the pots and pans. She didn't have to answer any of Jim's questions. Maybe he'd talk himself out and go home.

"How long do you think this thing between you guys will last? I mean there's some complicated issues between you two, starting with your age and ending with his career. Look at him. He's young and successful. Adam has the world by the tail. He could have anybody. Why would he hang with you?" Jim shook his head and laughed out loud. "It must be a mother complex."

Furious, she slammed the dishwasher door shut and turned on Jim. "Get out. It's time for you to go."

"No problem. I'm going." He placed the glass in the sink. "But don't be mad at me. I'm only saying what everybody else is thinking."

Wynn led him to the front door. With her

hand on the doorknob, she said, "Before you go I've got something to say to you."

Frowning, he leaned against the opposite wall. "What?"

"The other night Kevin asked me if I was getting married."

"Oh."

She stuck a finger in his face and said in a solid, determined voice, "Don't upset my kids with your mess again."

Indignant, Jim straightened. "What mess?"

"I don't want you telling them stuff about my relationship with Adam. That's for me and Adam to do. Not you."

"Hey, I was trying to do my job as a parent."

Wynn snorted. "Since when? If you wanted to do your job you'd pay child support on a regular basis."

"This conversation is not about child support."

"You're right. It's not. But it is about my children and my relationship with Adam. Don't frighten them again. I won't have that."

"I wanted them to have a heads-up on what might happen. They need to know and understand that things might change and they have to change with it."

"If that's the case, I'll be the one to explain the situation. Should I marry anyone, I will discuss it with my children. Not you with your speculations and half truths."

Jim puffed up like a bagpipe ready to explode. "I don't lie."

"You don't always tell the truth, either."

"That's not fair," he stated.

"Life isn't fair. Get used to it."

"I didn't say anything that they didn't need to know," he defended.

Wynn countered, "Actually you said more than you should have." She drew in a deep breath and let it out slowly. "You don't know jack about us."

"I want my sons to know that they can always depend on me. That I'm available whenever they need me."

She laughed nastily. "And when would that be? If my memory serves me you left your family alone when you went off with another woman. Were you anywhere near Jimmy or Kevin when you packed your bags and moved out? How much could they depend on you then? We didn't have a clue where you had gone."

Panting, she turned away. *I've got to calm down.* Wynn shut her eyes and willed herself to focus. "Look, Jimmy and Kevin were upset. They thought I was going to run off with Adam and leave them. They are young children who are recovering from a traumatic event. Please don't cause any more problems in their life."

"You're trying to say this is all my fault. Well, it's not."

"Jim, listen to me."

"What do you plan to do? Are you going to marry him?"

"When Adam and I make a decision on our future, we'll let you know. In the meantime, my children will not be coming to live with you. I have custody of them. They will be staying here.

And no, they don't want to come and live with you and Lorraine. They're happy here."

Wynn jerked open the door and pointed a finger toward outside, gazing expectantly at him. "Good-bye."

Shaking his head, Jim stormed out of the house, calling over his shoulder, "I never could talk to you."

"Have a nice day," she sang pleasantly, shutting her door and leaning against it. She felt as if she'd just fought a battle in the ring against Laila Ali. And Ali won.

Chapter 15

My baby has gone all out for this event, Wynn acknowledged, standing in the patio doorway of Adam's West Bloomfield home. The Carlyle and Evans families stood, sat, and gathered together, getting reacquainted after years of separation. Adam's dad and his girlfriend were among the visitors along with Mrs. Carlyle and her new husband.

A little more than two weeks ago, Adam had called her with barely concealed excitement in his voice. His sister, Sherry, planned to come home for a visit and he wanted to have a get-together for both families. Wynn had misgivings about Sherry's visit. Apart from the fact that she hadn't seen her friend in years, Wynn wasn't sure how Sherry would handle the relationship between Wynn and her little brother.

From that point, preparations swung into overdrive and the end results were pretty spectacular. To be fair, Wynn had offered to help. Adam had politely thanked her with a quick kiss and told her that he had everything under control. He expected her to come to the picnic and enjoy herself like the rest of the guests. Shrugging, she agreed and waited to see what he would come up with.

With two weeks to prepare, he'd done an excellent job. Wynn shook her head, smiling as her gaze touched on all the stuff he'd organized to make his home comfortable and welcoming.

The unmistakable scent of charcoal and roasting meat permeated the air. Staff from the catering company Fantastic Feasts stood behind a huge grill, cooking chicken, hot dogs, steaks, and beef ribs on Adam's perfectly manicured lawn. A second food station offered cold cuisine like salads and wraps. At the edge of the patio sat a third station devoted to mixed drinks, alcoholic beverages, and sodas.

Wynn focused on Sherry. Her childhood friend stood near the privacy fence, hugging her ten-year-old daughter April while talking with Peg and Jim Evans. Fifteen years older than her brother, Sherry was a female version of Adam with her shoulder-length auburn hair and tall, chunky figure. Sherry's eyes had widened in disbelief before narrowing to razor slits after Adam reintroduced Wynn and explained how they bumped into each other at the New Center One building.

Wynn sighed. She should have been prepared for Sherry's reaction. The Carlyles were a close-knit family who didn't allow many people into their circle of friends. Sherry had always been possessive of her younger brother. Any woman, not just Wynn, would have a battle getting past Sherry.

Adam's strong arm wrapped around Wynn's

waist and drew her against the length of his body. Smiling, Wynn melted into Adam's warmth and rested her head against his chest. His lips caressed the sensitive spots along the slope of her neck, making her quiver and moan softly in response. She loved his touch and found it nearly impossible to resist him.

"What are you doing in here? The party's outside." He nibbled the exposed flesh at the junction between her neck and shoulder while his hand moved to her waist. His fingers slipped beneath the waistband of her shorts, stroking the tender skin there. The sensations made her eyes slowly drift shut.

Barely able to think, Wynn panted. "You need to stop before someone sees us."

Adam removed his hand and spun her to face him. Warm and inviting, his hands rested on her waist and drew her close. "Maybe I'll try something else."

"Oh really? Like what?"

Gently, he touched his lips to hers and then slipped his tongue between her lips. For the second time Wynn moaned, sucking on the tip of his tongue. Lost in the feel and taste of Adam, her surroundings faded.

Someone cleared their throat, penetrating Wynn's passion-filled mind. Breaking away, Wynn's gaze collided with her mother's laughing brown eyes.

"Excuse me," Peg Evans said from the opposite side of the doorway. An amused grin spread across her face.

Embarrassed, Wynn brushed a lock of hair from her eyes. "Sorry."

Peg chuckled, poking her thumb toward the backyard. "It's fine with me. But you guys should remember that you're in plain sight."

"We get it. Come on, sweetheart. It's time to mingle." Adam took Wynn's hand and led her out of the kitchen and out the patio door.

Adam and Wynn moved off the wooden stairs and through the backyard, stopping along the way to visit with their guests. They chatted with everyone. Standing among his colleagues, Adam quickly got pulled into a deep discussion of office politics with Christophe and Tia. After a few minutes of listening intently, Wynn begged off and moved on.

Hands shoved into her back pockets, she looked around the backyard. Her gaze settled on a shady corner where the kids were enjoying the antics of the clown Adam had hired. She decided to see how her boys were doing. Wynn removed her hands from her pockets and started across the lawn to where the clown performed, twisting colorful balloons into animals as the children cheered. She never made it.

Sherry intercepted, stepping into Wynn's path before she reached the group of kids. "Hey, Wynn."

"Hi." Wynn eyed the near-empty glass of wine in her friend's hand.

Adam's sister waved a hand around the backyard. "This is quite the party."

"Yes, it is. Give Adam full credit. He put everything together. I offered to help, but he turned me down." Wynn noticed the dangerous gleam in Sherry's eyes. The hairs at the back of Wynn's neck stood on end.

"That's my *baby* brother." Sherry drained the glass. "He loves to be in charge."

Wynn heard the emphasis placed on the word *baby* and knew there were comments she might have made. She decided to ignore the slight. Everyone was having a great time and she refused to allow Sherry to ruin the afternoon by creating a scene.

"How long have you been kickin' it with my little brother?"

"Kickin' it" reduced their emotional connection to raw animal lust. This wasn't going to be a pleasant conversation. Wynn ran a hand through her hair and glanced around the huge backyard, considering different locations for this discussion. "We've been seeing each other a few months."

Sherry nodded. "Where's your husband?"

"My *ex*-husband lives in Southfield with his girlfriend." Wynn shoved her hands into the pockets of her shorts, resisting the urge to strangle Adam's sister.

"How's he taking you and my brother?"

Wynn let out an audible sigh. Sherry didn't plan to let it go. "It doesn't matter what Jim thinks. This is my business, not his."

Bristling, Sherry stood up straighter. Her lips pressed together as her hand tightened around the wineglass, turning her knuckles white.

Sherry's spoiling for a fight, Wynn thought. *Not on my watch.* Instantly, she launched a diversion. "How about another glass of wine?"

Before Sherry had a chance to respond, Wynn grabbed Sherry's elbow and steered her toward the patio. If she got Adam's sister a drink and then inside the house, no one would need to know what was going on between them.

After the bartender replenished Sherry's glass, they entered the house and stood in the center of the kitchen. Turning to face her former friend, Wynn leaned against the island. "Okay, Sherry. We've got a little bit of privacy here. What's on your mind?"

"For starters, you and my brother. When did you become a cradle robber?" Sherry placed her drink on the island and folded her arms across her ample bosom. "You two were always close. There were times when I thought you were closer to him than I was and he liked you better than me."

It sounded so childish. *He liked you better than me.* What was rolling around in Sherry's head? "I'm not a cradle robber. I like your brother and he likes me. We reconnected with a chance meeting."

"So you're saying that you and my baby brother are screwing?"

Slowly shaking her head, Wynn thought, *What a crude phrase for such a pleasant experience, especially with Adam.* "Wow! I don't know what to say to that." Lifting a hand into the air, Wynn added, "Actually, I do. Ask your brother."

Sherry's head snapped back as if she'd been hit. "I'm asking you."

"And I'm saying take it to your brother. Let Adam answer all your questions. In the meantime, don't cause a stir. He's put entirely too much time and effort into this party. Don't disappoint him by causing a problem."

"Why are you focusing on Adam?" Sherry's voice contained a cool edge of disapproval that ground on Wynn's nerves. "My brother has his whole life ahead of him. Can't you find someone your own age to kick it with?"

"None of this is your business."

"You and Adam together." Lips pursed, Sherry shivered, wrapping her arms around her middle as if she'd caught a chill. "Disgusting."

Wynn shrugged. "You're entitled to your opinion. But it doesn't change a thing between Adam and me."

"You should be ashamed of yourself. How do you think this looks?" Sherry swayed unsteadily on her feet. "You may not know this, but I'm sure people laugh at you all the time. Old woman with that young man. It's ridiculous."

I'll let you have your rant for a moment or two more. Once you finish this time, I'm not going to take any more of your crap, Wynn thought.

"You're a forty-three-year-old woman with kids. What could my brother possibly offer you beyond sex? Maybe this is an attempt to relive your youth. Fill in the things you missed when you got with Jim."

"Sherry, enough. This is not the time or place to have this discussion. It upsets everyone. If you insist on stirring up trouble, you'll just hurt everyone and cause unnecessary problems."

She huffed. "You don't tell me what to do. I'm Adam's sister. I have a right to say what needs to be said."

"And what is that?" Adam asked from behind Wynn. She whirled around and found him entering the kitchen from the hallway leading to the front of the house. Had he been listening to their verbal tug-of-war? He stopped inside the door glancing from one woman to the other.

Sherry immediately took the lead, smiling engagingly at her brother. "Hey. Just talking with Wynn about you guys."

His eyes narrowed. For a quick second the similarities in the gesture united the siblings in Wynn's mind, making her feel like an outsider. "So I heard."

"Sorry. We got a little carried away." Sherry pushed past Wynn, heading to Adam. She slipped her hand through the crook of his arm, pulling him against her side and away from Wynn. "Help me understand why you've gotten involved with someone as old as me. Honey, I know you must meet women all the time. Women your age."

Adam followed Sherry. Wynn watched the pair talking with their heads together. "I do."

"Then why this?" Sherry waved a hand toward Wynn.

"I've got the woman I want." Turning to Wynn, Adam gave her a quick wink. "I want her in my life, not some generic woman that you're producing for me."

Wynn's heart swelled with feelings for this man. Adam had made it clear that he knew what he wanted.

Sherry's tone changed. "I'm worried about you."

"Big sis, I don't need you to protect me. If

I can manage the legal department of a major automotive company, I'm pretty sure I can take care of my love life." He untangled himself from Sherry's clutches and moved to Wynn. "I appreciate your concern. I'm happy with the woman I have. Wynn and I are doing just fine."

"I - I - I," Sherry stammered.

He halted her with a sweeping wave of his hand. "Let me finish. This is my life. I'm an adult. I don't need you to take care of me."

"Baby boy, you've got your whole life ahead of you. Why are you doing this?"

"Because I want to. Because she's the one I want to be with."

Confusion spread across her face. "I don't understand."

Laughing, Adam wrapped his arms around Wynn's waist and pulled her against his body. "It's not for you to understand. Trust me. What we have works for us."

"I don't want to see you hurt," Sherry whispered.

"Honey, I can handle it. I'm a grown man. I'll survive. But I do want and plan to be with Wynn."

"And you're telling me, Wynn is who you want in your life."

Adam grinned, looking at Wynn with a mixture of tenderness and passion on his handsome face. "Yes." His admission made her blood soar. Adam gave her a quick squeeze and then released her, crossing the floor to give his sister a huge bear hug. When he stepped away, he cupped her cheek. "Be happy for me. I'm going to hope that you meet someone who makes you feel as complete as Wynn makes me feel. I want you to be happy and have someone as wonderful in your life."

Tears filled Sherry's eyes. "I want that, too."

"Then it'll happen for you, too," Adam stated confidently, reaching out a hand to Wynn. She grabbed his hand and squeezed.

Chapter 16

The Monday following the cookout, Wynn entered the offices of Nursing Solutions to quiet. The silence halted her in her tracks. For once, the CD player sat in the off position. No Mozart, Beethoven, or Kenny G serenaded potential customers. Confused, Wynn pursed her lips together, stepped out of the room, and glanced at the name plate beside the door before reentering the room.

In the outer office, Helen sat at her desk with the receiver attached to her ear, furiously taking notes on a pad. She hung up the phone. "What are you doing?"

"No music. I thought I was in the wrong office," Wynn teased. "So I had to check. Make sure I was in the right place."

"Ha-ha. You're so funny. Good morning."

"I try." Smiling, Wynn crossed the carpeted floor and dropped into the visitor's chair next to the desk. "Good morning to you, too. What's up with the music?"

Helen shrugged. "Nothing. I just haven't had time to find a good station."

"I'm sure that'll change soon."

"Yeah. Probably. I just have one thing to say to you this morning."

Wynn's eyebrows rose. "Oh?"

"Mmm-hmm. Your boyfriend can really throw one hell of a party."

Laughing softly, Wynn placed her purse on the edge of Helen's desk and her briefcase next to her chair. "Yes, he can. What happened to you? You showed up pretty late."

Helen grimaced. "I had some problems at home. The hot water tank died and I had to call a plumber."

"Yuck! Is everything okay now?"

"Fine. New hot water tank and a major expense." Helen grunted. "I don't want to talk about that anymore. You tell Adam that I said he can invite me to any party he gives. Any time, any place." Helen closed a green file and tossed it into her out-box. "The food was great, company was entertaining, and everyone seemed to be having a wonderful time."

"The clown surprised me. Adam hadn't told me about that." Wynn stretched her legs in front of her. "I was wondering how we were going to keep the kids entertained. But he had it covered. I guess that's why Gautier pays him the big bucks."

Nodding, Helen picked up her mug and drained the final drops of coffee. "Correct me if I'm wrong, Adam's parents and your parents were neighbors. Right?"

"You've got it." Wynn dipped her head.

"The tall woman was Adam's sister?"

"Yes. Sherry."

Helen nodded. "She's not happy about you and Adam, is she."

Surprised, Wynn stared at the older woman. "You saw that?"

"Sherry's body language said it all." Helen chuckled. "Dislike and distaste filled her face each time she glanced your way. Right now, she's in hate-you mode."

"Yeah, she is." Wynn sighed, feeling the same sting of disappointment. "I feel bad for her. But it's not my problem."

"Weren't you girlfriends growing up?"

Nodding, Wynn added, "The best of friends. We covered for each other when we snuck out and helped each other in school."

"What's her problem?" Helen rose from the desk and stepped into the small kitchenette. She returned with a chocolate doughnut, biting into it as she sank into her chair.

"Sherry hates the fact that I'm going out with her baby brother. She called me a cradle robber."

Frowning, Helen munched on her doughnut for a minute. "I don't think you robbed anything. Adam came after you. It was his choice. And if I hadn't encouraged you to go out with him that first time, you guys wouldn't be together."

"Things were a little tense at first. I thought Mrs. Carlyle was going to have one of those Fred Sanford heart attacks." Wynn clutched her chest with her hand and cried, "I'm coming to join you, Elizabeth."

Laughing, Helen joined in. "I'm coming to

join you, Elizabeth, my son's involved with an older woman."

Giggling uncontrollably, Wynn waved a hand. "Stop! Stop! Seriously, I felt like a freak for the first few minutes. Thank goodness it didn't last. Both families settled down and let the day happen."

"Except for Sherry?"

Wynn nodded. "Except for Sherry."

Leaning back in her chair, Helen folded her arms across her chest and asked, "What are you going to do about her?"

"Nothing. It's her problem, not mine."

"True. Here's how I see things. You can take them for what they're worth or leave them. It's up to you. What you and Adam do is your business. You don't need anyone's approval to have a relationship."

"I agree with all of that. But Sherry got me to thinking."

Frowning, Helen asked, "About what?"

"What in the hell am I doing with Adam? There's no future with him. We're sort of like friends with benefits. Am I setting myself up for a painful breakup?"

"I don't know," Helen responded. "Are you?"

"I like him a lot." Wynn leaned forward and fidgeted with the strap from her purse. "And I'm afraid that I'll get too wrapped up in him and eventually end up with my feelings hurt."

Helen laid her hand on top of Wynn's, halting her nervous movements. "That's a possibility in any relationship. Anytime you open your heart up there's a chance of getting hurt. Honey, that's called life."

"I guess you're right," she replied reluctantly.

"I know it's difficult for you to trust after what Jim did to you. But I've always said that Jim was an idiot. He didn't recognize what he had and now he has nothing. And that's what he deserves. I think Adam knows and appreciates what he's got in you. He's not influenced by what others think. Adam makes his own decisions. No one tells him what to do. He chose you, didn't he?"

Wynn licked her dry lips. "So what are you suggesting?"

"If your feelings are involved, so what. I told you before, enjoy. Let Adam take care of you for a little bit. You deserve a little fun, games, and pampering."

"All of that is fun and I've really enjoyed it."

Helen tipped her head a tad and studied her friend and boss. "When you and Adam first started seeing each other it was supposed to be sex, dates, and fun. You had all of that and you were enjoying things. So what's changed?"

"My feelings?" Wynn answered uncertainly.

Helen pointed a finger at Wynn. "Exactly. How do you feel now? What do you want from this relationship?"

Wynn shrugged. "I don't know. I like how things are now. But I still have my sons to consider."

"Yes, you do. There's one other person you need to consider, too."

Puzzled, Wynn asked, "Who?"

"Adam. How does he feel? What does he want? When I saw you and Adam together Saturday afternoon, I thought you looked perfect. Happy, content, comfortable with each other and thrilled to be together."

Wynn felt all warm and fuzzy as she thought about Adam and the time they shared. "Sometimes things are perfect." A chill swept through her. "I just don't think it'll last."

"Get real. Nothing lasts forever, Wynn."

"I know. This pessimistic streak keeps me from believing Adam and I will be together forever."

"Honey, whatever the outcome, you've got to let it run its course. Whether you're in love with Adam or just friends with benefits, enjoy."

Nodding, Wynn rose from the chair and headed to her office. She placed her briefcase on the desk and sank into her chair. Staring out the window, Wynn allowed Helen's comments to churn in her head.

She had to admit that she'd never felt like this about anyone, not even Jim. She'd loved her husband, created two beautiful children, and would have stayed with him, if he'd wanted to continue their marriage. But as the years passed, she had to admit that she wasn't happy and made the best of the situation because of her kids.

Unfortunately, Jim never sparked the kind of emotions that surged through her when Adam entered a room. Maybe it was the younger man thing, but she sure loved having him in her life, being with him, and spending time with him. Her only reservation concerned their future.

Did Adam truly love her? Or was he living out one of his fantasies? Wynn couldn't compete with the young women parading through his life on a daily basis. What about children? Did he

want them? There were so many issues that
needed to be addressed if they were going to
have more than a fling.

"I'm going to put all of those questions on the
backburner and concentrate on having fun,"
Wynn decided, speaking out loud as if it would
settle all of her worries. "I'm going to live for the
moment and be with Adam as long as things between us are good."

Chapter 17

The Latin rhythm of Kenny G's "Sax-o-loco" swirled around the car as Adam pulled through the Harbortown security gates and navigated his way along the maze of townhouses. Wynn swayed back and forth to the beat, humming to the music.

"Tell me again," Adam said. "Why am I here?"

Wynn laughed and leaned over the transmission gear to plant a quick kiss on his cheek. "It's a party, Adam."

"Yeah. For girls."

Try as she might, Wynn couldn't repress the laughter that boiled up from her gut. Adam was so cute when he pouted like a little kid.

Annoyed at her, he gave her one of the looks he reserved for bad service or idiots. "What's so funny?"

"You."

"What's that supposed to mean?" Adam made a left at the next intersection. Her laughter must be infectious because Wynn noticed a hint of a smile shining through Adam's pretend snarl.

"You sound just like Kevin and Jimmy. The big difference is I know you like women."

"I like one woman," he whispered in a soft, enticing tone. His hot and intimate gaze rested on the sway of her breast as the car moved through the parking lot. The heat of unquenched passion burned from his gray eyes. His expression was anything but childlike.

Wynn flushed as her body responded to him. Her nipples hardened to tight buttons against her silk top. Adam made her feel so precious. So loved. Since they crossed the intimacy threshold, they had become incredibly close. She'd never experienced anything like what she had with Adam. After more than ten years of marriage to Jim, she'd never been as close to her husband as she felt with Adam after only a few months.

She had to constantly remind herself that this was an affair and that Adam couldn't possibly love her. But boy, did he do a great impression of caring for her and her children. Speaking of her boys, she had to really be careful. Adam was making it more and more difficult to keep Adam away for her kids. Friday night he popped in with a board game, cheeseburgers and fries for the kids, and chicken marsala for them. It had been a wonderful family evening. If she didn't watch out, she might just fall in love with this man. Wynn gasped as her hand flew to her mouth. *Ohmigod! Did I just think that? You cannot let this happen.* Although she tried to keep some distance between her children and Adam, it was getting harder and harder to not succumb to Adam's charms.

"Brennan and Krista are your colleagues." She squeezed his hand resting on the transmission gear. "Not mine. They invited us and that's why we're here."

He grunted. "You are just too happy today."

She giggled and shrugged. "What can I say?"

"Not much. Wait!" He pointed a finger at a clay-colored brick townhouse. "There's their place." He slowed the car and stopped, waiting for a car to pull out before smoothly sliding into the spot. After cutting the engine, he slipped out of the car, ran around the hood, and helped Wynn out, taking a minute to retrieve their gift from the backseat.

Wynn waited beside Adam while he rang the doorbell. Minutes later, the door swung open and Brennan stood in the doorway.

"Hey, man! Come on in."

"Can I come in, too?" she teased.

Embarrassed, Brennan flushed red under his collar. "Sorry, Wynn." He bowed deeply and waved a hand at the house's interior. "Please come into my humble abode."

She laughed and stepped into the air-conditioned interior. Music and women's giggling filled the air.

Brennan pointed to a room off the foyer. "That's where all the ladies are. Adam, we're on the deck."

Adam handed Wynn their gift and followed the expectant father down the hall to the back of the townhouse. Left standing alone, Wynn decided to find her own way. She followed the female voices to the living room.

Krista emerged from the opposite way. "Wynn!" Krista gave her a one-arm hug. "I was wondering if you would make it."

"Hi, Krista."

The pregnant woman practically waddled into the living room with a tray of appetizers. She set the food on the table and plopped down in a Queen Anne chair. Wynn doubted Krista would be able to get up without some assistance.

"How are you?" Wynn asked.

"Tired. I can't wait to get this baby out of me."

Wynn knew exactly how she felt. She glanced around the room. She knew one or two of the ladies, but not all. Tia and Cathy worked at Gautier and Wynn had met them both at different Gautier functions.

Krista waved a finger at the remaining women that Wynn didn't know. "This is Tia's sister Nia. The lady with the busy little boy is my sister-in-law, Liz. Let's not forget the bundle of energy in her arms. That's Joshua. Everyone, this is Wynn Evans. She's Adam Carlyle's friend."

A chorus of hellos and welcomes erupted in the room. Wynn wasn't certain who had said what. Everyone appeared to be in a good mood, so she responded positively.

The toddler broke free from his mother's arms and raced across the room. He halted in front of Wynn and lifted his arms. Surprised, she gave Liz a questioning look before picking him up and placing Josh in her lap.

Liz laughed. "Krista, look. Josh just found a new woman to charm." She smiled at Wynn. "My son loves women. You're just too pretty for him to pass up."

Embarrassed, Wynn ducked her head and brushed a lock of hair behind her ear. "Thank you."

Tia rose from the sofa and handed Wynn a name tag and a penny. Wynn rubbed the square piece of paper on her top and then frowned skeptically at the penny. "What am I supposed to do with that?"

"It's part of one of the games we're going to play."

"The penny game will make you crazy. But it's a lot of fun," Nia added.

Liz reached for the gift on the floor next to Wynn. "I'll put this with the others. There's munchies in the dining room and Brennan is grilling chicken and steaks for later."

Josh wiggled off Wynn's lap and hurried after his mother.

"Food," Krista explained. "He saw his mother going toward the kitchen and he didn't want to miss out on any food that might come his way."

"Oh!"

Liz returned with a mixing bowl, wooden spoon, and a bag of cotton balls. She placed the bowl and spoon on the coffee table before tearing open the bag of cotton balls. "This is our first game. We're going to blindfold you and you have to take as many balls of cotton from the table and place them in the bowl."

Pointing at Wynn, Tia said, "She arrived last. Let her go first."

Oh Lordy! Wynn thought. She scooted to the edge of the table. "I'll go."

On the deck, Adam, Christophe, and Steve sat listening to R&B. Brennan slipped through the sliding door onto the deck and shut it. He handed a frosty green bottle to each man. "Friends, drink up. There's plenty more where that came from."

Chuckling, Steven twisted the cap off the bottle and tossed the cap in the trash near the grill. "Speaking of drinking up, make sure you get plenty of sleep. Once that baby gets here, that will be a lost cause. If you're lucky, you'll sleep when the baby sleeps. It's not your life anymore."

Grunting, Brennan admitted, "Yeah. I've been thinking about that. I'm not sure how that's going to go."

Steve rose from his chair and patted his brother-in-law on the back. "Liz and I will be here to help you."

Adam tossed the bottle cap in the air and caught it. "Family will make everything easier."

"Hey, Brennan, what are the ladies up to?" Steve stretched out on the patio lounger.

"Liz just started the first game." Brennan said, lifting the top of the grill and reaching for a fork. "I think they've got about six to eight lined up to play. It'll go on for hours."

Steve lifted the longneck bottle to his lips. "Good. What time does the Pistons game start?"

Studying his watch, Brennan answered, placing chicken and steaks in a blue roaster pan. "In about thirty minutes. Let me get this meat inside and then we can head to the family room."

"Cool!" Adam said. "They've been hot all season."

"They have. The family room is all set up. I've got a new HD 50-inch flat screen television. Man, you get every detail on that baby."

This isn't so bad, Adam thought, allowing the chatter around him to go unnoticed. When Wynn had asked him to come along, his first instinct had been to say no. But now that he was here, he was having an okay time. Swapping stories with the guys and drinking beer worked for him. It was good to see people in a nonwork environment having a good time. Adam leaned back in the chair with his beer, enjoying the gentle breeze floating around him.

"So what about you, Adam?" Steve broke into Adam's introspection.

"What?" He swung one leg over the arm of the chair and swung it back and forth.

"You've been with Wynn awhile. What's up with that?" Brennan closed the top of the grill. "Are you two getting serious?"

Not sure if he liked the direction this conversation was taking, Adam shrugged. "It's all good."

"But is it better than good?" Christophe asked.

Although Adam knew Christophe had been listening to their conversation with rapt attention, he didn't expect the Frenchman to ask such a personal question. Adam smiled, thinking of all the time he'd recently spent with Wynn. No matter how much they were together, he wanted more. He loved being with Wynn, her sons, and even Wynn's mother, Peg. Although he preferred being around Mrs. Evans in very small doses. "Yeah. It is."

Christophe took a swig from his bottle and gazed directly at Adam. "What are you going to do about it?"

Eyes widening, Adam studied the other man. Christophe seemed to be everywhere these days. He studied everything and everyone. But he kept his opinions to himself. This was the first time the man had made his presence known.

"I haven't planned on doing anything about it," Adam stated, rising from the chair to retrieve another beer.

"You don't want Wynn to get away, do you?"

Hell, no! swept through Adam's thoughts. *She's mine.*

Noting the expression on Adam's face, Christophe chuckled. "She's very attractive. At the launch, I noticed quite a few men eyeing your lady. You better watch your back. Someone's bound to try to take her from you."

"I'll take that under advisement," Adam answered in a nonchalant tone that hid the fear creeping into his soul.

Christophe saluted Adam with the beer bottle. "When it comes to a beautiful woman, never take anything for granted. You can look up and someone has swept her away. Don't let that happen."

"I don't plan on it."

"Good. Stake your claim."

Adam sat back in his chair. Christophe was right. It was past time for him to put his mark on

Wynn. She meant more to him than anyone in his life.

"What about you, Adam? Do you want kids?" Steve asked, finishing off his beer. He set the bottle on the floor near the grill and picked up another.

Adam nodded. He loved being with Wynn's boys. They were bright, intelligent, and quick-witted. "I would like a kid or two. Three would be okay with me. I don't think any kid should grow up alone. It's difficult and lonely."

"Yeah. I agree with you on that. I want at least one more," Steve admitted. "But Liz isn't ready for another one just yet. She feels Joshua should be on his way to school before we try again."

Brennan slapped his brother-in-law on the back. "I'm glad to hear it. I don't think this complex can take three small children from the Gillis and Thomas families. Let's give the cousins a chance to bond before adding a third baby to the mix."

Steve laughed. "The management would put us both out."

Adam sat quietly throughout this exchange, going over the comments of all three men. Today had opened his eyes to what he truly wanted for his future. He didn't want to lose Wynn. He loved her and her family. One question remained. What did he plan to do about it?

As usual the lyrical notes of Mozart filled the air outside Nursing Solutions. Wynn marched into the office and found the front desk empty. "Helen?"

The administrative assistant emerged from Wynn's office. She gripped the ever-present coffee mug in her hand. "You're back early."

"The meeting at Michigan didn't go real well." Wynn stomped across the office, dropped into the chair behind the front desk, and kicked off her pumps. Flexing her nylon-covered toes, Wynn explained, "They wanted me to practically give them the nursing staff for free. We're not doing that. Our nurses deserve a decent wage. ICU and CCU is hard work. Plus, they always want our nurses to act as charge nurses. They are going to be paid appropriately if that amount of work is expected from them."

"You know they think they're important. After all, they are the University of Michigan."

"I don't care. Michigan is going to pay for the

proper services like everyone else. What have you been up to?"

Helen refilled her mug with fresh coffee and took the guest seat at the reception desk. "Filling orders. It's been really busy today. We had quite a few calls this morning."

Impressed, Wynn patted the older woman on the hand. "Good. Did you make enough money for me to go on vacation for a few days?"

"I'm working on it."

They both laughed. Wynn rose from the desk and grabbed her shoes. "I'm starving. What do you want for lunch?"

"I don't know. Give me a minute."

The outside door to the office opened and Wynn turned in the entrance to her office to see who had arrived. She was surprised but pleased to find Adam filling the doorway.

As usual, he looked sexy and yet professional in a black tailored suit. A cream shirt and black-and-white tie completed his wardrobe and provided a nice contrast. At that moment, she felt pride that this man was in her life.

"Good afternoon, ladies," he greeted, shutting the door after him. "Have you guys had lunch?"

"You know, we were just discussing that," Helen replied easily.

He crossed the carpeted floor and kissed Wynn's lips. She responded instantly.

Smiling down at her, he said, "That was worth the trip."

Without hesitation Wynn cupped his cheek. "Yes, it was. What brings you to my end of town?"

"I wanted to talk with you." He revealed a brown Panera bread bag. "And I brought lunch."

Helen rose from her spot at the desk and removed the bag from his hand. "You are the best." She opened it and glanced inside. "What did you get?"

Without taking his eyes off of Wynn, he answered, "Chicken or tuna salad. Take your pick. Or turkey breast on whole wheat. There are chips, apples, and chocolate chip cookies to round out the meal."

"You're my hero. What do you guys want to drink?"

"Cup of coffee," Adam answered, strolling into Wynn's office. "Can we eat on your worktable?"

"Sure."

Wynn reached for the pink messages on the reception desk. "Would you mind setting up the table, Helen? I want to check my messages before I sit down."

She picked up her mug and headed to Wynn's office. "Sure. Adam brought food. I'm all in."

Adam rolled his eyes and then smiled, following Helen into Wynn's office.

Each time Wynn saw Adam, her feelings for him grew. She never planned to get so involved with him, but she couldn't help herself. He was kind and gentle. It scared her how important he'd become to her. She knew she should protect her heart and control her feelings. It wasn't possible when he was so close. She loved having him near her.

Shaking her head, Wynn warned silently, *Get yourself together.*

Minutes later they all were seated around the round worktable in Wynn's office. Helen distributed the food and everyone got down to the business of eating their lunch.

"What made you think of us?" Helen asked between bites of her chicken salad sandwich.

"I wanted to talk to Wynn," he answered, shaking potato chips out of the bag.

Her pulse accelerated. What did he need? Wynn gazed at Adam. "About what?"

"A trip. Vacation. Time away from everyday life. Take your pick."

Wynn placed the sandwich on the napkin and shut her eyes for a moment. Her heart beat faster. *All of the above,* she thought. She'd love to go someplace romantic and spend time alone with Adam. *Okay, slow down. Pump the brake,* she warned silently. Get the details before you let your imagination run away. "When and where?"

"Where, Mexico. Cozumel, to be exact. When, the first of next month." He glanced at the calendar on the wall. "In two weeks. What do you think? Can you make it?"

The word *yes* hovered on her lips. Her sons came first. Wynn nibbled on her bottom lip as she considered the logistics of this trip. To give herself a little time to think the situation through, Wynn hesitated, "I'm not sure."

Disappointed, Adam asked, "Why? What aren't you sure of?"

"Why are you headed to Mexico?" Wynn asked.

"I have to be in Mexico to finalize a land deal and I thought it would be nice to add a vacation to the end of it." He reached across the table and captured her hand within his. "I'd like you to come with me."

Wynn wanted to go with Adam. They hadn't had a period of time alone in quite a while. How could she work this out? She needed more information. "Adam, how long would we be gone?" she asked, holding on to his hand.

"About a week."

Wynn grimaced, grinding her teeth together. A week was an awful long time to expect others to pick up her slack.

She felt powerless to resist the gleam in Adam's eyes. It begged and enticed her to come with him. His expression made her go warm all over and she didn't want to say no, but she had others to consider. With a sinking feeling, Wynn realized there were too many complications to sort out before she gave him the answer he wanted to hear. "I can't say yes just yet."

The light went out of his eyes. Wynn found herself anxious to see it return. "I've got to find someone to keep the kids for a week. That's a long time to expect someone to take them back and forth to school, help with homework, feed them, and keep them. Plus, there's Nursing Solutions to think about. I've got appointments set up for the next few weeks."

"I'll take care of Nursing Solutions," Helen volunteered, finishing off her sandwich. She picked up her coffee mug and drained it. "I can rearrange your schedule. That's part of my job. If you want, I'll work with your mother on keeping the kids. Maybe I can keep them a couple of days and then Peg won't have so much pressure on her. Whatever you like."

The tight knot in her belly began to unwind. Hope replaced disappointment. "Are you sure? I know you've had the boys for a day or two. Are you sure you want to do this?"

"Anything for true love," Helen chanted. Her head bobbed from side to side.

"Oh, please. Calm down," Wynn suggested.

"Thank you, Helen. You're a lifesaver."

"Of course I am."

Wynn and Adam groaned.

Chapter 19

"Hi, Mom." Wynn stepped aside and gave her mother room to enter the house. It was three days before her trip to Mexico. Hopefully, Peg didn't plan on a long visit or serious chat. Wynn didn't have time for it. "What brings you here?"

Peg Evans shut the door and braced herself against the wooden entrance. "I wanted to talk with you before you take off on your trip."

Ding! Ding! Ding! Ding! Alarm bells went off in Wynn's head. This didn't sound promising. What did Mom really want? "Sure. I'm doing laundry. Come on back."

Peg trailed after Wynn to the laundry room and leaned against the doorjamb, watching Wynn stuff clothes into the washer.

Peg tilted her head to one side and listened before asking, "Where are my grandsons?"

Wynn glanced up from the pile of laundry. "Softball practice until seven."

"Oh. I forgot."

Wynn added laundry detergent and bleach, and

switched on the machine. She moved to the dryer and began to remove and fold clothes. "What's going on?"

Peg hesitated for a moment. Her expression shifted through a series of emotions before settling on determination. "First of all, don't get mad."

"Why would I get mad?"

"I'm not sure how to broach this subject with you. I don't want to upset you," Peg answered.

Frowning, Wynn straightened and studied her mother. "Then don't."

Shaking her head, Peg added, "I wish it was that easy. But I can't let this go. It wouldn't be right."

"Go ahead." Heart pounding, Wynn waited. Peg planned to have her say whether Wynn wanted to hear it or not. The best thing she could do was get it over with.

"As you probably already guessed, this is about Adam."

Wynn shut her eyes and counted to ten and then counted a second time before asking cautiously, "What about him?"

Fidgeting with the strap of her purse, Peg continued, "Do you really think this relationship is a good idea? Is there a future for you and this young man?"

Shaking her head, Wynn said, "Wait. Wait. Wait. You were fine with us at the party. What's changed?"

"The party made me take a cold, hard look at you and Adam. I started considering your future and the kids."

Wynn's stomach twisted into knots. She paused an additional minute to make certain her words came out firm and steady. "It can't be any worse than the years I spent married to Jim."

"That's another point. Do you really believe this young man will marry you?"

Wynn could tell that this line of thinking had been brewing for a while. "Mom, I'm not looking for a husband. Been there. Done that. Adam and I are enjoying being together, spending time together. We're not talking about marriage."

"Maybe you should be. Do you have any idea what this man plans for you?" Peg moved into the room and touched Wynn's arm. "Honey, you're not the kind of woman that flits from man to man. You need and want a stable relationship with one man who will cherish and love you and your sons. At the most, Adam is a passing fancy that will burn itself out. He'll move through your life with the life expectancy of sperm and then move on to the next woman."

Shocked, Wynn exclaimed, "Mom!"

"Oh, come on." Peg rolled her eyes and waved a dismissive hand at her daughter. Exasperation tainted her words. "Please. We're adults. Besides, that man is all over you. He can't keep his hands to himself."

"My sex life is not your business." Wynn wagged a hand in her mother's direction. "I'm not talking about this with you."

"Why not? It's not like I don't know about sex. Heck, you have two kids. They didn't get here through osmosis. And while we're on the subject of kids, Adam's young enough to wants some of his own. Are you willing to have more babies?

And here's a bigger problem—can and should you have more at your age?"

Wynn couldn't deny that her mother made a great case for caution. All were excellent queries. Thoughts that had flirted through her mind from time to time. Needing time before answering Peg's questions, she reached into the dryer and pulled out an armload of clothes. Her hands shook as she placed them on the countertop and turned her back on her mother, concentrating on folding Kevin and Jimmy's softball uniforms.

"Don't make light of what I'm saying." Agitated, Peg's voice rose as she marched across the room and removed the blue slacks from Wynn's hands. "I want to help."

Spinning around to face her mother, Wynn exploded. "You call this helping? Explain that one to me."

Sighing, Peg forged ahead. "Wynn Evans, you are not the kind of woman who gets involved with a man for purely sexual reasons. You want love."

Trying not to smile too broadly, Wynn thought, *That's exactly why I got involved with Adam. But, I'll keep that revelation to myself.* "You don't know that. Anyway, my relationship with Adam is private. Hint, hint."

Ignoring Wynn, Peg forged ahead. "Yes, it is. You're so tenderhearted. I'm afraid you're going to get hurt. You'll get all wrapped up in this man and he'll tear you apart. I don't think you're up to this. Honey, you're not as strong as you'd like to believe you are."

"That's not going to happen. I know what I'm doing."

Chuckling sadly, Peg shook her head and took Wynn's hand between both of hers. "You think you do. But you don't. I see it in your eyes already. That happy, sparkle-plenty gaze that you can't hide from anyone. Baby, your experience with men has been pretty limited. You had a total of three boyfriends in high school. Jim was the only serious one. And you dated him in college. Adam is the first man you've been with since your divorce. In some ways, you are as naive as any middle schooler."

"Mom. Stop. I understood the ground rules when I started going out with Adam. We understand each other."

"I'm your mother and I love you. When Jim nearly destroyed you I kept silent. Adam has the potential to finish the job." Peg grimaced, cupping Wynn's cheek. "Oh, baby girl. Do you really know what you're doing? Adam is a handsome, powerful man that women take note of. What happens when he turns to someone else?"

Wynn felt as if she'd been struck in the head with a hammer. Okay, she knew that she'd have to accept the end of their relationship at some point. Hopefully that would be an issue in the very distant future. Did her mother have to shove the whole mess in her face this way?

"What about the boys? How do you expect them to handle the end of your relationship with Adam? Don't forget their father walked off with another woman. What if Adam does the same thing? How are you going to explain that?"

"I've got it under control. Adam and the boys don't see each other that often and I don't encourage Kevin and Jimmy to get too close to him."

"What about your feelings? How close are you?"

"I'm fine. I know what I'm doing. This thing with Adam is fun, a good time, and time together." *No, I can't say that it's purely sexual.* Yes, her feelings were involved. She might even love Adam. That was her little dirty secret. No one else's. *Mom would have a fit if I admit it.*

"Is that why you agreed to go to Mexico? To have fun?"

"Partly," Wynn answered. "Why?"

"How long do you think the fun will last?"

"Long enough. Mom." Wynn slumped against the utility table. "Why are you doing this? Is this your way of saying that you don't want to keep the boys while I'm away?"

"No. Not at all. Your father and I love having Kevin and Jimmy. But I'm more concerned about you."

"Concerned? Why? I'm fine."

"Honey, you're far from fine. You just don't know it. I know Adam is charming and there's a hint of power that draws all women. But you're not equipped to handle a man like him. His life is the way he wants it. Do you really think he wants a woman with two children in his life permanently?"

Wynn took a closer look at her mother. Peg's face was etched with concern; she was not kidding about her feelings. Wynn dropped the clothes she was folding and moved to where her mother stood. She engulfed Peg in a big bear hug. "Don't worry. I promise I won't let Adam take me down."

Getting revved up, Peg began, "I worry so. The

kids. You. Your life. I don't want you to waste another moment with anyone that might hurt you—"

"Mom! Mom! Mom! Stop. Stop."

"But what about—"

"No. I appreciate your concern, but it's time to let it go. "

Tears welled in her mother's eyes.

Wynn wrapped her arms around her mother. How could she make her mother feel better about Adam? "Come on. Let's get a cup of tea."

Wiping her eyes, Peg agreed. Wynn stretched an arm around the older woman and steered her toward the kitchen. She pushed her mother into a chair and then grabbed the teakettle.

Wynn busied herself with preparations for tea, retrieving mugs and adding sugar and cream to the table. All the while her thoughts kept returning to her mother's worries. Facing the window, she allowed her mask to slip away and let out a shaky breath.

First Sherry and now Mom. Did people see something she didn't? How many more would tell her that she was making a mistake with Adam?

Chapter 20

Everyone needs a vacation like this at least once a year, Wynn decided. She tipped the waiter and picked up her glass of Riesling from the tray.

This is paradise, she thought, taking a sip from the frosty glass. The bright sunny days, moonlit tropical evenings, and intense lovemaking were making her forget her responsibilities and family at home.

For the past week, she had been pampered, stroked, and loved beyond her most daring dreams. The pampering and stroking were the products of the resort staff. All of the loving had been provided by Adam. It was heavenly to wake up each day with him snuggled against her side. The last thing she felt at night was his arms wrapped round her waist drawing her against the warmth of his body. Adam's scent tickled her nostrils the first thing in the morning. Yes, indeed, she was living in paradise.

Adam had been the perfect partner and lover. Pampering began with the limo ride from her Beverly Hills home to Metro Airport. The flight to Cozumel had been conducted in first class. Adam had filled the time with kisses, chocolate, champagne, and fun. Once they had reached their destination, Adam escorted her through the resort lobby to the presidential suite. It was a wonderful dream-come-true vacation. A place where she could show Adam her love and forget everything else.

Eyes shut, Wynn stretched along the recliner, shaded by a palm tree. A large male hand rode up her leg, caressing her skin before resting on her thigh. A spark of excitement filled her. Wynn opened one eye and found Adam sitting next to her on the lounger. He stroked her upper thigh below her shorts.

"Howdy." Adam smiled at her, taking the glass from her hand and swiping a swig.

His nearness made her senses spin. "Hi," Wynn replied, leaning forward and stealing a quick kiss. Unable to resist, she stroked his cheek. She wanted to stay connected to him. His tantalizing scent swirled around her, bringing back memories of their lovemaking. "How'd your meeting go?"

"Same crap, different day." His voice held a note of frustration. "But we're close to completing the deal. I don't want to think about that right now," Adam dismissed, reclaiming her lips in a second hot, passionate, and very satisfying kiss. His lips pressed against hers and then gently covered her mouth, demanding a response.

His touch, firm and persuasive, invited more. When he released her, her body tingled all over, making her wish that they were back in their room.

"Tomorrow is our last night," Adam reminded, handing the wineglass back to her.

Body still humming from the intensity of his kiss, Wynn took a minute to comprehend what Adam was saying. She shook her head and tried to clear her thoughts. Wynn hated to leave this place, but she knew living in paradise had to come to an end at some point. Her voice, though quiet, held a sad note, "Yeah. I know."

"How about we do something special? Memorable."

"Like what?" she asked.

"I've got a couple of ideas," he said with a special glint in his eyes and a lift to his voice.

Intrigued, Wynn leaned close. "Like what?"

"Dinner, dancing, maybe a walk on the beach. A few other ideas might come to mind once the spirit hits me. Maybe a little surprise at the end of the evening."

"I'm in."

"Good. Then we're on for tomorrow. Wear something sexy," he suggested. His gaze lingered on her breasts for a moment too long.

"You're a bad man."

Eyebrows raised, Adam suggested, "Come back to the room with me and you can see how bad I can be."

"No," she teased. "I'm going to lay here and soak up some sun."

"Be that way." Adam rose. "I'm frying. I can't stay out here in these clothes. I'm going in to change. See you later."

Whistling, Adam swung his jacket over his shoulder and started for the hotel. Wynn swallowed the remains of her wine, lifted her sunglasses, and watched the enticing movement of his rear. Her thoughts turned to the perfect time they had this morning before he left for his meeting.

Wynn rose from the recliner and raced after him. She called. "Adam!"

He turned, watching her rush toward him. "What's up?"

Her gaze did a slow, leisurely study of his body. "You, I hope."

Adam grinned, linking her arm with his. "Come on. Let's see what kind of trouble we can get into."

"Plenty, I think."

Another beautiful evening, Wynn thought, sighing as she strolled arm-in-arm with Adam. Their night started with a wonderfully prepared meal of surf and turf in the hotel dining room, followed by slow dancing cheek-to-cheek in the nightclub. Adam capped their evening with the suggestion that they take a moonlight stroll along the beach.

They dropped their shoes on the white sand near an empty lounge chair and took off down the shore. Music from the band playing on the deck faded as they strolled farther away from the hotel. Wynn and Adam went to the water's edge and dipped their feet in the water, washing away the white sand. Wynn sighed contentedly against Adam's side.

He gazed down at her, playing with her gray lock of hair. "You okay?"

Smiling, she nodded. "It's been a while since I've been anywhere without my family. I didn't realize how much I needed the break from kids, work, and my life until we got here. This has been a perfect vacation."

Adam squeezed her arm and then ran his hand up and down her sensitive skin. "Yes. It has." Leaning close, he closed his lips over Wynn's, drinking in the taste of her.

"Thank you for asking me, insisting I come with you. It was touch and go for a few minutes. I didn't think I'd be able to work out the details so smoothly." A lump formed in her throat. "The kids didn't want me to leave them and I wasn't sure if I'd be able to find someone I trusted to keep them for a whole week." She exhaled a long sigh of contentment. "Everything worked out and that's the most important part. Mom and Helen are sharing the kids and Helen's got what she's wanted for a while."

"What's that?"

"A chance to run the business solo for a few days."

"How do you think that's going to go?"

Wynn hesitated and then answered truthfully, "Probably better than I want it to. Helen's a great employee. She'll handle everything. It's all good."

Adam hugged her against his side and kissed her forehead. "Yes, it is."

With a sense of peace Wynn hadn't felt in several years, she moved along for several minutes. Adam stopped, turned to face her. "Wynn?"

Frowning, she studied his features. A disturbing note entered his tone. It held her captive and at the same time made her feel uneasy. "Yes?"

"I love you." He cupped her face between his large hands and planted a soft kiss on her lips.

The words seemed to linger in the air. Joy

bubbled inside her and threatened to explode. Wynn had hidden the truth from herself for far too long. Now that he'd made his declaration and revealed his feelings, she felt confident enough to reveal her own. She lifted his hand to her lips and kissed the palm. "I love you, too."

The beginning of a smile tipped the corners of Adam's mouth and then turned into a grin. He wrapped her in his embrace and hugged her close, whispering into her ear, "You had me worried for a minute."

"Don't worry. You've been in my head and heart for a while. Until you said those words I didn't want to admit the truth."

"So, what happens next?" he asked, dropping a sweet kiss on her lips.

Returning the kiss, Wynn shrugged. "Enjoy being in love. Get to know each other better."

"I can do that," he responded, sweeping her into his arms and kissing her. His tongue slipped between her lips, seeking her nectar.

Wynn moved closer to Adam, allowing her breasts to brush against his chest.

Moaning, Adam rested his hands on her hips and pulled her against him. "I've got an idea." He tipped his head toward the water.

Laughing, Wynn checked the beach for other guests. "Skinny-dipping? That's what you're suggesting?" Shrugging, she said, "I like that idea."

Adam's eyes twinkled. His eyebrows rose above mischievous eyes as he gazed toward the water. "Want to give it a try?"

Grinning, Wynn checked to the left and then the right. The beach was empty. "It could be fun."

"Well?" he asked.

"I'll show you mine, if you show me yours."

"I've already seen yours."

She did a double lift of her eyebrows and her voice turned sultry. "But not underwater."

Taking up the challenge, Adam laughed loud and hardy. He stripped his Polo shirt from his body and tossed it toward the shoreline. Next came his belt. He drew down the zipper.

Butterflies danced in the pit of Wynn's belly. She loved seeing him in his natural form. Clothes enhanced his wonderfully sculpted form, made him into the urban professional she first met. His body was lean and well toned. Adam stepped out of his trousers, revealing fitted black briefs. Smiling smugly, he waited, giving her an "I dare you" look.

Confident that Adam would protect her throughout this adventure, Wynn pushed the spaghetti straps off her shoulders one at a time and allowed the bodice to drop to her waist. She shimmied out of the dress, tossed it away from the water's edge, and stood in front of Adam in her panties.

His gaze touched her breasts with a savage inner fire. Instantly, her nipples responded, hardening to pebbles. A corresponding tingle started between her legs and seconds later her panties became damp.

Taking her hand, Adam urged her forward. "Come on."

Hand in hand they ran into the water.

Chapter 21

Our last night together, Wynn thought as they made their way back to the hotel suite. A sense of wonder filled her as she waited at the entrance to their suite. This was their last night in Cozumel before heading back to Detroit.

Adam slid the key card into the slot and waited for the green flashing light. He turned the doorknob and entered the hotel suite, stepping aside to let Wynn sashay past him into the living room. A huge full moon beamed through the balcony window, filling the living room of the suite with light.

Stretching her arms toward the heavens, Wynn unwrapped the black-and-white shawl from her shoulders, revealing a black strapless top and matching skirt. She tossed the shawl on the sofa and sank onto the spot beside it, leaning forward to kiss him lightly on the lips. "Thank you for a perfect evening."

"You're welcome." Adam dropped to his knees in front of her and removed one silver sandal and then the other, propping her foot on his knee. Curious, Wynn watched as he began a gentle kneading of her foot. Moaning softly, she leaned back, sinking deeper into the plush tan-and-purple pillows. "More!" she encouraged. "That feels heavenly."

"That's where I want to take you," he said, concentrating on his work. "Relax. You've been on your feet most of the day." He worked the tight muscles and tendons.

"I relaxed real well earlier tonight," she reminded in a seductive tone.

Grinning, Adam continued his work, but took a moment to gaze at her. His eyes sparkled as they touched her. "Yeah. We did."

Adam's hands explored the texture of her bare ankle before moving farther up her leg to massage her calf. His magic hands made love to her calves as he caressed and stroked them. The gentle massage sent currents of desire surging through her.

Sighing, Wynn shut her eyes, giving herself over to the incredible sensations Adam was creating. The stroking of his fingers sent pleasant jolts through her. "Your hands are wickedly sinful," she complimented, finding herself relaxing as Adam's hands approached her thigh. She opened one eye, watching as he lifted her skirt and massaged her thigh.

"I aim to please." He planted a tender kiss on her knee.

"What am I going to do once we get home?" Wynn whined. "No nightly lovemaking or massages. I'm going to miss having you in my bed every night."

"Doesn't have to be that way." His hands moved higher.

Distracted by his change in direction, Wynn opened her legs. Adam moved between them and his hands began a lust-arousing exploration of her soft flesh. His wandering hands crested the top of her thighs, mere inches from her panties. Adam's nimble fingers stroked the silk-covered mound. Her eyes popped opened and her pleasure-filled mind focused directly on the man. "What are you doing?"

"Helping you."

Now both of his hands were under her skirt, exploring her thighs and then moving up. Every so often his fingers brushed against her crotch.

Adam hooked one finger inside the band of her panties, teasing the soft curls with his finger. Gasping, Wynn reached for his hand, holding it against her. His fingers moved under the band and drew them down her thighs, along her long bare legs, and off her feet. He tossed the scrap of fabric on the floor and returned to his position between her legs.

This time when Adam touched her, he had a completely different agenda in mind. His fingers gently traced the slit between her legs, grazing it. His touch was so soft that she barely felt it. But it was enough to send her heart into a gallop while her flesh eagerly waited to see what he planned to do next. "You like?"

Nodding, Wynn moved restlessly against the pillows, meeting the enticing movement of his fingers. "Adam!" His finger slipped between the folds and found her nub. Using his thumb, he flicked back and forth across the hot flesh.

"Yes?" he answered, lifting her skirt and ducking his head under the garment. Instantly, she felt his questing tongue against her slit. He licked up and down the seam, tasting it like an ice-cream cone. His tongue replaced his thumb, toying with her flesh. It felt heavenly, forbidden, and so right. She was powerless to do anything beyond ride out the sensations.

As Adam's tongue loved her slit, his hands moved from under the skirt and found her breasts. He palmed their weight through the fabric of her blouse, stroking and massaging her nipples to hard peaks. He stroked her nipples with tantalizing possessiveness. Seeking more, he fisted a handful of black fabric and pulled the top away from her body, freeing her breasts. A grunt of satisfaction followed. His hands lightly touched her hardening nipples, rolling the peaks between his forefinger and thumb. Her body hummed and she squirmed, working her way to his questing tongue.

As his tongue stroked her clit, his hands followed the same pattern on her breasts. Wynn was on fire. She didn't know how much more she could take before she exploded. But she wanted everything he had to give.

"Oh Lordy!" she cried, unconsciously placing her hands on his head to keep him there.

The gently lapping of earlier was gone. He sucked strongly on her nub, drawing every sensation from her body. Adam's tongue explored and tasted her, giving pleasure beyond words. Instinctively, she arched against his tongue. His hands stroked her nipples, teasing, squeezing, and caressing them as he sucked her dry.

Wynn's interior walls began to tremble, quivering as she drew closer to exploding. His tongue slid lower and dipped inside her canal.

Wynn exploded, practically screaming her release. Quivering in the afterglow of her powerful orgasm, she laid against the pillow, fighting to recover. With another lick of his tongue, she exploded into another orgasm.

Completely sated, Wynn lay on the sofa, watching him through tired eyes. Adam rose from the floor. He scooped her into his arms and headed for the bedroom.

"We're not done," he announced, laying her gently on the bed before stripping his clothes from his body and then turning his attention to hers. Once they were both completed naked, he slid into the bed beside her, pulled her into his arms, and kissed her thoroughly. She could taste herself on his lips. The erotic fragrance filled her with renewed hunger and she reached for him. "No. We're not done."

Late into the night, Wynn dosed contentedly with Adam at her side. She smiled, thinking how perfect their last night in Cozumel had been.

Adam scooted against Wynn's back and wrapped an arm around her waist, pulling her against his body. He stroked his hand over her bare arm. "Sweetheart, I love you."

Cocooned within the warmth of those special words, Wynn answered, "I love you, too."

"Let's get married," Adam whispered into her ear.

Wynn's eyes popped open. Caught off guard, Wynn stayed quiet for a moment. Had she heard him correctly? She shifted in his arms to face him. "What?"

"I said, let's get married. We can do it right here, right now. Stay an extra day or two and get married in Mexico."

Lost for words, Wynn opened and closed her mouth several times. No words came out. Marriage? Where had that idea come from? This was not the time to make such a serious move.

Kevin and Jimmy were already worried about her relationship with Adam. The boys had cried and begged her not to go on this vacation. Jim's comments on Adam had hit a bull's-eye with the kids. How much damage would she do to her children if she came home as a newly married woman?

A tense, thick silence filled the bedroom. Adam waited calmly for an answer. She didn't have one.

"Well, are you sure you're not getting caught up in the moment?"

Restless, he moved a bit away, trying to see her face in the darkness. "What do you mean?"

"We're here in this exotic locale." Using her most persuasive tone, Wynn waved a hand around the room. "And we've been together constantly for over a week. Maybe you think marriage would be more of the same."

He laughed unpleasantly. The harsh sound grated on Wynn's nerves and twisted her belly into knots. "Noooooo! I know what I want."

"Do you? Do you really?"

His body stiffened against her and a hard edge entered his voice that had never been directed at her. "Why don't you say what you really mean?"

"Don't get mad. Just listen," Wynn pleaded.

"Who do you think you're fooling? There's something more." His eyes glowed like hard glass in the darkness of the room. "What are you not saying?"

"Adam." She reached for his hand. He shook it off and shifted away. She felt the chill as surely as if he had drawn the blanket away. "I've got to think about my sons."

"This isn't about Kevin and Jimmy. I asked you to marry me."

Wynn shook her head. "You are wrong." She emphasized each word. "Any decision I make involves not just you, me, but my sons as well. Everything, everything I do involves my kids."

Adam scoffed, turning on his side away from her, facing the opposite wall.

She touched his shoulder. "Adam, don't turn away. I thought you understood. My life is not my own. I have two boys that depend on me. Whether I go to the movies or have dinner with a friend after work, there are ripples that affect their lives."

The disdain and touch of anger in Adam's voice broke her heart. "Are you telling me that you have to go home and talk to your kids before you can make a decision? Marry me?"

"I'm saying I have to consider everyone before I make a decision. I can't get married here and expect to go home. Everything is not going to be perfect."

Adam's agitation was clear. He tossed the blanket back and sat on the end of the bed. "You're saying that you don't want to get married."

Wynn climbed out of the opposite side of the bed and turned to face him. "I'm saying let's not rush. Jim's been filling my kids' heads with all kinds of terrible stuff. It's my job to take care of that."

Nude, he stood with his arms folded across his chest and demanded, "Give me an example."

"Remember the grief the kids were giving me when you picked me up at home?"

Shrugging, he nodded.

"We can thank Jim for that. On his weekends with Jimmy and Kevin, he starts in on our relationship. He assures the boys that he'll always be there for them. They can come live with him. There's always room at his house for them."

"What do you say to them when they tell you about this?"

"They don't come to me. I have to force the info from them. Probe until they finally admit that they are worried."

Adam grunted, flapped his arms in the air like a fluttering bird. "What's next?"

"I need time. I have to talk with my children. Their fears must be calmed or we won't get any peace. I can't come home with you on my arm."

Nodding, he moved around the room, picking up his clothes. "Your answer to marriage is no."

Wynn rushed around the bed and held Adam's hands in hers. She cupped the side of his head, forcing him to look at her. "My answer is not yet. I'm asking you for time. Let me prepare my children."

His gaze cut away from her.

Wynn's heart ached for Adam. "This isn't the end of us."

"So you say. Look, I need to think. I'm going to take a shower," Adam announced in a flat, "don't bother" tone, leaving the bedroom and shutting the bathroom door behind him.

Chapter 22

The persistent shrill of the telephone jerked Wynn from a restless sleep. She stretched an arm across the nightstand, fumbling for the receiver. "Ahh," Wynn muttered, picking up the line and growling a crabby, "What?"

"Good morning," began the chipper automated voice. "This is your wake-up call."

Wynn dropped the phone back into the cradle and turned on her side, plumping her pillow and intending to go back to sleep. She reached across the bed to shake Adam. Confused, her eyes popped open. His side of the bed was empty. Adam hadn't come to bed last night.

She threw back the covers and swung her legs over the side of the mattress, reaching for her robe. On the lookout for Adam, she padded barefoot out of the bedroom into the living room. Knocked out and completely dressed, Adam laid prone on the sofa, asleep.

Relieved, Wynn sank into a chair and watched Adam sleep, reviewing and discarding several approaches to make him listen. Their talk last night hadn't gone very well. Hurt and upset, Adam refused to acknowledge the truth of her words. He hadn't displayed any concern or understanding regarding her children. She refused to marry a man who ignored her children's needs.

Wynn sighed, rubbing her throbbing forehead. What was she going to do? She loved Adam and wanted him in her life. They had to reach a compromise. There had to be a way to reach him, for him to see reason.

Adam stirred, stretching and yawning. Slowly, he opened his eyes and focused on her.

"Morning," she whispered.

His closed and unapproachable expression chilled her. Wynn rubbed her hands up and down over her arms.

Tears were seconds away, but Wynn held them back with superhuman strength. Adam seemed so distant. The man she'd spent the last seven days with had vanished, replaced by this cold person. Their relationship was finished, done. Wynn drew her tongue across her dry lips and fidgeted with the silk belt of her robe. "How are you feeling this morning?"

"Okay," he answered, rubbing his hand across his five o'clock stubble.

"Do you want to do breakfast?" Wynn asked softly.

Shaking his head, Adam frowned and rose from the sofa. "No. Maybe I'll call room service."

Wynn bit her lip. "Can we talk about last night?"

Ignoring her question, he asked, "You got a taste for anything in particular?"

"No. Please don't pretend you didn't hear me."

Standing, he faced her. "There's nothing to talk about."

"I think there is."

Adam snorted. "Like what?"

"Our future. Our relationship. Our love," she reminded.

"Our future together didn't mean much to you last night. Why should we rehash the pitiful scene this morning?"

Standing, Wynn moved across the room and stood in front of Adam. "Because I don't think you understand me."

He chuckled. "Oh, I understand all right. You don't want to marry me."

"That's not what I said."

"Then what?"

"I need time. My kids need time."

"You think time will make everything better between us."

"I don't know. I know my boys are not ready."

Disgust appeared on his face, but he kept silent.

"I want you to understand my mind-set. Where I'm coming from concerning my sons. Think about it, my kids don't truly know you."

"Whose fault is that?" he practically yelled.

Swallowing hard, she tried another approach. "I have to protect them. That's my job."

"From me?" Adam demanded.

"From anything that could hurt them," she shot back.

Shaking his head, he snatched up the blanket and folded it into a neat square. "I don't agree with anything you've said so far. I would never hurt them."

"That's probably true."

His tone dipped to a chilly note. "Probably?"

"I'm sorry. That didn't come out right."

He dropped the blanket on the sofa and placed his hands on his hips. "You're damn right it didn't."

"What I meant was I can't bring you into our home permanently without there being some connection." Wynn's hands moved aimlessly as she sought the correct words. "Comfort level. Jimmy and Kevin must trust and respect you if you're going to be a stable part of their lives."

He nodded. Wynn recognized the attorney in him was on the attack. He intended to plead his case. God help anyone who got in his way. "How is that supposed to happen when you keep me from getting to know them? Each and every time I come by your place, you work incredibly hard to keep the distance between us." Hands shoved deep into his pockets, Adam paced the length of the room as he spoke. "We have to spend time together for them to get used to me. We've only been out a couple of times as a foursome. How many times have I suggested that we go out and have dinner or go to a movie?"

Adam had just put her on trial. He might be the attorney but Wynn refused to let him get away with it.

"Adam, I can't have a parade of uncles in their young lives. They need stability, not different men in and out of their lives at every turn. We just went through a terrible divorce."

"That's not what I'm offering. I'm the man who wants to marry their mother and be a father to them."

"And that's another thing. Do you truly believe you're ready to be a parent, get married, and have a ready-made family?"

"I wouldn't have asked you to marry me if I didn't plan on doing my job."

The pain in Wynn's head pounded, causing spots to float in front of her eyes. She massaged her forehead. "Adam, I didn't know where this relationship was going. I certainly didn't expect you to say the 'M' word."

"What did you think we were doing, Wynn?"

She shrugged. "I went into this believing this was a fling. Good sex that would run its course and then I would return to my normal life. I took it as sex and fun. One day you would move on and that would be that."

Jaws clenched, Adam scoffed. "Good to know that you thought so highly of me."

Wynn felt the urge to be close to Adam. She cautiously approached his side and touched his arm.

Instantly, he jerked away as if she'd stuck him with a needle. He stepped away, putting some distance between them.

"If we plan to make our relationship work, you got to visit more often with the kids. Do things with us."

Ignoring Wynn, Adam returned to the sofa, sat, and shoved his feet into his shoes. "I expected you to understand my position. I thought we had more of a connection. Obviously, I was wrong."

"Don't be that way. What *do* you expect?"

Tense and uncompromising, his face took on that closed expression once more. He marched to the door. "You know, I think I'll go downstairs to the restaurant for a bite. See you later."

"Adam!"

With a hand on the door, he inquired, "Yes?"

"It's not going to go away. We have to talk this out."

"I'll be back in a bit. Make sure you're ready to leave about two." He opened the door, hovered in the doorway for a minute, as if he had something he wanted to say, and then stepped out of the suite.

Emotionally exhausted from the exchange, Wynn sank into the chair. The tears that had been threatening to fall during their argument finally arrived. She couldn't hold back anymore.

Chapter 23

I refuse to take this any longer. I want an answer and Adam's going to give me one, Wynn vowed as she entered the elevator. Her stomach twisted into nervous knots as she traveled to the thirty-eighth floor of the 600 Tower of the GM Renaissance Center with Tia Edwards at her side.

Determined to talk with Adam and resolve their issues, Wynn had made a trip to Gautier's office. Security halted her when she entered the executive wing of the tower. Always the dutiful executive assistant, Tia had popped down to the lobby, retrieved Wynn, and escorted her to Adam's office. Along the way Tia talked nonstop, explaining that Adam had gone to lunch but was expected back any minute. Wynn sensed Tia's uneasiness and nervousness. Had Adam confided some detail to Tia about their trip to Mexico?

Tia installed Wynn in Adam's office and then returned to her ringing telephones, leaving Wynn standing before the ceiling-to-floor windows watching the People Mover cruise above Tom's Oyster bar and DuMouchelle Auction Gallery. Was this the best place to have such a private and life-changing conversation? Probably not. This way the discussion should be short, sweet, and to the point.

Since they returned from Mexico, Wynn had received the silent treatment from Adam. No phone calls, e-mail, or cute text messages. Before she could move ahead with her life, she needed to have Adam state the obvious. If they were over, she wanted to hear it from his lips. Not this silence that could mean anything and be interpreted any number of ways.

Wynn shuddered at the thought of losing Adam. They were so close to having their happily-ever-after and now she found herself on the brink of ending their relationship. A big part of her hoped they'd find a way to salvage things and make another attempt to be together.

She rubbed a hand across her forehead. Lordy, she didn't want their relationship to end. Not yet, not with anger, misunderstanding, and pain between them. She wanted to stay in Adam's life and keep him in hers. Marriage remained a mystery, an unanswered question for them to sort out. But she felt certain about two things: she loved Adam, and Kevin and Jimmy needed time to acclimate and accept Adam before he became part of their family.

Yes, she admitted it was her fault that Adam and her sons weren't better acquainted. But it wasn't an insurmountable problem. A bit of quality time as a family would remedy that easily.

Before the trip to Mexico, it had become Adam's daily ritual to call. Sometimes he'd reach her at Nursing Solutions or at home after she'd gotten the boys to bed. They'd chat about their workdays. Or Adam would ask about her plans for dinner, or what funny or interesting tidbit the boys had revealed over the evening meal.

"I brought you a cup of tea, Wynn." Tia crossed the carpeted floor and set the tray on the corner of the desk.

"Thanks, Tia."

"No problem."

Telephones continued to ring incessantly. Tia frowned and turned toward the door. "Excuse me. I need to get back to my desk. I'll be right back." Tia hurried from the office, closing the door after her.

Voices were getting closer. It sounded as if they were right outside the office. The silhouette of a man and woman appeared through the frosted glass. Wynn instantly recognized Adam's unconscious movements. His hand tucked into his pocket, the tilt of his head, and his commanding stance were his trademark gestures.

"No. No. You're wrong." Vivian stated confidently. Her hand glided along the edge of the lapel of Adam's suit jacket.

Frowning, Wynn groaned. *That woman always stirs up trouble between Adam and me.*

Laughing, Adam leaned into her touch. "I don't think so. I know my seafood. The wait staff served you ocean perch, not lake perch."

"How do you know?" Vivian challenged, planting a hand on her hip while maintaining a hold on his lapel with the other hand.

"I'm the boss. I always know," he stated self-assuredly.

So that was why Wynn hadn't heard from him. He'd been spending his free time with Vivian. *No, Wynn, that's not fair,* she chastised herself. *All you really know for sure is they shared lunch today.*

Vivian stroked a finger along Adam's jawline. "I'll bet you dinner at Big Fish that I'm right."

Rage surged through Wynn's blood. How dared that woman put her hands on Adam! The rational side of Wynn's brain kicked in, reminding her that Adam could do whatever he wanted and it didn't have to be with her.

Betrayal pierced her heart. This was far worse than when Jim told her he was leaving her for Lorraine. In that case, although she was hurt and worried for her children, she hadn't loved Jim in years and a sense of relief accompanied his confession that he was moving on and leaving so that she could get on with her life.

When it came to Adam, her feelings ran deeper, were stronger, more intense. The last thing they needed was this monkey wrench thrown into their already-wounded relationship.

"What else will you give me?" he asked provocatively.

"Anything you want."

"Interesting. I'll have to think on that one."

"I'll make it good," Vivian promised.

Enough! I've heard enough. Lowlife son of a bitch. No wonder he hasn't called, Wynn thought, placing her cup on the tray, and then marched across the room and snatched open the door. She folded her arms across her chest and glared daggers at Adam.

Adam turned toward the door with a frown on his face. Shocked, his eyes widened. "Wynn!" He took a step away from Vivian, putting some distance between them. "What are you doing here?"

Filled with anger and humiliation, she answered, "I came by to talk with you. I was wondering why I hadn't heard from you. Now I know."

Adam slipped into the office, stopped in front of her, and took her hand in his. "Is everything okay?"

Wynn flinched away from his touch. "I'm fine."

"How long have you been here?"

She looked toward the door and found Vivian watching them. Wynn moved across the carpeted floor, shut the door in Vivian's startled face, and then turned to face Adam. Her body language changed. Wynn swayed her hips seductively as she moved toward him and caressed the lapel of his suit jacket. "What else will you give me?" she mimicked.

Embarrassed, Adam looked away as his cheeks flared scarlet, hastening to say, "That didn't mean anything. Really. It's not what you think. We were teasing."

"Mmm," she grunted. "I believe that one."

"Umm, umm," he stammered. "This isn't what you think."

This was the first time she'd seen Adam at a loss for words. If the situation hadn't been so painful, she almost would have laughed. Of course it was what she thought. "No? Then what is it?"

He pointed a finger to the door. "We went to lunch and were joking around."

"Interesting. So that's what it's called now."

"Come on, Wynn. You know better than that."

Taking in a deep breath, Wynn headed for the door. She faced him with a hand on the doorknob. "I thought I did. But maybe I don't."

"Wynn!" Adam tried to take her hand. "Don't. We do need to talk."

"I think we're past that now." She swallowed the bitter taste of hurt and despair, shook off his hand, and opened the door. *I won't cry. Adam won't see tears,* Wynn silently promised. She mustered all the dignity at her disposal and stiffened her backbone. Head held high, she marched out of the room, past Tia's desk where Vivian stood.

Wynn blindly made her way through Gautier's executive offices to the elevators. Holding herself together by sheer force of will, she punched the button to call the elevator. "Come on. Come on," she mumbled urgently, jabbing the button and hoping it came quickly and took her away from this terrible scene.

Tia Edwards touched the older woman's arm. "Wynn?"

Wynn jumped, running her hand across her throbbing forehead. "Oh, Tia. You scared me. I was a million miles away. Hi."

Tia gave Wynn a gentle smile. "I got that. You okay?"

Nodding, Wynn answered, "Mmm-hmm." But tears pooled in her eyes and Wynn feared the flood gates would open and she'd be unable to control herself.

"Wait. Let's get out of the hallway. Come with me." Tia grabbed her arm and gently led her away from the elevator.

Tia guided her down the hallway to the executive washroom. They entered the elegant room and the young woman pushed Wynn onto a sofa, and then sat down beside her. "Is there anything I can do?"

Wynn shrugged. "It's not your fault. This was between Adam and me."

"Yeah, but I knew he'd left for lunch. I just didn't know Vivian was with him."

"Again. It's not your fault." Wynn let out a shaky breath. "We had things that we needed to be resolved. It's been done."

"Adam's not seeing her, you know."

"It doesn't matter."

"Yes, it does. I know Adam cares about you. Vivian can be bulldozing and overpowering at times. She's very insistent." The cell phone in her pocket began to ring. "Excuse me a minute." Tia checked the display and rose from the sofa.

I need to get myself together, Wynn thought, rising from the sofa and heading to the vanity. *Maybe a little water on my face will make me feel better and clear my head.*

She ran water into the sink and splashed a bit on her face. The cool water revived her and she began to feel better. She picked up a hand towel and patted away the wetness. *I'll survive,* she thought, looking at her sad face.

Quick, clipped steps followed the opening of the door. Seconds later, Vivian stood next to her in the washroom.

"Oh!" Vivian exclaimed. The smirk on the attorney's lips made Wynn want to slap her.

Great! Wynn thought. *I can't get away from you today to save my soul.* She opened her eyes and gazed into the mirror at the other woman. For several tense moments they glared at each other. No one spoke. The room was loaded with suppressed emotions and fury.

"Closed any more doors in people's faces?" Vivian broke the silence, brushing a finger across one eyebrow and smoothing the hair into a neat curve.

"Only in yours." Wynn replied sweetly, facing the other woman.

Vivian smiled dropped. Fire burned brightly in her eyes. "No biggie. I've got everything I need. Adam was mine before you came on the scene."

Disbelief surged through Wynn. "Yours! Did you buy him at Kmart?"

Shocked, Vivian took a step back, demanding, "What are you talking about?"

"He's yours? Unless you purchased him, I'm pretty sure he's a free agent."

"Nobody cares what you're saying. You stole him from me. So now you've got your feelings hurt. That's the way things work. You should have stayed in your place."

Wynn's voice dropped a furious octave. "You need to check yourself. I don't steal anything, including men. Adam chose me. He asked me out."

"Pfff." Vivian dismissed with a wave of her hand. "You've been after him from the start. As you can see, he came back to me."

"Did he?" Wynn questioned in a skeptical

tone. She rubbed her hands together, acting as if she was considering Vivian's response. "Hmm. Someone very close to Adam told me that you bulldozed your way back into his life. He can't get away from you. And that you were the one who insisted he go to lunch with you today."

The younger woman's posture stiffened as her eyes narrowed to dangerous slits. Her voice dripped ice. "Let me give you a word of advice. Don't mess with me. You're playing with the wrong girl."

Wynn took a step closer and smiled, lowering her voice to a rasping whisper. "It's time for me to make myself clear. You're on the top of my list of people to mess with. Unless you want your feelings stomped down, I suggest you stay out of my face. Go someplace, sit down, and pretend that Adam wants you."

"Bitch!"

"Maybe. But that doesn't change the facts."

Vivian opened her mouth to add something.

Wynn raised a hand and announced, "We're done here." She pushed past the young attorney, leaving her standing in the washroom.

Chapter 24

Wynn took the Woodward/John R exit off I-94 of the freeway. Turning right, she flew down John R Street toward Warren Avenue, humming along to Mariah Carey's *Butterfly*. The cell phone in her purse began to ring. She fished the silver item from her bag and answered, "Wynn Evans?"

"Wynn?" Adam said.

Who else would it be? she thought. "Yes."

"Can we get together? I'd like to talk with you. Clear the air. Talk about what happened at my office."

She shook her head as though he could see her. "I don't think so."

"Please." He paused. "Give me a chance to explain."

"No." She disconnected the call.

Her cell phone immediately rang again. She sighed. Adam refused to give up. If she didn't answer he'd start texting her any minute. Since the encounter in his office, Adam had constantly called, trying to convince her to agree to a meeting. Phone calls, text messages, e-mail, calls to the office and to her home were part of his campaign. He'd stopped by Nursing Solutions on several occasions, but she'd been out on appointments so he had missed her.

Maybe the time had arrived to have that talk and settle their differences. Hopefully she'd be done with him and could move on with her life. She hit the Answer button and chanted, "Wynn Evans."

"Don't hang up."

"I won't. Say your piece."

"Meet me. I promise if we can't work things out, I won't bother you again."

Silence followed Adam's promise. Wynn weighed her options. If she took thirty minutes and talked with him now, she'd finally be done. "Okay. When? Where?"

"Great!" A slight tinge of wonder filled his voice. But Adam instantly seized the moment. "Now. Where are you?"

"Detroit Medical Center." She turned into the parking structure attached to Harper University Hospital and snatched the ticket from the machine.

"I'll meet you at Union Street Bar on Woodward near Alexandrine. Okay?"

Wynn pulled into the parking structure and nailed a spot on the first floor near the entrance. "Make that an hour. I'm just going into a meeting. I'll see you at three."

Fifty-five minutes later, Wynn entered Union Street Bar and Grill. Dark wood and a bar that stretched the length of the main dining area made up a large portion of the interior. Framed San Francisco Union Street posters lined the beige walls. A hostess escorted Wynn across the small room to where Adam sat with a can of Coke and a glass of water in front of him. As they approached, he rose, waiting beside his chair for her. His eyes said it all. They were rimmed in red and it looked as if sleep had evaded him for days. Good! That's what he deserved.

The hostess stopped at the round table and placed a menu and wine list on the surface before quietly leaving. Wynn and Adam stood awkwardly gazing at each other.

Only weeks before they would have hugged, kissed, and held hands as they shared a meal and talked about their days. Their relationship had truly changed.

The change in Adam's expression eyes made her body quiver in response. Hunger, hot and intense, glared back at her from his brown eyes. At that moment, she wished that she'd refused his offer to talk and gone about her business.

Adam cleared his throat. "Thank you for coming."

She nodded.

He held Wynn's chair politely before returning to his spot. "Can I get you anything?"

Shaking her head, Wynn shifted in her chair. She wanted this meeting finished as quickly as possible. "I'm fine."

"Coffee? Maybe a cranberry juice?"

"No."

Arms folded protectively across her chest, Wynn leaned back in the chair and eyed the man across the table. A part of her wanted to reach out and stroke his cheek, draw him into her embrace, and assure him that they would survive this period and come out on the other end stronger, wiser, and more secure in their relationship.

Wynn loved Adam. She truly did. But she'd taken her last step backward where men were concerned. He would need to do a boatload of kissing Wynn's feet before she allowed him back into her life. If at all.

Younger, older, it didn't matter. No man would get away with treating her like she didn't matter. She deserved better and expected it.

"Okay, I'm here," Wynn announced. "Say what you have to say."

For once, Adam lacked his confident persona. It fascinated her to watch. He picked up the glass of water and took a quick sip. "Wynn, I'm sorry."

"And that's supposed to change things how?"

"Please believe me. I don't want to lose you."

"Really. You were doing a great imitation of it when I came to your office." Wynn linked her fingers together and slowly placed them on the table. "What do you call that hot mess you pulled with Vivian?"

"I wouldn't have slept with Vivian," he hurried to explain.

"How do I know that?" Wynn shot back. "And why should I believe you?"

"Up until that day at my office, have I ever given you a reason to doubt my actions or feelings? Do you think I've cheated on you?" Adam asked in a harsh, raw voice. His direct, unflinching gaze told her everything she needed to know. He may have taken a few missteps, but she never felt as if he'd taken their relationship for granted.

"No."

A long, audible breath escaped from his lips. "Thank you for that. There's no excuse for what you saw. I was hurting. When we flew to Mexico on vacation, I expected to come home with a fiancée."

She speared Adam with burning reproachful eyes. Her voice rose an octave before she caught herself and hissed, "This is not about me."

"That's not what I'm saying. Let me explain. I felt pretty low and Vivian was everywhere, in my office constantly and on the phone calling me about one crisis or another. That woman made it almost impossible to avoid her, especially because we were having problems. I was the center of her world and I enjoyed the attention. I'm almost ashamed to admit it. But Vivian stroked my ego. She made me feel like Mr. Big Man."

Wynn understood what Adam was saying. She remembered the night they first made love and Vivian's frantic call to Adam's house. For the first few weeks of their relationship, Vivian practically stalked the poor man. The young attorney inserted herself in every possible situation she found and called Adam at every turn for advice on every little detail on the work she should have been able to handle.

But that didn't excuse him from stepping in a direction that could cost him a relationship that he claimed he valued. In the end, his decision opened the door to Vivian.

Shaking her head, Wynn reminded, "I told you

we could work things out. You were the one that got the attitude, not me."

"I know." He took a sip of Coke. "It's my fault. I screwed up. I'd never proposed before. When you turned me down—"

"I didn't turn you down," Wynn fervently denied.

"I felt lost," he finished. "Vivian was available. Things got a little out of hand, but not to the point where we slept together. I wouldn't do that. I didn't want her that way. I love you, not her."

Her nostrils flared. "Pfff. It didn't seem that way to me. I'd say you were in your own version of heaven."

Snorting, he rubbed his forehead as if it hurt. "Hardly. Although I must admit my ego needed stroking. Are you satisfied?"

"No." Wynn leaned toward the table. "This is not a fun situation for me. But there are a few things you need to know."

Leaning closer, Adam questioned, "What?"

"I won't allow you or anyone else to treat my feelings so carelessly. I deserve better."

Head bent, he nodded and then gazed directly at her. "You're right. You do."

"Why should I believe you, Adam?"

"Because I love you," Adam stated simply and honestly. The look in his eyes, the expression on his face, and stillness of his body took her back to the day he told Sherry that Wynn was everything he wanted. The words were so simple and honest they couldn't be denied, made her believe him. There was nothing devious or false in his expression or words. He did love her. But did he love her enough?

He looked directly at her and Wynn felt his love reach out and wrap her in its warm embrace. "I messed up. Real bad. But I want to make things right. I'll do whatever it takes to put us back on track. Just tell me what you want."

"Adam, I love you and I do believe you about Vivian. You occupy more of my waking thoughts than I like to admit. But I've been married before and that man lied and deceived me. Jim cheated on me and our children with another woman." Wynn's voice broke. She shut her eyes and fought for control. After a couple of seconds, she continued, "I'll go the distance for the sake of my kids. Believe me, if the situation was different and I didn't have children, I wouldn't allow Jim anywhere near me. That should give you an idea of how important my boys are to me and what I'll do for them."

Saying the words hurt. Wynn felt as if she'd been cut open and left to bleed. On the brink of tears, Wynn couldn't control the huskiness of her tone.

"He took all of my trust, twisted it, and then destroyed it. I was embarrassed and left alone. I *won't* be used that way again. It doesn't matter how much I love you."

Wynn felt so conflicted. She wanted to stay, to race into Adam's arms and let him assure her that they were going to be okay. But if she did that, she'd set a precedent that she didn't want in a new relationship. If she gave in to him so easily, Adam would believe the magic phrase was

"I'm sorry." Everything needed to be talked out. "We still need to consider my kids. I have two young boys who depend on me and it's my job to raise them into young men. Are you willing to share me with them? Teens that constantly need my attention?"

"Absolutely."

She laughed. "You say that so easily. I wonder if you truly know what you're getting into." Wynn pressed her lips together and waited a moment before speaking. "As they get older, they're going to require more of my time, need me in different ways. When I have to focus my energies on them, what will you do then? Will you find a new Vivian and spend your time with her when you can't have all of me?"

"No." Bitterness laced his laughter. "I'll never do that again."

"Maybe you won't. Why don't you think about it for a few days and get back with me," Wynn suggested. She grabbed her purse and stood, leaving Adam at the table.

Chapter 25

A week after meeting Adam at Union Street Bar and Grill, Wynn stepped from the elevator and strutted confidently through Oakwood Hospital's lobby toward the front entrance. A self-satisfied smiled lifted the corners of her lips. The meeting with the hospital's nursing administration had gone excellently. Oakwood's vice presidents had signed a contract and requested long-term nursing support for two of their three daily shifts. Pleased with the outcome, Wynn was headed back to the office to work on filling the orders.

Her cell phone went off as she approached the sliding doors leading to the valet parking area. Wynn stepped out of the stream of people, found a solitary nook, and dug inside her purse for her phone. She flipped the phone opened and recited, "Wynn Evans."

"Are you sure?" came a familiar male voice.

Her body sagged against the wall. Adam! Her heart did a flip in her chest and she gripped the silver phone tighter. Wynn couldn't deny that she missed Adam.

Licking her dry lips, Wynn answered, "I'm sure."

"How are you?" he asked in a soft, sensual tone that brought back memories of them making love. The mental image of Adam licking the sweat from her body felt so vivid she shivered from the vision.

"Good. Busy. And you?"

"Same."

What in the world were they doing? This one-syllable dialogue was getting old really fast. Why had Adam called? What did he want from her?

Nibbling on her thumbnail, Wynn waited. Adam called her. He obviously had something he wanted to say.

"What are you up to?" he asked.

"Just leaving Oakwood Hospital after a meeting."

"Oakwood. That's in Dearborn, right?"

"Mmm-hmm." She twisted the strap of her purse around her finger while watching the crowd exit the building.

Where was he going with this? Adam had been raised in Detroit. He knew the city and its surrounding suburbs as well as she did.

He cleared his voice and said, "I just came out of a meeting myself. There were some suppliers we needed to hammer out a deal with."

"Oh," Wynn responded, hunching her shoulders.

"Where are you headed now?"

"Back to the office. I need to process this order from Oakwood."

"Does that have to be done immediately?"

Her forehead wrinkled into a frown. Why did he care? "No."

"Great! Have you eaten?"

"No." Wynn glanced at the display on her phone. Wow! It was close to two. She hadn't had anything to eat since she snatched a plain doughnut from the box on Helen's desk this morning.

"How about—" Adam stopped, hesitating over his next words.

Wynn heard the hope in his voice. It echoed the longing and yearning that filled her heart.

"Can I buy you lunch?" he finished.

Wynn felt like jumping for joy, or yelling out loud. Instead, she grinned and nodded yes. *Silly girl, he can't see you through the phone,* she thought. "I'd like that. Where?"

"My meeting just finished at the Hyatt on Michigan Avenue. Since we're both in Dearborn, you want to meet me here?"

"It works for me." Wynn mentally calculated. "It should be there in about fifteen minutes."

"That's fine. Park in valet and I'll settle up everything later. I'll be waiting for you in the lobby."

"Will do. See you in a few minutes." Elated, she disconnected the call and balled her hand into a fist, pulling her arm down triumphantly.

I need to talk to Helen before I do anything else, she thought, punching in the number to Nursing Solutions. If Adam had plans to discuss their problems, that might take a while. She didn't want Helen paging or calling her at a crucial moment.

Plus, Helen needed to get right on the Oakwood deal. Start making calls and line up their nursing staff.

The phone rang once before Helen picked up the line, reciting, "Good afternoon. Nursing Solutions. How may I help you?"

"Helen?"

"Who else?"

"Okay, smarty-pants."

"That's me. What's going on? How did Oakwood go?"

"Great." Proud of herself, Wynn added, "We got the contract."

"Excellent."

"I need you to start rounding up neonatal nurses. Oakwood wants nurses on afternoons and midnights."

"Are you on your way back?"

"Not for a while."

"Oh?"

There was no fooling Helen. Her radar for crap worked perfectly. It got straight to the heart of things—especially when you hoped it wouldn't. "Yeah. Adam called. I'm going to lunch with him."

"Good. It's time for you two to talk. Don't worry about the office. I'll take care of things on this end. Enjoy your lunch."

"Thanks. I'll see you later."

"Maybe. Maybe not," Helen said before hanging up.

Wynn snapped her phone shut and dropped it into her purse, heading for the front entrance. She waited outside for valet to bring her car around. Her heart felt full of hope. Adam had taken the first step. That was a good thing. Maybe he'd thought about things and realized that they needed to work together if they planned to continue their relationship.

The attendant stopped in the circular drive. Wynn handed the young man a hearty tip before climbing into her car. As she pulled away from the hospital entrance, she hummed the lyrics to Phyllis Hyman's 'You Know How To Love Me.'"

After dropping the keys to her car in the attendant's greedy little hand, Wynn strolled through the doors of the Hyatt, eagerly searching for Adam's handsome face. Butterflies must have laid eggs in her belly, because she felt as nervous as a pregnant woman worried over the delivery of her first baby.

During the ride to the hotel, she had considered and discarded several ways to address their issues. After mentally debating the pros and cons, she decided to let things happen naturally. When Adam felt ready, he'd bring up the topic. Until then, Wynn planned to enjoy a-pleasant and possibly expensive meal with and on the man she loved.

From the far end of the lobby, Adam emerged and sauntered toward her. Handsome and powerful, he slowly approached her, dodging hotel guests and staff to where she waited. He took her hands and brought one to his lips. "I'm glad you came."

"Me, too," she admitted, fighting the urge to pull him close and kiss him thoroughly. It had been more than a week since they talked. She'd missed him deeply.

With a hand at her elbow, Adam guided Wynn through the lobby. He punched the button for the elevators.

"What restaurant are we going to?"

Adam hesitated. "I hope you don't mind. I got us a room so that we could talk privately." He rushed ahead, waving a hand toward the balcony where the Archimedes restaurant sat, saying, "If you don't want to do that, it's fine."

She touched his hand reassuringly. "It's a good idea. We really don't want curious bystanders to hear our business."

Adam relaxed against the back of the elevator. "Good. I didn't want you to misunderstand my motives."

"No problem." Actually, there was a problem. From the moment he touched her, she couldn't think of anything but being in his arms again. Unhurried, they stepped from the elevator and started down a long hallway. Adam's hand rested at the base of her spine, sending every nerve ending into overdrive. As they got closer to their room, images of them making love filled her head.

At a door marked 1503 they halted. Adam slid the card into the reader and within seconds they were in the room. The door slammed shut behind them. Something primal consumed Wynn. She took his face between her hands and drew his head down for a deep, passionate kiss.

Her tongue slipped between Adam's surprised lips. She tasted coffee and the essence of the man she loved. Not satisfied, her hands stroked his chest through the starched, pressed shirt. She felt the pounding of his heart against her hand. It matched the beating of hers.

Wynn brought her body hard against Adam, rubbing her breasts against him. He groaned, placing his hands on her hips and holding her against him. Fumbling with the buttons of his shirt, Wynn shifted her attention to his flesh against her own while working the shirt from his trousers.

A new idea popped into her head and she abandoned the shirt in favor of his belt buckle. Wynn unhooked the leather strap and drew down the zipper, slipping her hand inside the opening. She found him hot and hard. Quite pleased with herself, she squeezed him through the fabric of his briefs. Adam's moan of pleasure followed. Intoxicated by the power of having Adam at her mercy, Wynn stroked him through his shorts. Up and down she went against the hard ridges of his shaft.

Wynn gently untangled him from his clothing and his rod sprang free. She kissed him deeply, snaking her tongue inside his mouth and dueling with his.

Groaning, he ran his fingers through her hair. A moan rose from his gut as Wynn pumped his rigid shaft.

Ending the kiss, Wynn lifted her head, nibbling her way along the taut column of Adam's neck. Moving lower, her tongue licked his nipple through the cotton shirt, making him cry out. "Don't stop," he begged, caught up in the feel of her wet tongue heating his skin. She didn't plan to. Wynn suckled on one nipple, drawing on the pebble before blowing out cool air. He shivered.

Her tongue created a steamy wet line downward, leading to his erection. His flesh jerked, waving in the air. She kissed the smooth head of his penis, licking the sweet drops from the head as she held his gaze with her own. He bucked, surging into the hot recesses of her mouth.

Concentrating on her task, Wynn licked the flesh from base to head in a slow deliberate motion reminiscent of the way she licked an ice-cream cone before taking the tip into her mouth and sucking greedily on it.

"Jesus!" he growled.

She sucked on the head, lapping up the droplets while her empty hand shifted lower, finding and then fondling his sac between her fingers.

Adam swallowed hard, fisting his hands at his sides. "Oh, babe! I can't hold out much longer."

Obviously, Wynn didn't believe he needed to because she went down on him, taking him deep into her mouth. Sucking noises and his cries and moans were the only sounds in the room as Wynn took him to the edge, then drew back, sucking softly and swirling her tongue around his flesh.

The tension built with each draw of her tongue. Adam's head thrashed side to side against the wall. Each time she took him to the edge by sucking a tad harder, making him whine louder, beg her for more and then plead for her to end this torture. Passion soared to unbelievable heights as Wynn took him to the edge over and over but refused to let him leap.

Suddenly, she felt the tightening of his leg

muscles and knew he wouldn't be able to hold out much longer. Adam exploded in a sea of colors. His hands gripped her head, holding her close. Sensing the tension in him, Wynn's tongue worked faster, harder, greedily swallowing everything he offered. It seemed to go on and on until his body went slack. Adam released her hair and his hands flopped at his side. Drained, his organ slipped from her mouth and lay limp and wet against his trousers.

"You taste so sweet." Wynn drew her tongue across her lips, licking away any juice from her mouth, and then crawled up his body, settling within his embrace.

"Thank you."

Smiling at him, she tenderly kissed his lips. "You're welcome."

Adam's knuckle swept across her breasts. "Your turn." He swept Wynn into his arm and headed for the bed.

Chapter 26

Wynn stepped from the shower stall and dried herself with one of the fluffy towels provided by the hotel. Warm and content, she tossed the towel over the shower rod and wrapped herself in a white terry cloth hotel bathrobe. She moved out of the bedroom and crossed the floor to the living room, pausing in the doorway to watch Adam escort room service from the suite.

Dressed in a duplicate bathrobe, Adam smiled back at her as he closed the door. "Hey, you," he whispered in a soft, sensual rumble.

Each time he spoke to her in that tone, she felt herself go hot with desire and love. "Hey," Wynn muttered shyly, brushing a lock of hair away from her eyes. After all the things they had done together her shyness seemed a bit ridiculous, but she couldn't help it. She glanced at the table and found it set up for a meal. "What did you order?"

"We've got shrimp scampi over a bed of pasta, mixed greens with balsamic vinaigrette dressing, garlic toast, and turtle cheesecake."

"Mmm." Wynn's stomach rumbled loudly in response to the tantalizing offerings. Embarrassed, she said, "Obviously, I'm hungry."

"I got that." He chuckled, waving a hand toward the table. "We worked up quite an appetite. Come on. Let's eat."

She crossed the room and settled in the chair opposite Adam's, lifting the lids from the trays. The pungent aroma of garlic and seafood filled the air and she inhaled deeply. Wynn reached for his plate, spooning shrimp and pasta onto his plate and then added a healthy dose of salad before sprinkling it with dressing. "Tell me when."

"When," Adam muttered, watching her dish up the food.

"I've never eaten at the Hyatt before," Wynn mentioned, diving into her salad. "This is really good."

"Yeah, it is. I thought you might like it. Gautier does a lot of lunch meetings here."

Silence filled the room as they appeased their hunger. Stomach stuffed with pasta, Wynn pushed her empty plate away and reached for her glass. The sparkling wine went smoothly over her palate and down her throat, warming her blood.

She glanced toward Adam and found him watching her. A tense silence enveloped the room. A cold knot formed in her stomach, twisting the food. It was time to have the talk.

"I love you," Adam stated simply, reaching across the table for her hand. "And I don't want to lose you."

"I don't want to lose you, either," Wynn admitted, taking his hand and kissing the palm. But she couldn't leave things alone. She had to make him understand her concerns. "But I still have two kids who are my priority."

He let go of her hand and leaned back in his chair. His words were as cool and clear as spring water. "I'm trying to understand that. Honestly, I felt rejected when I'd offered you something that I'd never given to any other woman."

"I wasn't rejecting you. I love you. You're important to me."

"I hope so."

"You are." She nibbled on her bottom lip. *How honest should I be,* she wondered, and then decided he had to know everything. "Adam, I have to be honest. I didn't realize that you were planning to ask me to marry you. Your proposal took me completely by surprise." She paused, noting the blank expression on his face. *This isn't going well,* she thought. "I needed time to make the right decision. To do the proper thing for everyone who depend on me, my children, Kevin and Jimmy. Think back to when you were a child—your parents did what they had to for you. You and your sister always came first with your parents."

He sat quietly for a moment and admitted begrudgingly, "Yeah, I know. That's true."

"I'm just doing the same for my children. They deserve the best. I wasn't saying no to you forever. Just not yet. Not right now."

Picking up his wineglass, Adam sipped. He returned it to its spot on the table. "What do we do now?"

"What are you doing Sunday afternoon?"

Frowning, he hunched his shoulders. "I don't think I have any plans. Why?"

"Come spend the afternoon with me and my kids. I'll throw in dinner. Maybe the four of us can have that barbecue we talked about when I bumped into you at the New Center building."

He grinned. "Sounds good."

"Normally, Sunday afternoon is game day or we do a movie. Something fun for all of us. I want my sons to accept you as part of their life and eventually learn to love and respect you."

"I want this to work," he stated.

"So do I."

Wynn swallowed hard. One problem solved, another one to go. "There's a big white elephant in the room and I guess I should be the one to bring it up since it concerns me." She held his gaze with her own while fidgeting with the edge of her napkin. "What about my age?"

Frowning, he answered quickly, "What about it?"

"Good answer. But you know what I mean. I'm thirteen years older than you. That won't change. If anything, it'll get harder as we get older. Can you handle it?"

"I love all of you."

"Yeah, you do for now. But there will be a time when all of my hair is going to turn gray and then white. My body will sag and I'll probably have problems with my hearing and/or sight. Are you ready for that?"

"It's not about the outside package, although I love yours." His gaze did a slow check of her form and then his tongue slid seductively across his lips.

Wynn remembered him doing the same that last day in Cozumel when they returned to the suite and he tasted her. She went all hot and flushed. Adam was an expert at getting to her.

"To answer your question honestly—absolutely. Your age has never been a problem for me. If it had, I would never have asked you out the first time." He stood, moved around the table, and cupped her face in his large hands. "I think I would love you if you were twenty years older than me. Your body is hot and I love being inside you and making love with you, but that's not all I love about you."

He leaned down and kissed her tenderly, stroking a finger down her cheek.

"I also love more than your body. I love the woman that you are and the things that make you you. Like how you say no to me. It hurt my feelings, but you made your point. Let me say this, any other woman would have accepted my proposal even if they did have reservations about our future. You said no and you meant it. I didn't like it. But I can respect you and your decision."

"What about your job? You're a big man at Gautier. Are you sure you can handle the fallout from how it looks?"

Adam scoffed. "I don't care what people think about me. Never have and never will. I run my life. Not my job or the people I work with." He tapped his chest. "Me."

"Sounds good on paper but are you willing to back it up with actions?"

"I don't have a problem with it." He snagged the chair next to her and pulled it close.

"But I've got another question. Have you thought about having children of your own? I have two sons and the possibility of me having more is slim. Can you live with that?"

"Sure can. I don't have to be a biological father to love and raise kids. I'll have Kevin, Jimmy, and you. I don't need to produce offspring to make my life complete. You and our family will do that just fine for me."

Wynn sighed. Adam had all the right answers. Was he just paying lip service to her or were these his real thoughts and feelings? She didn't know. But she wanted to believe him.

He took her hands in his and gazed into her eyes. "Wynn, if you agree to marry me, I will do everything in my power to keep our sons safe and be a good husband to you and father to our sons."

She liked the sound of that. Our sons. It sounded right. Perfect. Maybe she needed to reserve judgment on that until later.

"I know you will. But it's not time for us just yet."

He blew out a hot puff of air. "I just have to tell you about me."

Her head snapped back. What was he talking about? "Tell me what?"

"I've never loved anyone the way I do you." He leaned forward and pressed his forehead against hers. His hands stroked her neck, sending a surge of awareness through her.

The mere touch of his hand sent a warming shiver through her.

"You're in my head as well as my heart, and sometimes it frightens me when I realize how much you are a part of me and how much you mean to me. I don't want to lose that. Over the last week, I've held on to that, because there wasn't much else for me to do. We have something special like I've never had in my life."

Each word made her heart fill with such joy. He'd revealed what was in his heart, openly and completely, regardless of the possible pain his admission might cause at some point in the future.

"Adam," she stated softly, enjoying the feel of his name on her lips. "I wasn't rejecting you. It was the situation."

"I can see that now. But not then."

"Let's take things slow and work through everything before we decide to get married." She held out her hand.

He took it and tugged, pulling her from her chair and seating her on his lap. She could feel the hard, stiff ridges of his erection pressed against her buttock.

Wynn wrapped her arms around his neck and leaned down, hungrily covering his mouth with hers. When she lifted her head, the start of a sensuous fire burned in the depths of his eyes.

"We done talking?" he asked.

She leaned down a second time and whispered, "For the moment."

Chapter 27

"I'm sorry," Wynn apologized from her office doorway.

Collating a stack of copies, Helen turned her face away, but failed to hide the smirk hovering on her lips.

"What?"

"Nothing," Helen responded with a tiny shake of her head. Her lips twitched as she held back a giggle.

Wynn strolled into the room and took the visitor's chair next to Helen's desk. She picked up the DMC's file and flipped through it, counting the number of nurses scheduled for the midnight shift.

"How's Adam?"

At the mention of Adam's name, Wynn's lips broke into a grin. "How do you know I was talking to Adam?"

"Please, girl." Helen leaned back in her chair and studied the younger woman. "Before you left for vacation, you two talked on a daily basis like teenagers. You couldn't get enough of each other. Then silence prevailed after you returned from Cozumel. The calls have started again since your meeting at Oakwood."

Smiling happily, Wynn silently conceded that no one fooled Helen. Pursing her lips, Wynn nodded. "Okay. You've got me. We talked for hours and then agreed to work out our problems. Adam and I are doing things together with my sons. Going to the zoo and stuff like that."

"Good." Helen stapled the pages together and tucked them in a manila folder. "Adam's a great guy and you deserve someone special in your life."

Choked up, Wynn couldn't push words out for a moment. She swallowed the lump in her throat and suggested, "Let's get back to Sparrow Hospital. I thought I'd make an appointment and then take a road trip to Lansing to talk with their administration. If they agree to work with us, we can set up a satellite office and recruit."

Helen's eyes grew large and round. "Gee! Are we ready to make that large a move?"

"Absolutely!" Wynn answered confidently. "The business is doing great. Contracts with Oakwood and St. John's Health System gave Nursing Solutions a real boost."

Ready for a fight, Helen folded her arms across her small chest and asked, "Does that mean I'll get a raise?"

"And a promotion to business manager," Wynn responded, taking the wind out of Helen's sails.

"Yes. That's what I'm talking about," Helen said, balling her hand into a fist and pulling down jubilantly.

The door opened and both women turned toward the entrance. Jim Harrison stood in the doorway.

Shocked, Wynn stared. What was he doing here?

"Hi, ladies." Jim gave them his most engaging smile and then shut the door.

Helen grunted and got up from her desk, grabbing her mug and marching away. She picked up the coffeepot and poured a cup of java.

Since the divorce, Jim had never taken the time to show up at her place of business. Wynn was suspicious of what madness brought him to her door today.

Wynn rose. "Is something wrong, Jim?" It was a moot question. Her mother or the school always contacted Wynn if there were a problem with the kids.

"No. Everything is fine."

Puzzled, she stared at her ex-husband, waiting for an explanation for his visit.

Strolling across the reception area, Jim halted next to the desk. He studied Helen as she brewed a fresh pot of coffee, inclining his head in the direction of Wynn's office. Jim asked in a cool tone, "Can we talk in your office?

"Sure." Wynn dropped the file on the desk and led the way. Once they entered the room, she continued across the office.

Jim shut the door and leaned against it. Intimidated, Wynn's gaze flew to the closed door. She didn't want Jim to see how his actions had affected her.

"What can I do for you?" she asked, rounding

the desk and sinking into her chair, feeling a certain comfort at placing some distance between them. She didn't trust Jim one little bit.

Jim strolled about the office, checking out her décor. "You've done a nice job here."

"Thank you." She tilted her head, waiting and hoping her ex would get to the point and then get out.

He weighed her with a critical stare and then asked smoothly, "How was Mexico?" His expression was crafty, too knowing.

Jim was full of surprises. How did he know about her trip? She knew the answer. The kids or her mother had told him. He always pumped both kids for info about her private life.

Wynn flushed, picked up her pen, and tapped it against the desk before answering, "Nice trip. We had a good time."

He picked up the photo of the kids from her desk and then returned it to the exact same spot.

Wynn frowned, feeling the edge of agitation pulse through her. His inability to state his reason for being in her office really bugged her.

Was he nervous? Did he have an agenda?

"How's the boy?" Jim sneered.

Wynn's eyes narrowed. "Boy? Which of our sons are you talking about? Jimmy or Kevin?"

"You know who I'm talking about."

If Jim wanted to play games, that was fine with Wynn. Shaking her head, she leaned back in her chair and said, "Actually, I don't."

A momentary look of uneasiness crossed his face and then he recovered. "You're not going to answer my question, are you?"

She replied, "No."

"Okay." He began to pace.

Wynn checked her watch. So far Jim had managed to do or say nothing. If he continued to waste her time by not getting to the point soon, she intended to usher him out of her office pretty darn quick.

"Do you ever think about us?" he asked suddenly.

Think about them? Ah, no. "What are you talking about?"

"Us. As a couple."

She laughed harshly. This man was crazy. "No."

Jim rubbed a hand across his chin. "I've been doing a lot of soul searching lately. Reviewing the stuff I've done in the past and trying to figure out what I'm doing with my life."

Wynn drew in a deep breath and shifted uncomfortably in her chair. Maybe he'd get to the point soon and then leave.

"Anyway, I realize that my family should have always come first. That nothing should come before them."

"You're right." A note of disdain entered her voice. "Jimmy and Kevin should always be first in your life. They are in mine."

He shrugged off Wynn's comment and then said in a low composed voice, "I know things haven't been good between us. But there was a time when we were in sync. When our home was happy."

Sick of Jim's pitty-pattering, Wynn blurted, "What do you want, Jim?"

Instead of answering, he grabbed the back of

the guest chair and dragged it around the desk to where Wynn sat. He dropped into the seat and took her hand. Surprised, Wynn tugged. But he held on tight.

"Stop. Let go of me," she demanded, pulling on her hand.

"Wynn, listen to me."

She let her hand go limp. If listening to his tale of woe would get him out of here, that's what she intended to do.

"We've had some rough times. I've made a few mistakes. But I've never stopped caring about you."

Wynn's heart began to race. She didn't like the direction this conversation was taking. "Don't do this."

Jim ignored her. "Do you think we can try it again?"

Oh, hell, no, Wynn thought, jerking her hand from his. "No!"

"Don't make a decision right now. Think about it. Our kids would love having us together again."

"No!"

"Come on. You're not being rational," Jim stated in a calm, superior tone that infuriated Wynn. "This is the best thing for our family. After all, Jimmy and Kevin are your top priority."

"They are." Wynn rose from her chair and headed around the opposite side of the desk. "But us you and me together is not going to happen."

"I don't think you're being fair to me or the kids."

She shrugged and turned toward the door. "Don't care what you think. We are not going to get back together. Our days as a couple are over. Stick a fork in me. We're done."

"No," he yelled.

The fury in his eyes made her jump. *I need to get this fool out of here,* she thought.

"I want to come home!"

"You can't," Wynn countered, moving toward the door. If she could get to the door and call Helen, she'd call security.

Jim met her in the center of the room and took her hand. "We can do so much together if you'd let us."

Hoping to calm Jim down, Wynn asked, "What about Lorraine? Is she supposed to come and live with us, too?"

"Lorraine's in the past. That's done."

Her head began to throb. Jim was so cavalier about other people's feelings. When he left home, Lorraine was all he could talk about. She was his life. The kids meant nothing. Now, Lorraine and Jim were over and he spoke of her as if she were a DVD that he'd just returned to Blockbuster. Not going to happen. "You've forgotten Lorraine, just like you forgot about us? Packed up and left without a word being said. My answer is still no!"

Jim shook his finger at her. "That boy is behind this, isn't he?"

"I don't go out with boys."

"Adam!" Jim spit out the word as if it left a bad taste in his mouth.

"No. You're behind my decision. I don't want a man who doesn't have staying power. You're weak and undependable. I need a man who will be with me through the good as well as the rough times. You're not it."

A stain of red filled Jim's cheeks and then he came back with a verbal attack. "You really don't believe that that boy loves you. That he'll marry you." Jim chortled. "Come on, Wynn. Get real. He's young and one of the top execs at that auto company he works at. You are too old and you have nothing to offer him, except for two kids and a sagging body. He'll want a young, sweet thang on his arm. Not somebody like you with kids, a mortgage, and responsibility."

Jim's contemptuous tone sparked her anger. "Why do you want me if I'm so old and have too much responsibility? What's wrong with you?"

Tongue-tied, he stammered, "I - I - I."

Furious beyond belief, she marched across the floor, jerked open the door, and commanded, "Get out!"

Ready for anything, Helen ran into the room. "Are you okay?"

"Call security!" Wynn demanded.

"On it." Helen pivoted on her heel.

Jim waved a dismissive hand in the air and then started for the door. "Don't bother. I'm on my way out." He focused on Wynn and grinned broadly. "Hit a nerve, did I?"

Wynn picked up the phone. "Go."

"I'm leaving. But I'll promise you this. You'll be sorry." He strolled to the front door, turned to the women, and said, "See you soon."

Panting, Wynn sank into the guest chair before she fell down.

Helen raced to the door and locked it. "You need to do something about him."

"Like what?"

"I don't know. Get a restraining order. Something, because that man is crazy and I think he'll find a way to hurt you."

"I'll talk to Adam. He may have some ideas about what we can do."

"That sounds like a plan. Don't forget."

Wynn glanced at the door. "I won't. Something's going on with him and I don't want it to hit me in the face."

Chapter 28

Tired and worn out after a long day and ready to pick up her sons, Wynn pulled into her parents' driveway and shut off the engine. She glanced at the dashboard clock, noting the time. It was almost six.

Nursing Solutions had been incredibly busy today. Orders came in from a variety of locations. They had so much work that Wynn missed her afternoon phone conversation with Adam. On top of that, she hadn't had an opportunity to discuss the Jim situation. She really valued Adam's knowledge and skills and wanted to hear his opinion about what do about her ex-husband.

Wynn grabbed her purse and wrapped present and started up the drive, stopping at the garage door. She entered a code into the gray remote attached to the side of the house. The garage door hummed and slowly rose, allowing access to her parents' garage. Dad's car was missing. *The boys must be with Dad,* she thought, moving past her mother's Lincoln.

As usual, the door leading to the house was unlocked. Wynn entered the kitchen, where Kirk Franklin's religious voice serenaded from the compact disc player. Mom sat at the kitchen table, dressed in a baby blue jogging suit. Her rainbow-colored reading glasses were perched on the bridge of her nose as she flipped through the newspaper.

Peg Evans glanced up. "Hi."

"Hey," Wynn responded, shutting the door after her. "Anything good in there?"

"No." Peg folded the paper and sorted it into the proper sections, returning it to its original state. "I'm considering buying new living room furniture and I wanted to check out the sales."

Nodding, Wynn placed the gift on the table.

Peg eyed the brightly wrapped box. "What's this?"

"Gift from Mexico. I've been meaning to drop this off for the past two week. Per usual, life got in the way."

"That's for sure." Nodding, Peg reached for the box and tore the paper from it. She opened the box and removed the bottle. "Mmm. Tequila. Very nice."

"I know you're not a drinker." They both laughed. Peg rarely touched anything stronger than a glass of wine. "It's nice to have something alcoholic on hand to offer guests when you're entertaining."

"You're right," Peg agreed, taking a moment to read the label. "Your dad will like this. He likes a nip every once in a while."

Yes, Dad did, she thought. Smiling, Wynn

strolled across the kitchen and opened the refrigerator door. She peeked inside, searching for something to drink. "Can I have a drink?"

"Sure. Help yourself. I made chicken salad for lunch. Your dad didn't want anything. Help yourself." Peg pointed to the cupboard. "There are paper plates in that cabinet."

"Nah, I'm good. I just want something to drink." Wynn grabbed a Sunny Delight and returned to the table. She sank into a chair opposite her mother and ripped off the cover.

"How was work?"

Wynn took a sip from the plastic bottle. "Most of it was good."

Frowning, Peg asked, "What part was bad?"

"Jim came by the office today."

Frowning, Peg asked, "Jim? What did he want?"

Wynn shook her head, wondering if there was more going on with her ex-husband. "He asked me if we could get back together."

"You're kidding, right?" Peg laughed. "What was he smoking?"

"No. I think he was serious," Wynn took another drink from the bottle.

"What did you say?"

"Don't look so stricken. That ship has sailed and will never come back. I told Jim that I wasn't interested."

Peg let out a relieved sigh. "Good."

Wynn toyed with the almost empty bottle. "Where's Dad?"

"Went to the store. He should be back in a few minutes."

Finished with her drink, Wynn rose from the

chair and dropped the bottle in the trash. "Excuse me a minute. I'll be right back," she said, hurrying into another room. She grabbed the phone off the post and quickly dialed Adam's number. The sound of his voice would sooth Wynn.

Adam answered on the second ring. "Hello?"

"Hi, it's me," Wynn said in response to his greeting.

"Hey, you. How's my girl?"

I love that old-fashioned phase, Wynn thought. It warmed her heart to know that she was truly his girl. "Okay. Good."

Adam remained silent for a moment. "I hear hesitation and something else. What's going on?"

"I've been meaning to talk to you about this. But wc got sidctrackcd."

"Tell me now," he encouraged.

His concern found its way to her through the phone. "Earlier today Jim dropped by my office."

"Mmm. Is that something he does often?"

"No. Actually, it was the first time. Anyway, after some rambling and sort of apology, he asked me to reconcile with him."

"I assume you said no," Adam responded in a cautious tone.

Shaking her head, Wynn slowly strolled around the room as she spoke. "Calm down, silly man. I'm with you, remember?"

He chuckled. "Sorry. My 'this is my woman' side comes out every once in a while. Your ex-husband does that to me."

"Well, tuck him back in. I need your professional expertise."

"Tell me what you need. I'll do everything I can."

"Jim got a little crazy when I refused him. He started making threats, promising that I'll be sorry."

"What?" Adam's voice roared through the phone line. "I'm not having that. We'll get a restraining order against him."

"That's what I wanted to know. Is it possible? And what about my kids? Jim still has joint custody."

Adam was quiet for a moment as he considered the issue. "I can have some type of addendum or provision drawn up that will include where he picks up the kids. It can be at your mother's, if she agrees to it. Or someplace neutral that you and Jim agree to. If you want, I can be the point man. I'll drop off and pick up the boys myself. That way you won't have to see him at all. Matter-of-fact, I don't think I want you to see him if he's making threats."

"I don't want to see him. I'm concerned about Jimmy and Kevin."

"The kids are a concern. But I'm more worried about you. Jim wouldn't be the first man to hurt his ex-wife. We're going to find a way to keep you safe and still give him the visitation rights he's entitled to."

"I knew I'd talk to the right person. Thank you."

"I always aim to please."

"I'm at my parents' so I don't want to hang on the phone. I'll give you a call once I get the kids settled for the night."

"Do that. I'll work on the restraining order. Don't worry. We'll get this resolved."

"Okay. Bye-bye."

"Wynn?"

"Yes?"

"Love you."

Smiling, she answered, "I love you, too." Feeling better about the situation, Wynn returned the phone to its cradle. She went back into the kitchen and found both parents sitting at the table. Her father sat reading the label on the bottle of Tequila.

Confused, she moved farther into the room and asked, "Where are the boys?"

"Why are you asking me?" her dad replied.

"I came to pick them up."

Her father put down the bottle. "They're not on the porch?"

"No," Wynn said.

Flustered, Peg answered, "I don't know. They have some friends down the street, maybe they went down there."

"I didn't see them at all when I pulled up. I thought they were with Dad."

Wynn's dad shook his head. "I left them outside together."

Still not comprehending, Wynn touched her mother's arm. "Then where are they?"

Eyes wide with confusion and concern, Peg answered, "We don't know."

Her father rose from his chair and took charge. "Calm down. Don't work yourself up until we know what's going on."

"You're right." Peg started toward the garage

door. "I'm going down the street to see if my grand-children are down there."

"I'm coming with you." Wynn followed her mother.

An hour later, Wynn and her mother returned to the house. "It's going to be all right." Peg rubbed a hand up and down Wynn's arm. "They're here somewhere. They just forgot the time."

Wynn nodded, but remained silent. Frightened beyond words, she paced the floor. "We need to call the police."

"Sit down," Peg ordered. "Let's wait until your father gets back. He may have found them."

She obeyed her mother and literally dropped into a chair at the kitchen table. Tears were a step away and she fought to keep her emotions in check. No good would come from a bout of hysteria.

Wynn glanced out of the kitchen window and shivered. The moon sat high in the sky. *Where are Jimmy and Kevin?*

The back door opened and her dad hurried into the room. A boy about seven years old followed Wynn's father into the room. "I went to all the kids on the block that the boys play with." Her father pushed the child in front of him, placing his hands on the boy's shoulders. "This is Parker. Earlier today, he played with Jimmy and Kevin. Tell them what you told me."

Parker nodded, but he turned huge, fearful eyes toward Wynn's father.

"It's fine. You won't get in trouble."

Heart pounding in her chest, Wynn stepped forward and tried to smile at the small child. She took his hand between both of hers and said, "Please, tell me what you know. I'm worried about my kids. What happened?"

This time he did speak. "We were playing on the porch."

"Which porch? Yours or ours?" Wynn asked quickly.

"Mine," Parker answered promptly. "When this big car stopped."

"What color was it?"

"Red."

Wynn let go of Parker's hand, frowning. Red car?

"Then he called. Jimmy and Kevin went to him and they talked for a minute and then they waved at me and got in the car."

Wynn glanced at her father.

"Did you know the man in the car?" Wynn's father asked.

"Yeah."

Holding her breath, Wynn waited.

"Who was it?" her mother asked.

"Their dad."

Chapter 29

Wynn jumped from the sofa and yelled, "What do you mean you can't do an Amber Alert? My sons are missing!"

Officer Szymanski tucked his hat under his arm, rose from the sofa, and said in an infuriatingly even tone, "Calm down, Ms. Evans. Ranting won't help you get your children home."

"No, it won't. Get out of here and go find my children!"

A silent tower of strength, her father rose from the opposite side, draped an arm around her shoulders, and drew her against his side. He whispered close to her ear, "Don't worry. We'll find them."

Wright, the younger officer, took a step closer to the mayhem and spoke up. "We're sorry, ma'am. According to Michigan law, we can't issue an Amber Alert because your ex-husband has joint custody. The law states that it must be a noncustodial parent who has abducted the child. By law, he has the right to take the children anywhere he wants."

She studied one officer, dismissed him, and then turned to the next. Was she losing her mind? Or were these two men complete idiots?

"Not without my permission." Wynn snapped, doing a mental review of the details of her divorce decree. "I believe it's a provision in our divorce settlement."

"We'll need to see that, ma'am," responded Officer Szymanski, scribbling on his notepad.

"Your ex doesn't have a history of child abuse, sexual and/or domestic assault, or any victimization of children. The only thing we have on him is he didn't tell you that he has the children. That's an intricate part of the criteria used to determine if a child has been abducted." Officer Szymanski flipped to a fresh page in his small spiral notebook and took the chair opposite the sofa. "Let's get some more details."

With a gentle movement, her father urged her to sit down. He took the spot next to her, offering a steady hand.

"Does either child have any disabilities or illnesses that could put them in jeopardy?" Officer Wright asked.

"No. They're pretty healthy."

Officer Wright did a *tut-tut* with his tongue. "We can't use that angle. I'm sorry, ma'am."

Hands balled into fist, Wynn felt a frustrated scream bubbling up from the pit of her belly, but she kept her composure. Jimmy and Kevin's safety was on the line. "What can you do?"

"We're going to file a missing persons report

on each child. Put out an APB on your husband's SUV. If your ex is anywhere in Michigan, we'll find him," Szymanski promised.

Good. Wynn felt a tiny portion of her anger ebb. Finally, the officers were talking about things that made sense to her.

Officer Wright moved to the sofa and crouched down next to her. "Ms. Evans, we need pictures of the kids. Something recent that we can distribute. Also, what were they wearing when you last saw them?"

"I've got some," Peg volunteered, hurrying from the room.

The younger officer touched Wynn's arm gently. "What about your husband? Do you have a recent photo of him?"

"I don't think so."

Officer Wright smiled reassuringly and said, "We can't do an Amber Alert. But we won't give up. We'll bring your sons back to you. Here's what we need from you. Ms. Evans, you've got to work with us."

"How? What do you mean?" She locked her hands together to keep them from shaking uncontrollably.

"There are things you can do to help."

"Like what?"

"When you get home if there is a message from him or he makes contact with you, let us know. The more information we get the better the chances that we'll find him. Let's work together and bring your children home."

* * *

Completely exhausted and totally lost, Wynn opened the door to her house. Worried, her parents had begged her to stay. Declining politely, she'd insisted on coming home. She wanted to be in her house, surrounded by familiar things, including the kids' stuff.

Standing in the foyer, she waited, half expecting to hear the sounds of her children running to the front door to greet her. The silence smacked her in the face. Stomach tied into knots and her head pounding from the pressure of not crying her brains out, Wynn shut the door and dropped her keys and purse on the table in the foyer.

Headed to the kitchen for a glass of water and aspirins, Wynn moved listlessly down the hall. Far too tired and distraught to do anything, she entered the kitchen, switched on the light, and dropped into a chair at her kitchen table. Kevin's science project sat in the center of the kitchen table; the sweet potato growing in water had grown roots that were submerged. Jimmy's A+ spelling test paper hung from a magnet on the refrigerator. *I've got to get out of here,* her thoughts screamed. *There are way too many memories for me to cope with right now.*

Intent on her escape, she rushed from the kitchen, heading to the family room. The ten o'clock news would be on soon. If the news did a small story on the boys, maybe someone, possibly a good Samaritan, would come forward with information.

Wynn flopped down on the sofa and grabbed for the remote. Jimmy's green nerf football sat on the coffee table. She reached for it and cradled the styrofoam toy in her arms. Without realizing it, tears began to fall, burning a path down her cheeks. The fear of never seeing or holding her children overwhelmed her.

What was she going to do? It seemed almost hopeless to think that the police would find her boys.

In the distance, she heard the phone ring. Emotionally drained, she sat, waiting for the voice mail to pick up. On the third ring the machine kicked in.

"Um, Wynn?"

Jim! Her heart almost exploded from her chest. She jumped to her feet and raced around the room, tossing pillows and newspapers aside in her haste to find the telephone. "There it is," she exclaimed, breathing a sigh of relief, as she pushed aside the TV guide and snatch up the receiver.

"Jim! Jim! I'm here."

"Good. I almost hung up."

Remember, Wynn, she cautioned herself, *you need to listen for things that will tell you where he's at.* Afraid she'd frighten him off, she paused, collecting herself and quickly reviewing her options. "I'm home. Don't hang up."

"Didn't want to miss this call, did you?" Jim chuckled nastily.

"No. I didn't."

"Now you've got time for me."

Oh Lordy! *He's still mad. Of course, he is. You called security on him when he came to your office.*

Wynn licked her dry lips and went for what she hoped sounded casual. "So, umm. Where are you?"

"Wouldn't you like to know?"

Yes, I would, she thought. *And once I found you and my sons, I'd have your ass put in jail for life.*

"Well, we're not here," he replied.

Swallowing hard, she strove for light but concerned. "Are Kevin and Jimmy okay?"

"They're fine. They just had dinner and went to bed."

Work with him, she reasoned. *Don't upset him. He's not going to tell you much. But maybe you can get a few clues.*

"Are you taking them on a trip? Will you be back soon?"

"No."

Okay, try something else. "W-wh-when do you think you'll be coming home?"

He snorted. "Never."

Numb with shock, Wynn felt as if Jim had just shot her in the head. Silently, she prayed. *Please, God. Don't let this be true.* There must be a way to reason with him and get him to bring the kids home. Wynn decided to try another approach. Voice quivering and hands shaking, she asked, "Jim, the boys aren't used to being away from home for long periods. They get scared when they don't hear from me. Can I talk to them?"

"No."

"Please. Kevin is so young. Let me talk to him for a moment. I promise I won't say anything that will upset him."

"He'll be fine. They both will. They don't need you."

She couldn't help saying, "I'm their mother. Of course they need me."

"And I'm their father," he countered. "I told you that you'd be sorry. I bet you are now."

"I am. Very, very sorry. Tell me what I can do to make things right between us. To fix this."

"Nothing. It's too late."

"No. No," Wynn contradicted. "It's not."

"The only reason I called was to tell you that we're not coming back."

Wynn began to shake. Her hands were so nervous that she could barely hold the phone.

"We're out of Michigan and headed as far away as possible."

"What about your stores, Jim? Are you going to let them go?"

"Yes. I don't care about that. It's me and my sons."

Chewing on her bottom lip, she asked, "What about school? Jimmy and Kevin are going to miss their school and friends."

"It doesn't matter," he dismissed without a moment's hesitation. "The boys will make new friends."

"Where do you plan to go?"

After a moment of quiet, he answered, "South."

South! That didn't sound right. Jim didn't know anyone or have family in the southern states. "Why south?"

"You won't find us. If I get into the back hills, you'll never find us."

Oh Lordy! Wynn thought. *This man has lost his mind.* Jim could possibly disappear forever with her children.

"Why did you call?"

"To tell you to stop calling us. Leave us alone.

We're out of your life. After tonight, I won't answer."

No hovered on her lips, but she fought to stay calm; she didn't want to upset him more. "Then don't you think I deserve to speak with my sons to tell them good-bye? I've always allowed you to see them whenever you wanted. I deserve the same treatment."

"Dream on. You're not going to get it. I want you to know that you can have your 'boy toy.' But I won't let him or any other man raise my children. Do you understand me? Nobody."

"I understand. Please think about letting me speak to them to say good-bye. We both need this."

"Maybe," he taunted, and then hung up.

Wynn dropped the phone and covered her face with her hands. She felt so lost. What if he never called back or the police couldn't find him? She was in danger of losing her family for the rest of her life.

Stop! You can't let that happen. Fighting back the fear of never seeing her children again, Wynn picked up that phone and called the police. *I've got to let them know everything little thing he said. That's the way to get my kids home safe and sound. I'll cry later.*

Chapter 30

After tossing and turning most of the night, Wynn rose from the bed before dawn with a plan in her head. She dressed in a pair of denim jeans, a sweatshirt, and sneakers before getting in her car, determined to find a way to get her children home. A flicker of apprehension coursed through her as she considered the limited options she had for getting her boys back.

Once she arrived at her destination, she hesitated at the front door, mentally bracing for what she knew would be a torrent of questions. *I can't take this,* she thought. *There's no other place for me to go. The inquiries were going to come anyway.*

Seated at her desk, Helen glanced up, welcoming smile firmly in place for any newcomer to Nursing Solutions. That smile quickly folded into a concerned frown. For a beat Helen said nothing, taking time to study her boss. Her concern quickly turned to pity. "What are you doing here?" The surprised note in the older woman's voice, grated on Wynn's nerves. She didn't have the energy or the time to answer a bunch of questions and she didn't have to.

"I work here." Wynn moved into the outer office and shut the door. The expression of concern and pity on her employee's face bugged her. She brushed past Helen and headed for her office.

Halting, she turned back to Helen, uttering the truth in a desperate voice. "I couldn't stay home. I can't take the quiet. It's driving me crazy. Nobody's there." Her voice cracked and she covered her eyes with her hand. Fighting for composure, she drew in a deep, calming breath. *Focus, Wynn. Think of Jimmy and Kevin and how scared they must be. Do what needs to be done to get your children.*

"What if Jim calls? How will he reach you?"

Blinking, Wynn stopped and gazed at Helen, although she truly didn't see the older woman. Her thoughts were focused on what she planned to do. "I forwarded all the calls to my cell."

"That's good."

The constant pain and buzzing in the back of Wynn's head moved to the frontal lobe. She swayed unsteadily on her feet.

"You okay?"

Wynn nodded.

Today, Mozart's sonata was far from soothing. The music banged around in her head, intensifying the throbbing pain. "Helen, would you please turn down the music? I can't take it today. It makes my head hurt."

"Certainly." The administrative assistant picked up the remote, pointed at the sound system mounted on the wall, and dropped the volume on the compact disc player. "There, that should be better. Honey?"

"Huh?"

"Your mother called. She's worried and looking for you. Why don't you give her a call?"

Wynn started for her office. "Maybe. Sometime today, if I get some things done."

"Good." Helen took a swallow from her mug and then followed Wynn into her office. "If you're worried about Nursing Solutions, I can handle things until you're back. Don't forget, you might want to spend time with the boys once they get home."

"Maybe. Who knows." Wynn crossed the office. "Can you do me a favor?"

Helen replied. "Sure."

"Call my mother and tell her where I am." Wynn massaged her forehead with her fingertips. "I can't talk to her right now."

The older woman turned away. "I'll take care of it."

Minutes later, Wynn heard Helen's soft voice. The words were indistinguishable. Relieved, Wynn sighed. She didn't need either of her parents rushing to the office to insist that she go home.

"Thanks." Wynn sank into her chair, covered her eyes with her hands, and forced back tears. *Stop this right now.* There were things that needed her attention. Kevin and Jimmy were out in the world and they needed her.

On the hunt, Wynn went to her bookcase, searching for one particular item. Unable to locate it, she called, "Helen?"

"What?" she yelled back.

"Where is the Yellow Pages?"

"What?"

"I need the Yellow Pages." Wynn brushed a lock of hair from her eyes and turned to the closet. She might have put the book in the closet the last time she used it. After rummaging through an array of crap, she admitted defeat. It wasn't there. Where else could she look? She started for the desk. Maybe the book was hiding in the bottom desk drawer.

"Is this what you're looking for?" Helen stood in the doorway with the yellow tome cradled in her arm.

Wynn nodded, reaching for the book.

"What are you looking for?"

"I have to find a private investigator."

Helen placed the book on the desk. "Why?"

Wynn opened it and found the section she needed. "The police aren't doing everything. I need some help."

"Why don't you call Adam? He's got resources beyond anyone else you know. He can help."

At the thought of Adam, her stomach clenched into knots. She hadn't treated him fairly. She couldn't ask for his help. Shaking her head, Wynn studied the patterns in the wood grain. "I can't."

"Why not?"

"I haven't treated him right. When he tried to get close to the kids I always pushed him away. And now I need help. I can't do that to him. I have to find a way by myself to work out this mess."

"I think you're wrong," Helen dropped a hand on her hip. "Outside of the police, that man is the best shot you have of finding that fool of an ex-husband."

Wynn grimaced. The police were bound by the law. They hadn't seemed real interested in finding Kevin and Jimmy last night. "No. I'll work on this by myself."

"Okay. I'll leave you to it." Helen handed over the book and left the office, closing the door after her.

Wynn opened the book to the section on private investigators, searching for one that has experience finding exes. She reached for the telephone and dialed. Bert Wojochaski might be the one to help her. Wojochaski's credentials included work with finding lost family members. His phone rang a dozen times. No one answered.

An hour later, Wynn slammed the book shut in frustration. How was she supposed to find her kids if she couldn't locate a decent private investigator to do the job? She returned to the book, circling several additional listings. *I can't give up. My future depends on it.*

A shadow filled her doorway. She glanced up. Her heart skipped a beat. Adam!

"Hi, sweetheart," he said, leaning against the door frame.

"Hi."

"What are you doing?"

"Looking for something," she answered, sticking the pen inside the Yellow Pages and shutting the book.

He strolled into the office, knelt down next to her chair, and took her hand. "Why didn't you call me?"

The query was asked softly with no reprimand or recrimination. With a moan of distress, the tears she'd been holding back flowed like water from the faucet. "My problem."

"No, baby. Our problem. Tell me everything. I need to know," Adam urged, holding on to her hands.

"Who told you?" she asked.

"Helen."

Wynn started to rise. Helen had to stop telling Wynn's business.

Adam held her in the chair, saying, "Don't bother. I would have come anyway. What happened?"

She closed her eyes, her heart ached with pain. "You already know."

"No. I don't." He encouraged Wynn with a touch on her arm. "I need to hear it from you. Tell me."

"Jim took them. Kevin and Jimmy. They're gone."

"When?"

"Yesterday afternoon from my mother's." Tears rolled down her cheeks. She brushed them away with back of her hand.

Adam gently pressed on, using a soft, caring tone to draw the information from her. "Do you know where he's gone?"

Wynn shook her head solemnly. "Jim called last night after I got home."

"What did he say?"

"I tried to reason with him. Explain that the boys weren't used to being away from me that long. I begged him to let me talk to them. But he wouldn't."

She fell silent for a moment, reliving those horrible moments when she knew her children were within shouting distance, yet too far away to get to.

"He claims he's going south on vacation with the boys. He wants them to see some of the beautiful countryside. That statement pretty much blew my chances for an Amber Alert because he took the time to call and inform me of his plans." She couldn't hide the inner misery tearing her soul into a million pieces. Pieces that she didn't believe would ever come together again.

"I know it hurts to talk about this, but I need to know. You called the police, correct?"

"Yes."

"What did they say?" Adam probed. Using a gentle finger, he brushed her hair from her eyes.

"They said that although I'm the custodial parent, Jim had joint custody so they couldn't do an Amber Alert. In Michigan it must be a noncustodial parent. Jim could be taking them on a vacation but forgot to tell me." She snorted. "As if he would do anything for them."

"What do you think?"

Her short, intense bark of laughter lacked humor. "I think he's pissed at me for rejecting him. He's getting a charge out of having control over me and the kids. He can call the shots."

Adam thought about this for a minute. "That could be. Why are you here?"

"I need to find a PI. Get somebody on my side to help me."

Adam cupped her cheek and brushed away her tears with his thumb. "I'm on your side. And I'm here to help. Let me."

"How?"

"First of all, I'm going to drop you at your parents and then make some calls. Come here," he muttered, rising to his feet and drawing her along with him. He pulled her into his arms and held her close.

Suddenly, Wynn couldn't hold back the tears anymore. She held on tight to him and cried. Finding the kids gone from her parents', returning to the empty house, and the sheer ineffectiveness of the police were all too much for her to handle.

Deep sobs racked Wynn's insides. Yet Adam held on, stroking her back and whispering soothing words in her ears. He let her cry until all of her tears were gone and sadness took over, spreading through her body, leaving her drained and listless. With a tender touch, he mopped her face with tissues from her desk.

"Come on," he said, wrapping an arm around her and leading her to the door. "We're going to get out of here."

"And do what?" she asked.

Adam answered simply, "Find Kevin and Jimmy."

Chapter 31

After dropping Wynn at her parents' for a little tender loving care, Adam rushed downtown to the Gautier offices. He parked in the executive garage and navigated through the maze of towers connecting the Renaissance Center. He marched through the offices of Gautier Motors toward his suite. Ignoring the elaborately posh burgundy carpeting, beige walls stuffed with photos of the company's founding fathers, and office décor, Adam nodded appropriately at several colleagues as he passed their offices.

At the end of a long hallway, he opened the door to executive row and turned down a second corridor, leading to his offices. Adam entered, stopping in front of his administrative assistant's desk.

Tia rose. "Hi, Adam," she greeted in a cheery tone and held out a batch of pink slips. "Here are your messages."

With a strong sweep of his hand, he waved them away. "Later."

"Okay," she muttered, dropping the scraps of paper on her desk.

"I need you to get Ralph MacDonald and Mitchell Grimes up here ASAP. Tell them to drop whatever they're working on and meet me in my office."

Tia's brows creased into a puzzled frown. Without asking a question, she reached for the phone and dialed the appropriate extension. "Got it."

"Good." Adam continued to his office. Taking pity on his administrative assistant, he halted at the door and said, "I'll explain everything later."

Tia acknowledged his comment with a wave of her hand while completing Adam's request.

He crossed the floor, hung his jacket in the closet, and stood behind his desk. With his hands on his hips, Adam stood, studying the shoreline of Windsor.

Where are you, Jim? Adam wondered. *I'm going to find you. Once I get the boys back, you're going to jail for a very long time. You can put money on that.*

A knock at the door interrupted his maudlin musings. He turned, calling, "Yes?"

Ralph MacDonald hovered in the doorway. "You sent for me?"

"Yah. Come on in." Adam waved the older man inside. He watched the bow-legged, five-foot-nine investigator make his way across the carpet and stand near the desk. Slim built, the New York City transplant was one of Gautier's best investigators. Wild gray hair framed his long angular face and intelligent brown eyes. A bald spot the size of a silver dollar sat on the crown of his head. MacDonald's ordinary appearance masked the spirit of a true bulldog investigator. Ralph refused to let go until he undercovered everything. Nothing got by him.

No sooner had the greeting left Adam's lips than Mitchell Grimes appeared. Knocking on the door, Grimes peeked inside and noticed Ralph standing near Adam's desk. "Oh! My apologies. I didn't know you had company," Mitch explained in a deep southern drawl. He took a step back. "I'll wait out here until you're ready for me."

"No need. I'm ready now. Come on in. I want to talk to both of you."

Mitchell ambled his way into the office. "Sure."

Adam pointed past Mitchell and ordered, "Shut the door."

A southern boy at heart, Mitchell Grimes carried that soft-spoken gentlemanly manner throughout everything he did. At six-foot-five inches he had once had ambitions for a pro basketball career. A knee injury railroaded that career but led him to his true calling. Mitchell was as effective in searching out the truth as Ralph. Each man used different approaches to get the answers they sought. They were the best and that's what Adam needed for this particular assignment.

"Have a seat, gentlemen." Adam sank into his leather executive chair and pulled it close to his desk. He waited until both men were settled before going into his explanation.

"Ralph, Mitch, I know you were surprised by my call. I need your help in a matter that has absolutely nothing to do with work."

The New Yorker listened intently. He placed a yellow pad on his lap and removed a white pen from his breast pocket. Mitchell sat silently, absorbing Adam's words without taking notes.

"This is personal and confidential. I don't want to hear about any of it through the company grapevine. Understand me?" He glared directly at Ralph and then turned his cool gaze on Mitchell.

"Got you," Mitchell drawled.

Ralph nodded.

"Good. Now we'll talk. I have an assignment for you guys. I want you to coordinate your efforts because I believe it's going to take both of you to get this particular job done."

Mitchell shifted uncomfortably, glancing sideways at Ralph. There was an interesting rivalry between the two men. Normally, Adam tried to respect their differences. Today, he didn't care.

"Go ahead. Give me details," Ralph encouraged.

Generally, Adam kept his private life just that, private. Today called for something very different. He drew in a deep breath and began, "My friend Wynn Evans's children have been kidnapped by their father. Wynn's ex-husband may have taken them from the state. I need you guys to find them, bring them home by fair means or foul. I prefer that you stay within the letter of the law. But I know you have contacts that can make this investigation easier."

"Have the police been contacted?" Ralph asked. "Yes."

"Amber Alert?" Mitchell inquired.

Adam shook his head. "We're skating on thin ice here. No Amber Alert because Wynn and her ex have joint custody. He could be taking the boys for a long weekend and forgot to inform Wynn for all we know."

"Has the ex contacted Ms. Evans since he took the kids? What about a woman friend? Is he seeing someone who might know about his mind-set or whereabouts?" Mitchell eased to the edge of his seat.

"Can we talk to Ms. Evans? I'd like to interview her." Ralph scribbled frantically on his pad. "She may know more than she realizes."

"I agree." Mitchell added his approval. "That's our starting point."

Pleased, Adam rubbed his hands together. "Good. I'll pay you separately for this case. It's completely personal and needless to say there is some urgency attached to it. The sooner you get the boys back, the bigger your bonus."

"When can we interview Ms. Evans?" Mitchell asked.

"Let me check." Adam picked up the phone and dialed Mr. and Mrs. Evans' home. After a short talk with Wynn, he hung up. "This afternoon," Adam answered. He felt skeptical about letting too many people close to Wynn right now; she was fragile and needed as much protection as Adam could provide. He'd be at her side, making certain things moved swiftly while causing her the least amount of stress.

Mitchell and Ralph needed her input. Without it, they were flying in the dark.

Adam reached for a scratch pad and jotted down the Evans' address. "Here. Meet me there at three."

* * *

Wynn sat on the sofa in her parents' house between Adam and her father. Adam placed a protective arm around her shoulders and drew her close to his side. She eyed the two men sitting opposite her. They were like a weird Mutt and Jeff combination. One was so tall she wanted to ask him if he'd ever played professional basketball. The other had a strong New York accent that he had kept through his years in Michigan. Both wore serious expressions on their faces.

Adam nudged her shoulder and whispered close to her ear, "Go on. Tell them everything."

The New Yorker glanced at the man beside her, seeking permission. Adam nodded.

"Have you and your husband been at odds lately?"

Wynn hesitated. She didn't want to air her dirty laundry. What transpired between Jim and her was private, but she didn't have a choice. She wanted her kids back and soon. "Yes. He came by my office and asked if he could come home."

Peg gasped. "When did this happen?"

"A few days ago," Wynn answered, fidgeting under her mother's disapproving glare.

"You should have told me."

The tall man cleared his throat, bringing all eyes back to him. "I'm wonderin' what kind of business your ex-husband runs?"

"Jim has a chain of sporting goods stores. They're called Lucky Sports."

Ralph's eyes lit up as he leaned forward. "Are the stores in Michigan?"

She nodded.

"Mitchell, we need to check them out," Ralph said.

"I'm on it." Mitchell removed his cell phone from his pocket and hit a button. A second later, he rose and stepped from the room, speaking softly into the phone.

Ralph watched Mitchell for a moment and then turned his attention back to Wynn. "While he's working on that, tell me about his relationships. Does he have a girlfriend or significant other?"

"Girlfriend. Her name is Lorraine Howard."

"What does she do?"

"Lorraine works for Jim."

Ralph wrote on his yellow pad. "At one of the stores."

Wynn nodded.

"Ms. Evans, do you know who's running your ex-husband's businesses?"

"No. I don't have any information about that."

"What about your child support? Have you been receiving it regularly?" Mitchell asked as he returned to the room.

"Spotty at best," she answered. "I tried to discuss it with Jim, but he blew me off. Insisted that he'd sent the money to the Friend of the Court."

Mitchell glanced at Ralph. A silent message passed between them. "That's a sure sign that something is wrong. Plus, he asked to come home. Something was going on that he was trying to dodge."

She shut her eyes. She felt so stupid. How could she have missed the signs? *Easy,* she thought, *you were trying to get along for the sake of your children.*

Adam must have felt her tense up next to him. He gazed at her and asked, "You okay?"

She nodded.

"I pulled his driver's license and vehicle information." Ralph handed the sheets to Wynn. "Is this correct?"

Again, she nodded. The photo revealed a smiling James Harrison. The next photo was a picture of his red Jeep. The SUV he used to take her children. She was barely able to look at the man. Wynn quickly returned the photos to Ralph.

"Cell phone. Can we get his number?"

Wynn shrugged. "I've got it. But he refuses to pick up."

"Don't worry about that. We've got another reason for getting them."

"You going for the LUGS?" Adam asked.

"LUGS?" Mr. Evans asked.

"Phone records," Ralph offered. "We can learn who he's been talking to."

"Don't you have to have a warrant for that?" Mrs. Evans asked.

"Most times." Ralph grinned. "But I have ways of getting that info."

Pleased, Adam smiled. "Good."

Mitchell took a look at Jim's ID. "What about the GPS system?"

Ralph studied the vehicle registration. "It's a 2007. There's got to be some type of tracking device. OnStar or something. Maybe even LoJack."

"What are you going to do with that?" Mr. Evans asked.

"See if we can find him. Get a location. If OnStar

is working, GM can tell us where the car is,"
Mitchell explained.

"You can do that?" Peg inquired, eyebrows
raised.

Smiling, Mitchell confirmed, "Sure can."

Adam turned to Wynn. "You're far from help-
less. We can do a number of things where law en-
forcement's hands would be tied. But not ours.
Ralph and Mitchell will stay within the law. But
they can move around it a bit. They've got wiggle
room."

"When was the last time you heard from Jim
Harrison, Ms. Evans?" Ralph questioned.

"He called last night."

"What did he tell you?"

"That he was taking the kids on a trip and he'd
let me know when they got back," she recited.

Mitchell brushed a finger down the slope of
his nose. "I know we mentioned it before—do
you have any information about the shops?"

"No. Whenever I asked, Jim didn't seem very
concerned."

Handwriting at super speed, Ralph said, "What
else did he say?"

"That he and the boys were heading south.
That didn't sound right to me. Jim doesn't have
any friends or family in the southern states."

"He may be trying to throw you off. He's probably going north," Mitchell drawled, leaning
back in his chair with one leg resting over the opposite knee.

Adam rubbed her arm. "Was there anything
else? Something that seemed odd at the time but
you didn't have the time to evaluate?"

"I think he'll do anything to keep the kids away from me. He's enjoying the fact that I'm scared for them. This is all being done for sheer spite, revenge. Whatever. Before he hung up, he said, 'I told you that you'd be sorry.'"

Ralph stood. Mitchell did the same.

"We're not going to let that happen, Ms. Evans," Ralph reassured her.

Mitchell added, "I double that. We'll have those boys back with you real soon."

"One more thing." Adam gazed at Wynn's parents. "I don't want Wynn alone. If this is a vendetta, we don't want to give Jim a shot at you."

Peg gasped. "Do you think he'd do that?"

"I think he'll try anything because he feels that she's done him wrong," Adam answered.

"Oh, I don't think he'll bother to come after me." Wynn swallowed hard and added, "Jim knows that he's done his worst by taking the boys."

"Right!" Adam drawled sarcastically. "That's why he's got your children. Because he'll never do anything to hurt you. Honey, he's done nothing but. We're not going to give him another chance. Until this is resolved, someone will be with you at all times. I'll assign a bodyguard."

"No."

"Yes."

She stood, faced him with a determined expression on her face. "If you don't listen to me, I'll call all of this off and do my own search."

He opened his mouth to say something, but quickly shut it when he realized that she was completely serious. "Okay. We'll do it your way for now."

Chapter 32

Portfolio tucked under his arm, Adam shoved his gold Cross pen inside the breast pocket of his suit jacket and hurried from Reynolds Gautier's office. Tugging on his tie, Adam unhooked the top button of his shirt as he rushed to his next meeting.

This had not been a good meeting. He'd had to explain to Reynolds why two of his top private investigators had been pulled off their assignments to help Adam. Plus, the men designed to provide security for Wynn 24/7. He offered a brief explanation that the boss had bought. Reynolds had been sympathetic but suggested Adam complete this project quickly.

Adam marched down the hallway to his office. Tia glanced up from the work on her desk and smiled. "Hi. Good meeting?"

"No."

Tia grimaced, handing him his messages, and said, "Ralph and Mitchell are waiting for you in your office."

"Good." He opened his door and found the two men with their heads together. "Hello, gentlemen. What do you have for me?"

Their heads snapped up and separated. Ralph ran his fingers through his mixed brown and gray hair. Sucking on a tooth, Mitchell stretched his long legs in front of him while reviewing his notes.

"We know why Mrs. Evans hasn't been receiving child support payments," Mitchell stated.

Adam stepped into the office and shut the door and took his place behind the desk. "Tell me more."

Ralph took over at this point, "We sent a man to check out the stores. The downtown Detroit and Southfield stores are already shut down."

Adam leaned closer, mentally dissecting the implication of this material. "Shut down? I thought his businesses were doing well." With a hand stroking his forehead, he shook his head. "Wait. Step back a minute. Let me ask another question. Why is the store shut down?"

"Lack of payments," Ralph explained. "Jim Harrison was evicted for not paying his monthly leases."

"You're kidding!" Adam chuckled.

"No, sir." Mitchell scratched the side of his neck with a finger. "There are eviction notices on the doors."

Amazed, Adam sat back and chewed on this information. Lack of funds would explain why Jim wanted to returned to Wynn. Her business was highly successful. Plus, the added bonus of whisking her away from someone else must have given Jim a charge. Unfortunately, it didn't work out the way Jim planned. Wynn refused to sit at home, pining away for her ex-husband. Instead, she found a new man. He chuckled silently. A successful younger man. Her rejection must have been the last straw. No money. Rejected by his ex. It all made for a bad day that ended with Jim hatching a plot to hurt Wynn that would never end.

"There's more," Mitchell added. "Mr. Harrison's stores in Royal Oak and Southfield have been at the center of a hostile takeover by one of Jim's competitors."

"Didn't Jim have two more stores?"

"Yeah," Ralph answered. "There's one in Lincoln Park and the other is in Detroit."

"Yeah. That's what I remember Jim saying." Adam leaned back and tented his fingers. "Were they successful with the takeover?"

"Pretty much," Ralph answered, scratching an item off his list. "The Lincoln Park store is hanging on by a thread."

"What else did you find out?" Adam opened his portfolio to a clean page and began to take notes.

Ralph's voice held a rasp of excitement. "Mr. Harrison's in debt up to his eyebrows and sinking very fast."

Pen poised to write the dollar amount, Adam asked, "How much debt?"

"Over two million."

Whistling long and hard, Adam tossed down his pen, leaned back in his chair, and stared at the men. "You're kidding, right?"

Slowly, Ralph shook his head.

"Wow!"

Ralph's tone was coolly disapproving, "Yeah. That's what I thought."

"How did he get that way?"

Mitchell pulled the leg of his denims over his ankle and said, "He likes to live like a king. Mr. Harrison took two- or three-week vacations to Hawaii and Europe. Huge expensive dinners where he took all of his friends out. It looks as if when he left Ms. Evans, he went hog wild. Buying sprees for him and his lady friend. Whatever he wanted, he bought, and he did it with credit cards."

Adam shook his head. "Bad move. Childish actually."

"There's more," Mitchell added.

"Go on." Adam's voice hardened ruthlessly.

"For the past few weeks, he's liquidated all of his assets and turned them into cash."

"How much money are you talking about?" Adam strummed the desk with a pen. "It can't be that much cash if the man is in so much debt."

"Almost eight hundred thousand can go a long way. That's more than enough to disappear and start a new life somewhere else."

Adam took a quick breath of utter astonishment. He stared wordlessly at the two men. Eight hundred thousand dollars if used properly could take a person a long way. This wasn't good. Not at all. "We've got to find this fool ASAP. Are any of the employees left in the two remaining stores?"

"Just the girlfriend."

"What?"

"That's right. She was a clerk at the Lincoln Park store."

How humiliating for Wynn. Jim was a complete idiot. Not only had her ex abandoned his wife and children, he'd taken up with one of his employees. "We need to talk to her. Can you find her?"

"Already done. We're on our way to her place after we finish with you," Ralph assured.

"Good. I'm coming with you. I have to see this woman for myself." Adam picked up the phone and hit the intercom button. "Tia, I'll be out of the office for about three hours. Forward anything important to my cell phone."

Adam focused on the two investigators. "What about the GPS system? Any luck with that?"

"Not much. Mr. Harrison hasn't been paying the bill." Mitchell read his notes. "So the system was shut down. On top of that he removed the tracker manually a few weeks ago."

Adam snorted. "That figures. What about the LUGS for his cell phone? How are you doing with them?"

"Received them this morning," Mitchell drawled, waving the sheets in the air. "Lots of calls to the girlfriend. Few to creditors. But the interesting thing is the calls are coming from Canada. Ms. Evans was correct. Mr. Harrison was trying to throw her off the trail by saying he was going south."

"Give me your ideas on what Jim is doing," Adam demanded, leaning comfortably back into his chair.

"Mr. Harrison is calling from different spots in

Canada as he works his way toward Niagara Falls." Mitchell studied the list of numbers, shifting through the pages. "I think he plans to come back to the United States through Canada."

Adam's heart jolted in his chest. They couldn't allow that idiot to reach Niagara Falls. With the money, Jim could slip back into the country through New York. He could disappear for good and start a new life without regard to what he was doing to Wynn.

Adam rose from the desk. "Let's get on it."

Adam, Ralph, and Mitchell entered the shop together. Adam strolled to the counter. Ralph moved to the back of the store while Mitchell moved to the right, scoping out the store's layout.

"Welcome to Lucky Sports," A teen clerk chanted like an automated telephone recording.

Adam nodded in the girl's direction and moved around the store. The three men met at the rear. After conferring at the back of the store, they returned to the cashier and asked for Lorraine Howard.

The clerk paged her overhead and minutes later a woman sauntered confidently toward them. Her blue contact lenses were in direct contrast to her chocolate skin. Straight blond hair fell over her shoulders, down her back, to her rear end. Rings adorned her nose and bottom lip. Her blouse was opened, revealing deep cleavage.

Fascinated, Adam stared. Lorraine was completely different from Wynn Evans. He expected some great beauty who had possibly swept the married man off his feet with flattery and great sex. Looking at the seductive sway of her hips, Adam didn't doubt that great sex had been on the menu, but this woman was a far cry from what he expected. How could Jim have gone from being married to a queen to sharing living quarters with a peasant?

Lorraine Howard halted in front of them, surveying the unusual group. Remembering her manners, she plastered a fake smile on her face and asked, "What can I do for you?"

Ralph took the lead, offering his hand. "Ms. Howard?"

"Yes?" She offered him a limp handshake.

He removed a card from his pocket and handed it to the woman. "I'm an investigator from Gautier Motors."

Her gaze shifted from one man to the other. "Gautier? Those new French cars? What do you want with me? I don't have one of those cars." She giggled nervously. "I can't afford it."

"We're looking for the owner of this business. A Mr. James Harrison."

Lorraine took a step away from the men. "And?"

"He's fled the state. We need to talk with him."

"I can't help you." She placed the card in Ralph's hand. "I don't know where he is."

"When was the last time you spoke with him?"

"A week ago. Maybe longer. He hasn't been in for a while."

Mitchell stepped forward and asked, "Does he call? How are you conducting business? Payroll?"

The woman's demeanor turned hostile. "I think it's time for you to leave," she said with an arrogant twist of her shoulders. "Excuse me, I have work to do."

Adam interrupted. "Actually, I do mind. I have a few more questions before you leave."

Examining him thoroughly, she asked, "You're not the police. I don't have to say anything to you."

"No, you don't," Adam stated firmly. He crowded the woman's space and then saw the fear in her eyes. It was a hearty feeling that he planned to exploit. "But if I find out that you had anything to do with the kidnapping of Jimmy and Kevin Harrison, I'll make it my life's work to put you in jail for as long as the law allows."

Ralph took the moment to add his unique brand of persuasion. "Ms. Howard, we already know that you've been in contact with Mr. Harrison. If you have any influence with him, I'd suggest that you tell him to bring the children home."

"We're gonna get those babies home with their mama," Mitchell added.

Adam led the way out of the store. They stood on the curb, gazing through the glass door at Lorraine.

"Follow her. Check her calls. She knows something and I think she'll lead us to Jim." Adam shoved his sunglasses on his nose and started for the car.

Chapter 33

Lorraine is the key, Adam thought as he strolled into Gautier around three. *That woman knows a lot more than she's telling.* Adam felt it. Plus, her demeanor turned downright smug when she realized why they were at the store. She was a hard, tough cookie who refused to budge an inch. He stopped and added a note to his growing list. Putting a tail on her might reveal some much needed information.

Preoccupied with finding a way to learn everything Lorraine knew, Adam opened the door to his office suite and glanced up. Wynn sat with Tia. The two women were talking in low tones.

Pleasure surged through him at the sight of Wynn in his realm. "Hi," he greeted softly. Eager to be near her, he moved across the room and leaned down to plant a kiss on her cheek.

Pain still lingered in Wynn's eyes. "Hey."

"What brings you here?" For the second time today, he wondered what kind of fool Jim was. Here was the most fantastic, beautiful, sexy woman. Yet Jim went for someone completely different. If he had to turn a phrase, he'd say Jim leaned toward the Ghetto Fabulous. Obviously, beauty was in the eye of the beholder.

"Got a minute?" she asked.

"Five for you," he teased, leading the way to his office. "Maybe more if you treat me right."

"I know you're busy. I won't need much more than that," she promised.

He called over his shoulder, "Tia, hold my calls until I say otherwise."

"Got it," Tia stated, shifting through a pile of paper on her desk.

Adam allowed Wynn to go into the office ahead of him and then shut the door once he'd entered the room. He urged her forward and placed her in a chair. Once they were both seated, Adam got a whiff of something unpleasant going on. He sensed a problem. "Wynn?" he prompted.

Sitting stiffly in her chair, she shifted uncomfortably and said, "I want you to call them off."

Damn! She figured it out. *I'm going to plead ignorance and refuse to admit a thing unless she makes me.* "Call off? Who?"

Directing the evil eye in his direction, she answered, "The security people you have on me."

"I—" Adam began.

Instantly, Wynn lifted a halting hand. "Don't bother telling me a lie. I'm far from dumb."

That was true. He'd ordered security to keep an eye on her the moment he realized that she might be in danger. Jim's profile had changed. He was capable of anything. Desperate people did desperate things.

Adam couldn't lose Wynn. He refused to lose her.

"Okay," he conceded. "I did put a guy on you. It was for your safety."

"I'm fine," she insisted.

"No. You're not. Wynn, Jim Harrison is a dangerous man. Look what he's done so far. He left you and your kids for some woman and now he's kidnapped the boys to hurt you."

She snorted, folding and unfolding her arms. "Too late. Jim's already hurt me. There's not much he can do to me."

"I don't know that and you don't either."

Tears pooled in her eyes. Her voice held firm and true. "I'm already on the edge. Having some strange person watching my every move is not the way I want to live my life. Call them off."

Adam rose from his chair and circled the desk. He scrunched down next to Wynn. "Honey, I'm afraid for you."

"I need normal. Right now my life is completely abnormal. I don't have much control over what's going on around me." She stopped, lowering her head to study her linked hands. Although she tried to control it, her voice wobbled. "Everything is out of control. I can't go to work, shopping, do anything without looking over my shoulder. I know you mean well, but call them off."

Adam searched for another approach. He needed a way to convince her.

"Call them off," she insisted louder, more firmly.

Her near hysteria frightened him. If this situation didn't resolve itself soon, she might slip over the edge. He couldn't have that. "Okay."

She sighed. Her body sagged against the chair. "Thank you. I appreciate your concern. I really do. But I need my space."

Looking up at her, he realized that he'd done the right thing. He didn't like leaving her open to anything but she needed some control in her life. An idea hit him. If she refused security, maybe he could do the job himself. "How about you come and stay with me for a while?"

Her head snapped up. "At your house?"

"Yeah." He rose from his spot on the floor and offered her an engaging smile. "Get away from your place and all the reminders. This will give you some space and time to clear your mind. I'll have you close if my investigators need a piece of information from you."

Nodding, she evaluated the idea.

He waited, certain she'd agree if he let her make the decision without putting pressure on her.

"Okay. I think so."

"Good. We'll drop by your place and pick up some of your clothes and then go to my house."

"All right." Smiling gently, Wynn added, "I like that idea."

So do I, Adam thought. This would provide the freedom she needed while allowing him to keep an eye on her.

"Have you heard anything?" she asked in a hopeful tone.

Wynn needed to know. He returned to his place behind the desk. "Honey, Jim is in a lot of trouble. He's up to his ass in debt. Ralph and Mitchell found that two of Jim's stores are in foreclosure."

"What?"

Adam nodded. "Yeah. I was quite surprised. Also, the two remaining stores are in the middle of a hostile takeover. That's why you haven't been receiving your child support."

Her forehead furrowed into a frown as she absorbed this information. "How could this be? When we divorced, his businesses were in great financial shape. My attorney subpoenaed his books."

"Since the divorce, your ex has lived a lavish lifestyle. Jim and Lorraine Howard have taken expensive trips and meals at lots of highbrow restaurants. He's blown a lot of money and not focused on his business."

"What else have you learned?" she asked.

"You were right. We believe he's in Canada."

Frowning, she repeated, "Canada? Why?"

Adam didn't want to tell her this part. But if they didn't get the boys back, she'd demand to know why he hadn't told her the complete story. "We're surmising he's headed for Niagara Falls."

She shrugged, shaking her head. "I don't understand."

"I think he wants to cross back into the United States through the U.S.–Canada border."

"What good would that do?"

"Jim could disappear with the kids and be back in the U.S. to start a new life," Adam whispered softly. He didn't want to frighten her.

Her eyes grew large with fear and she sagged against the chair. "He can't do that. I'd never see my boys again."

Adam jumped to his feet and hurried to her. He

wrapped her in the warm cocoon of his embrace. "I won't let that happen. I promise. I won't."

Moonlight shone through the bedroom window, casting large shadows on the walls. Relieved, Adam gazed down at the woman in his arms. Finally, Wynn had drifted to sleep after crying most of the night. She'd tried to hide it, excusing herself and lurking in the bathroom. When she returned her beautiful, soulful brown eyes were red-rimmed, displaying her hurt, pain, and worry. Her cheeks were puffy and stained with dried tears. He wrapped her in his arms and rocked to and fro until she slipped into an exhausted slumber. Adam wanted to take her pain away. Unfortunately, he'd used up his options. He felt as if he'd failed her.

Unable to resist the need to touch her, he brushed a wayward lock of hair off her forehead. Wynn was so appealing in sleep. The urge to lean down and kiss that spot overwhelmed him. She was just so adorable. A deep shudder raked her body before she snuggled close to his warmth. "It's going to be okay. I'll find them," he promised, massaging her back through her nightgown. He truly hoped those words would come true very soon.

After they prepared dinner and Adam had urged her to eat, they had settled down in the family room to watch a movie. For most of the evening movies played on the Blu-ray disc player, but neither Wynn nor Adam had been able to focus on them. She sat, staring blankly at her cell phone. Each time it rang, the renewed hope flashed bright in her eyes, only to be dashed when she answered the call and found it wasn't Jim on the other end.

Adam hated seeing her this way. Yet there wasn't much more he could do. Ralph and Mitchell were working nonstop to find Jim and they offered the best hope they had at the moment. Yet Adam felt as if he had failed in his job of caring for Wynn, let her down. He should have done more, protected them better.

He snorted, pulling her limp frame more tightly against his side. From everything he'd learned, Jim had been hiding money problems and living way beyond his financial means for a long time. Who would have believed Jim would have lost his mind and run off with the boys.

The ringing of the telephone broke into his thoughts and Adam reached for the phone to silence it before it disturbed Wynn. "Carlyle."

Mitchell drawled, "Adam?"

Instantly, Adam became fully awake. "Yeah?"

"We've found him," Mitchell announced in a self-satisfied tone.

Adam shut his eyes and uttered a silent thank you to God. "Where?"

"Just like we thought. He's staying in a small town outside of Niagara Falls."

He let out a soft sigh. "Good." He glanced at Wynn. Her eyes were still shut. He didn't want her to hear his next question. "Are the boys with him?"

"The hotel clerk said he saw two small children in the truck when he checked in."

Adam let out a breath that he hadn't realized he'd been holding. "I'm on my way."

"Mr. Gautier lent us the company plane. We're

fueling up right now. Shouldn't take more than a couple of hours to get there."

Gratitude replaced the worry filling his heart. Reynolds always came through when Adam needed it. It was one of the reasons Adam felt such loyalty toward his boss. "I'll be there within the hour. Do you have somebody on Jim? In case he decides to make a move."

"Yeah. I've got a buddy up there that's keeping an eye on them. We're okay on that front. I'm ready to get those kids and put that fool behind bars."

"I'm with you on that."

"Oh, by the way," Mitchell added.

"Yeah."

"Ms. Howard is with Mr. Harrison. She showed up an hour ago."

Adam held his tongue. But he had a few choice names saved up for that woman. "I'm not surprised."

"Me, neither. Anyway, we'll see you soon."

"Mitchell, good job!"

"My pleasure."

Not wanting to wake Wynn, Adam gently placed the phone on the nightstand and threw back the covers. Silently, he crept out of the room and entered the bathroom down the hall. After a quick shower, he dressed and returned to the bedroom with a note explaining his destination. He didn't like leaving Wynn without talking to her first. But if he returned with the kids, he felt certain she'd forgive him.

Entering the room with a note in his hand,

Adam stopped short when he found Wynn sitting on the side of the bed fully dressed.

Hands linked together, she glared at him with a look of determination. "I'm coming with you," she declared.

He'd hoped to avoid a confrontation like this. He licked his lips and began, "Sweetheart, this could be dangerous. I don't want you in harm's way."

Ignoring Adam, she reached for her purse sitting behind her on the bed and stood. "They're my children. I'm coming."

"Wynn, Jim could see you and hurt someone just to get back at you."

"Doesn't matter. I'm coming," she responded instantly.

Fierce anger surged through him. How could she be so naive about this man? For God's sake, he'd kidnapped her sons and told her that she'd never see them again. Hardening his heart, he stated, "I think he's capable of anything."

"You're probably right. But, I'm coming anyway."

"Wynn—"

"Adam—"

They both stopped. The room filled with silence.

Wynn recovered first. She strolled to Adam and placed her hands on top of his. "I know you're trying to protect me."

He opened his mouth to speak. To tell her that she needed to wait here for him to return with the boys. She raised a hand and placed it over his mouth, effectively ending any discussion.

She smiled, showing all the confidence she had in his abilities. A beautiful curve of her lips that made him feel as if he could do anything and that she trusted him with her life. Even the lives of her sons. "We're a team, right?"

Sensing a trap, he nodded slowly.

"This is where I come in as part of the team. You have to let me do my part."

Smiling gently at him, she removed her hand, waiting for him to state his case. He kept quiet, letting her talk.

"Your people found them. And I'll be forever grateful for that." Choked up, she blinked rapidly. Steadying herself, she continued, "Now, it's my job to be there for my children. Kevin and Jimmy are going to be scared, afraid. They've been away from home for three days. They don't know your investigators. Your men will probably storm in, take their father away, and leave them with nothing. I need to be there so that they are not frightened beyond belief. So that they have a parent to turn to. I don't want my sons traumatized by this incident."

Adam gazed down at this extraordinary woman and nodded. He'd never been more proud of her than he felt right now. She'd gone through hell but maintained her dignity and focused on what mattered most. Her sons.

"You're right," he answered gently, drawing her into his arms for one final hug. When he released her, he took her hand and they strolled from the room. "Let's go get our boys."

Chapter 34

Through most of the flight to Niagara Falls, Wynn sat staring out the window. Traveling among the pre-dawn clouds, she listened to the roar of the engine. Without delay, they had boarded the small plane and cut a smooth path from the United States to Canada. The accommodations were in line with a regular commercial plane, although somewhat smaller. The ride was pleasant and un-eventful. But Wynn still felt uncomfortable and nervous. The whole small plane thing didn't sit well with her.

Her throat closed up each time she considered the consequences of this ordeal. Focused on her children, Wynn sat quietly. There were going to be a lot of questions once this ordeal ended. She wondered how she would explain Jim's actions to his sons.

Seated ahead of her, Ralph and Mitchell con-versed in low tones with their heads together. The two men were debating the best approach to get-ting in and out of the hotel room with the least amount of fuss. Wynn only half listened as she struggled with her own thoughts. She didn't understand the details of what they were discussing and soon tuned them out. All she wanted was her children to come home. Wynn didn't care how they got the job done, as long as it got done and her boys were safe.

Adam sat at her side through the complete flight with a watchful gaze. Forehead crinkled into a frown, he directed his concerned gaze to her many times during the ninety-minute air time. Finally, he linked his fingers with hers and asked, "You okay?"

Biting her lips, she looked away. "Yeah. I'm not used to small planes and I'm worried about my kids."

He brought her hand to his lips and kissed her palm. "From what we've learned so far, they're fine. Ralph and Mitchell have someone watching them."

Soon after that remark, the plane began its descent and landed on a private airfield. The crew hustled everyone off the plane. Two limos waited side by side near the runway. Adam ushered her into the backseat of one. Ralph and Mitchell climbed into the second car. Confused by this turn of events, she pointed at the pair. "Why aren't they with us?"

Adam turned his head and glanced out the back window. "They're working on a plan to get into the room without any problems."

Her heart rate accelerated. "What kind of problems?"

"We don't want to lose Jim."

Her hands grew sweaty with uneasiness. "I don't understand."

"Basically, they want to be prepared for any contingency." Adam's voice was velvet edged and strong, telling her nothing and hiding a lot. "If he tries to climb out of a window or hide somewhere in the room, we want to know every spot that he can sink into."

Secretly wishing Jim would disappear forever, she nodded. Regardless of how the evening ended, it wouldn't be a perfect solution. This situation wouldn't have a clear, happy ending. Jim would probably end up in jail. Jimmy and Kevin would lose their father. The best- and worst-case scenario involved Jim getting probation. That would keep him in their world, allowing him to cause additional trouble and wreak more havoc.

Damn Jim. His selfishness hurt everyone. It put her, the kids, and even Adam in an awkward and unpleasant position. When the dust finally settled, everyone would be branded a loser.

The limo rolled to a stop at the Niagara Motel. Confused, Wynn glanced at Adam. "This can't be the place."

"I'm afraid it is," he stated, frowning at the neon flashing sign crackling with electricity. Several missing letters appeared in the word *Niagara*. It reminded her of those old hotels on Woodward Avenue in Detroit that specialized in by-the-hour room rentals.

Jim loved the best of everything. The Niagara was a long drop from a four- or even three-star hotel. Wynn's blood ran cold. She didn't want her children in a place like this. It looked like a hole for unsavory activities. Her sons were innocent. What had Jim been thinking?

"I'll be right back." Adam patted her knee and then climbed out of the car, shutting the door after him.

Peering through the window, Wynn waited and watched, not sure she liked the idea of being left out of things. From her car window, she saw Adam conferring with Ralph and Mitchell. The three men strolled to a small compact car facing the rear of the motel. The driver got out. This man reminded Wynn of Ralph. A small, average man with graying hair, he pointed to a spot at the back of the motel. After a brief discussion, the foursome headed for the motel lobby.

Getting more nervous by the minute, she waited. Adam returned to the limo and got in beside her. "Okay. We're going in. Mitchell got a pass key. I'd like you to stay in the car until I bring the kids out."

"No," she stated, reaching for the door handle. "I'm going with you."

"You can't." He placed his hand over hers.

On fire, she demanded in a biting tone, "Who do you think you're talking to? I don't work for you. Those are my kids and they need me." Her voice rose an octave. "I can do whatever I want. You can't stop me."

Resigned, Adam leaned into the leather seat and studied her. For the first time Wynn recognized the strain he'd been under since this ordeal began. "Yes, you can," he responded in a reasonable tone. "I'd like you to take a minute and listen to me. Put your emotions on the back burner and give me all of your attention."

Adam's tone stopped her cold. His efforts had put her children within her reach and gotten her to this point. She owed him. Without him she'd still be begging the police for an Amber Alert. Instead, she was yards away from her children and would soon be taking them home with her. She reached out and cupped his cheek. "I'm sorry. This has been a stressful time for us both. Go ahead, I'll listen."

"I understand your feelings. I want them at home, too. But we have to handle this very carefully. Remember, you and Jim have joint custody. We're in a foreign country. If we don't do this right, we'll all end up in jail."

She digested that info without comment. Lord knew Jim liked to cause as much trouble as he possibly could. Things might turn ugly.

"Let us get the boys out of there quietly, without a lot of noise and fuss. Trust me. I promise that I will bring them to you."

Trust. The word resonated with her. It was time for Wynn to show some faith in Adam. He'd been at her side throughout the entire situation. He'd provided private investigators who led the search. Heck, without the company plane they would be traveling by car for more than eight hours. She owed him this.

"Okay. I'll wait."

He leaned his forehead against hers and said, "Thank you. I won't let you down."

* * *

Jim went down with a minor struggle. He surrendered within minutes of encountering the combined force of Ralph and Mitchell.

Lorraine Howard turned out to be a completely different matter, screaming like a banshee. The Canadian investigator, Jack, slipped into the room and held her at bay until Ralph returned. He gave her a firm shake to quiet her down. Lorraine glared at Ralph with venom in her eyes. He took it with a shrug as he escorted her from the room and into the hallway.

Jack began searching through Jim's luggage.

"Hey!" Jim protested from the doorway. "That's my stuff. Don't touch it."

"Yeah, right. That's going to happen." Duffel bag in hand, Jack unzipped the bag and pulled out a handful of documents.

His find included fake passports for Jim and the kids, a New York State driver's license, and birth certificates with new names for all three.

"That's what we need to turn over to the police. This is exactly what we need to make our case," Adam said, shifting through the array of material. He didn't want Wynn to see some of this stuff. She'd flip out. He shut his eyes, thanking God. Another day and they might have been too late.

The Gautier investigators had been right. Jim had purchased everything he needed to start a new life. Maps of Niagara Falls with designated routes to Buffalo, New York, were ready for a trip back to the United States. Hotels, rental apartments, and schools were included on Jim's list.

All that noise must have disturbed the kids, Adam thought. He quietly opened the bedroom door and peeked inside. They were so still. Were Kevin and Jimmy alive? Fear ripped at his heart. Adam held his breath as he approached the bed.

Kevin laid curled up against Jimmy. Both boys were asleep. Kevin moaned and turned on his side.

Adam stood next to the bed for a moment, silently thanking God that they were unharmed. He touched Kevin's shoulder. The little boy's eyes opened slowly. After a moment recognition filled his gaze.

"Hi, Mr. Adam."

"Hi, Kevin."

"Is my mommy with you?" he asked, sitting up.

Adam dropped onto the bed next to the small child. He grinned at Kevin and said, "Yes. She's outside in the car."

"Good! I miss my mommy." His eyes brimmed with tears.

He reached for the child, held him in his arms, patting him on the back. "It's okay. I'm going to take you to your mother. She's missed you, too." Rising from the bed with Kevin in his arms, he touched Jimmy's arm.

Instantly, the boy opened his eyes. Warily, he studied the man. "Where's my dad?"

"He needed to leave. Your dad called your mother and she came to pick you up," Adam improvised.

Eyes narrowed, Jimmy glanced around the room. "Then where's my mother?"

They're baby parrots, he thought, tilting his head toward the window. "In the car outside. Come on." He reached out a hand to the boy. "I'll take you to her." Adam held his breath. Kevin was an easier kid to handle. Jimmy was older and more suspicious of any newcomer to his life. The boy scooted off the bed and reached for his shoes. It looked as if the boys had been living in the same clothes since they left home three days earlier. After Jimmy tied his sneakers, he took Adam's hand. With Kevin in his arms and Jimmy at his side, they exited the room, made their way to the front of the building, and Adam led the boys to the limo.

The limo door opened and Wynn practically leaped from its interior. She ran across the driveway with her arms open, eager to hold her children. Adam found it difficult to decide if Wynn was happy or sad. Crying tears of happiness and laughing at the same time, she raced toward her children.

Jimmy saw her first. "Mom!" He dropped Adam's hand and ran to his mother. She fell to her knees with open arms and Jimmy raced into them. The child held on to her, squeezing her. "I missed you," he muttered into her neck. "Missed you."

"Me, too. Me, too. I missed you." For minutes, they rocked back and forth and then Wynn let go long enough to look him over, check him out, and make sure he was okay.

Adam watched them. He still couldn't figure out if Wynn was crying or laughing. Maybe she was doing a little both. "You've lost a little weight. Why? Haven't you been eating?"

"Dad doesn't cook as good as you," he explained, stroking her hair.

"As well as I do," she corrected absently, preoc-

cupied with his weight loss. "What kind of foods
have you been eating?"

"Mom!" Jimmy exclaimed.

Laughing, she hugged him. "Okay. Okay. I'll
let it go for now. When we get home, I'm going
to fix you all your favorites."

"Pancakes?" He asked hopefully, eyes beaming.

"Absolutely."

"Cool!"

"I need to check out your brother." She rose
from the asphalt pavement and hurried to Adam.
Jimmy followed at her side. Adam held Kevin
against his shoulder, rocking the child back and
forth.

"Kevin woke up for moment and then went
right back to sleep," Adam said, turning so she
could see her son's face.

She stroked the child's cheek and then grinned.
"He's knocked out. Kevin always did sleep through
everything." Her voiced brimmed with pleasure.
"The house could blow up and he'd wake up in a
new locale and be fine with that."

Adam asked, ready to hand over the small
bundle, "You want to hold him?"

Wynn reached for her son and then suddenly
drew back. Shaking her head, she said, "No.
You're doing just fine."

Turning to Adam, she touched his free hand
and whispered. "Thank you."

Those simple words, said with such heartfelt
sincerity, made him feel ten feet tall. "My pleasure. You're welcome."

Jimmy took that moment to yawn. He covered
his mouth with his hand. Looking embarrassed,

he gazed at his mother, saying in a small voice, "Sorry."

Wynn hugged him a second time. "That's okay. Come on. It's time for us to go home. I'm tired, too." She reached for Adam's hand and tossed an arm around Jimmy. They strolled across the drive and entered the limo.

Chapter 35

A week later, Wynn and Adam sat in Wynn's family room. They had just finished watching *Iron Man* and the latest Indiana Jones movie.

The display on the DVD player flashed 11:45. "Guys," Wynn reminded, "it's time for you to go to bed."

"Ah, Mom! Do we have to?" Jimmy whined.

Unperturbed, Wynn answered, "Yes."

"Can't we stay up a little longer?" Kevin picked up his blanket and started to the hallway.

The boys dragged themselves and their blankets and pillows toward the stairs. They left a trail of un-eaten popcorn on their way to the stairs.

"One more movie?" Jimmy questioned.

"Nope. Don't forget to brush your teeth," Wynn reminded.

Adam remained silent throughout their ex-change. He chuckled. "Go through this often?"

"All the time. They never go to bed without a struggle. They whine and delay as much as possi-ble, but in the end they still have to go to bed."

Wynn grabbed used napkins and paper plates. "I'll give them a few minutes and then head upstairs to make sure they're in bed."

Nodding, Adam stood, picked up the empty pizza box and soda cans. "I'll toss this stuff while you're taking care of the boys."

Wynn ran a hand down his arm and grabbed his hand, squeezing it. "Thanks, Adam."

"No problem."

Adam moved down the hall in the opposite direction as Wynn headed for the stairs. With a happy beat of her heart, she climbed the stairs. Adam had been a saint since their return from Niagara Falls. He made certain they arrived in Michigan and got home safe.

In addition, he'd help produce the legal framework that would keep her sons safe. Concern for Wynn's children had driven Adam to produce a document that kept Jim out of jail but forced the courts to reevaluate his joint custody status.

Wynn made her first stop in Kevin's room. Her younger son was already in bed. She sat on the edge of the mattress and tucked the blanket around him.

After receiving her nightly kiss, she said, "Good night."

Kevin caught her hand and began to play with her fingers. "Mommy?"

"Hmm?"

"I like Mr. Adam. It's okay if you want to marry him."

Shocked, she stared at her child. "Well, thank you. I like Mr. Adam, too. I'll keep that in mind if he ever asks me."

Puzzled, he titled his head to one side. "Why wouldn't he, Mommy? You're perfect. Great!"

"You're biased." Wynn rubbed her nose against Kevin's.

"What's biased?" he asked.

"You like me better."

"Yeah, that's right."

"Have you thought about the fact that Mr. Adam may not want to get married?"

"Nah. He likes you, Mommy."

"Yeah. He does." At the entrance, Wynn switched off the overhead light, leaving the night-light burning. "Good night. I'll see you in the morning."

"'Night, Mommy."

Wynn crossed the hallway to Jimmy's room and opened the door. *Oh Lordy!* She thought, *I forgot to knock.* She found her son tossing a pajama top on.

"Mom!" he cried, quickly pulling the cotton top over his hips. "I was getting undressed."

"Sorry." Holding back a grin, she repeated. "I'm sorry. I thought you were already in bed."

Jimmy definitely was heading toward puberty. He demanded his privacy. Even Kevin wasn't allowed to barge into Jimmy's domain without knocking. She felt a certain amount of apprehension. Her baby was growing up. This was a major step to becoming an adolescent and eventually a man.

"Ready for bed?"

Her oldest son nodded and crawled into the upper bunk of the bunk beds. Standing next to the bed, she tucked him in. "Can I still give you a kiss good night?"

Jimmy thought it over and then nodded.

"Thank you," she offered before planting a big sloppy kiss on his forehead. "Good night."

"Mom?"

"Yessss?"

"Mr. Adam is cool."

"Yes, he is," Wynn agreed. *What's with my kids?* she wondered. They both had Adam on their minds. They must have talked together and decided to add their vote of approval.

"I like him. He's not my dad. But he's okay."

"Nobody can take your dad's place. He'll always be your father. Just remember, he does love you. But he's made some mistakes that he has to pay for. That's why he can't see you by yourself. Okay?"

Jimmy's head bobbed up and down.

Wynn stole a second kiss and headed for the door. "Time for bed. Good night and I'll see you in the morning." Trotting down the stairs, her thoughts returned to her conversations with her sons. Adam was an accepted part of their lives.

During the search for Jimmy and Kevin, Adam had provided support, investigators, and the company plane from Gautier. Each time she lost her mind with grief and wanted to do things her way, he gently steered her in the correct direction. Adam had been her rock and she was grateful for everything he'd done to get her children home.

Before Jim ran off with the boys, Wynn and Adam's relationship had been questionable. Maybe it was time to take it out of the slow lane and move them into the fast lane.

Wynn entered the family room. Adam sat with

a glass of wine in each hand. She snuggled against him and took the glass he offered.

"Let's make a toast."

She held her glass, waiting for him.

"Here's to having your children home safe and sound." He touched her glass to his. "And to more happy times."

They both took a sip from their glasses.

Wynn faced the television and sat quietly for a moment. *Go ahead. Talk to him,* she silently egged herself on. "Adam?"

"Hmm?" he muttered, watching the Lifetime Channel movie.

"I want to thank you for everything you did for me and my sons."

"No problem." Focused on the television screen, he tossed an arm around her shoulders and drew her against his side.

"It was a big deal. I want you to know that."

Adam smiled.

It's now or never, Wynn thought, taking in a deep breath. "Remember when we were in Mexico."

Frowning, he turned to her. "Yeah?"

"You asked me to marry you?"

His body went rigid against hers. He shifted and stared into her eyes. "Yes?"

"I said that I couldn't give you an answer because my children didn't know you?"

"Yes," he answered for the third time.

"Kevin and Jimmy think you're great. They told me it was okay for me to marry you."

"Did they now?"

She smiled and took his hand in hers. "Yes, they did."

Adam shrugged. "I'm glad to hear it."

"Adam Carlyle, I love you. And I want to spend the rest of my life being with you." Wynn shut her eyes, searching for the strength to do this. She opened them and gazed into the eyes of the man she loved. "Will you marry me?"

The biggest grin spread across his face. He pulled her into her arms and kissed her deeply.

When Adam released her, Wynn said, "That was real nice. But you haven't answered my question."

Laughing, he replied, "Yes!"

Epilogue

"And they lived happily ever after," Wynn chanted, closing the book. "Now, it's time for you to go to sleep."

"I don't want to. I'm not sleepy."

Sitting at Wynn's side, Adam added in a stern voice that quickly softened. "It's time, young lady."

"Please?" Peyton whined, turning big liquid brown eyes on her father. "Just one more story."

Kevin gently tugged on one of Peyton's pigtails and stood. "Good night, Peyton."

In his sock-covered feet, Jimmy slid across the hardwood floor. He leaned down and tickled his sister behind the ear. "Sleep tight, Pey-Pey."

"You two get ready for bed," Wynn ordered.

"Ah, Mommy!" Kevin moaned.

Jimmy asked, "Do we have to?"

Laughing, Wynn shook her head. No wonder Peyton moaned and whined like her brothers. She heard the same thing every night. Her boys were still the same. Nothing changed. Bedtime at the Carlyle household was full of drama.

Adam opened his arms.

Jimmy hugged his stepfather. "Night, Dad."

"Night, son. Kevin?"

The boy wrapped Adam in a big bear hug. "Night, Dad."

"Maybe we can read one more," Adam amended, turning to his wife. "What do you think? Just a short one?"

Wynn laughed and opened the book, flipping through the pages until she found a two-page story. From the moment Peyton Leigh Carlyle pushed her way into the world, corporate giant Adam Carlyle had been wrapped around her baby finger.

Being a pregnant middle-aged woman hadn't sat well with Wynn. After her first visit to the doctor to confirm her suspicions, she'd realized her baby had been conceived during her afternoon delight with Adam at the Hyatt Hotel. There were so many issues to consider. She had a new marriage and two growing boys to thing about.

Until the doctor told her that she was pregnant, Wynn believed her baby-making days were behind her and she was looking ahead to grandchildren once her sons graduated from college and got married. A new baby was the last thing she expected to deal with.

Of course, Adam had been thrilled. Since the incident with Kevin and Jimmy, Adam had grown very close to her sons. The boys respected and looked up to their stepfather. Through Adam, Kevin and Jimmy had found a true father figure.

Becoming a father for the first time, Adam had vowed to become the authority on childbirth and rearing. He could hardly wait for the birth of his first child. He'd refused to listen to Wynn when she tried to tell him the sex of their child, claiming instead that he wanted to be surprised. And then went on to plan a couples' baby shower so that he could invite his friends.

Kevin and Jimmy were happy with the idea of having a sibling. They talked nonstop about the newest member of the Carlyle family.

Peyton's birth had gone on without a hitch. The little girl arrived one afternoon and went home two days later.

Adam tugged the book from Wynn's hand and started to read. His deep, sexy drawl made Wynn go all soft inside. The years had been good to and for them. Their family was happy and content.

Wynn smiled. Who would have thought that an accidental meeting would turn her life around so thoroughly?

She refocused on her husband's voice in time to hear Adam announce, "And they lived happily ever after."

Wynn reached for Adam's hand. She squeezed it and gazed into the eyes of the man that had changed her life so drastically. *My own Prince Charming*, she thought, *living our own fairy tale*. And she planned to continue to live happily ever after for the rest of their days.